ISBN 978-1-330-91089-4
PIBN 10120331

English
Français
Deutsche
Italiano
Español
Português

www.forgottenbooks.com

Mythology Photography **Fiction**
Fishing Christianity **Art** Cooking
Essays Buddhism Freemasonry
Medicine **Biology** Music **Ancient**
Egypt Evolution Carpentry Physics
Dance Geology **Mathematics** Fitness
Shakespeare **Folklore** Yoga Marketing
Confidence Immortality Biographies
Poetry **Psychology** Witchcraft
Electronics Chemistry History **Law**
Accounting **Philosophy** Anthropology
Alchemy Drama Quantum Mechanics
Atheism Sexual Health **Ancient History**
Entrepreneurship Languages Sport
Paleontology Needlework Islam
Metaphysics Investment Archaeology
Parenting Statistics Criminology
Motivational

EDINBURGH:

PRINTED BY JAMES BALLANTYNE AND CO.

THE

OLFE OF BADENOCH

A HISTORICAL ROMANCE OF THE

FOURTEENTH CENTURY.

BY THE AUTHOR OF " LOCHANDHU."

De cornada de ansaron
Guarde Dios mi corazon.
Spanish Proverb.

VOL. I.

EDINBURGH:

PRINTED FOR CADELL & CO. EDINBURGH;

AND SIMPKIN & MARSHALL, LONDON.

1827.

PRELIMINARY NOTICE.

THE WOLFE OF BADENOCH was advertised in June 1825, at which time it was ready for the press. Since then, certain circumstances, easily guessed at, have subjected it, with many a more important Work, to an embargo, from which Critics may very possibly say it should never have been liberated. The Author himself had forgotten it, until now that it has been unexpectedly called for; and this must be his apology for that want of revision which he fears will be but too apparent.

The Author has been accused of being an imitator of the Great Unknown. In his own defence, however, he must say, that he is far from being wilfully so. In truth, his greatest anxiety has been to avoid intruding profanely into the sacred haunts of that Master Enchanter. But let it be remembered, that the mighty spirit of the Magician has already so filled the labyrinth of Romance, that it is not easy to venture within its precincts, without feeling his influence; and to say, that in exploring the intricacies of these wizard paths, one is to be denounced for unwittingly treading upon those flowers which have been pressed by his giant foot, amounts to a perfect prohibition of all entrance there.

In the WOLFE OF BADENOCH, the Author has adhered strictly to historical fact, as far as history or historical character has been interwoven with his story. He has felt, indeed, that this scrupulosity has considerably fettered his invention; and had circumstances permitted the Public so to judge of his former production, some of the remarks thrown out upon it would have been spared.

ERRATA ET CORRIGENDA.

Page   2, line 16, *for* day-*read* gay.
—— 21, line 2 from the bottom, *for* vale *read* nale.
—— 23, line 5 from the bottom, *for* foeman *read* foemen.
—— 24, line 1, *before* 'tis *insert* but.
—— 73, line 8 from the bottom, *for* coarcted *read* coarted.
—— 133, line 2 from the bottom, *for* butt-horse *read* batt-horse.
—— 144, line 7, *for* paukers *read* pankers.
—— 155, line 11, *for* alunes *read* alures.
—— 169, line 13, *for* carriers *read* couriers.
—— 173, line 7 from the bottom, *for* risks for *read* risks of.
—— 188, line 6 from the bottom, *for* Gad-a-mercy *read* Gra-mercy.
—— 216, line 12, *for* topinage *read* tapinage.
—— 258, line at the bottom, *for* hither *read* thither.
—— 261, line 5, *before* climbed *insert* they.
—— 327, line 1, *for* cheerily *read* charily.
—— 332, line 3, *for* bywoxan *read* bywoxen.

THE
WOLFE OF BADENOCH.

CHAPTER I.

It was in the latter part of the fourteenth century, that Sir Patrick Hepborne and Sir John Assueton—two young Scottish knights, who had been serving their novitiate of chivalry under the banners of Charles the VI. of France, and who had bled their maiden lances against the Flemings at Rosebarque—were hastening towards the Border separating England from their native country. A truce then subsisting betwixt the kingdoms that divided Britain, had enabled the two friends to land in Kent, whence they were permitted to prosecute their journey through the dominions of Richard II., attended by a circumscrihed retinue of some ten or a dozen horsemen.

" These tedious leagues of English ground

seem to lengthen under our travel," said Sir John Assueton, breaking a silence that was stealing upon their march, with the descending shades of evening. "Dost thou not long for one cheering glance of the silver Tweed, ere its stream shall have been forsaken by the last glimmer of twilight?"

"In sooth, I should be well contented to behold it," replied Hepborne. "The night droops fast, and our jaded palfreys already lag their ears from weariness. Even our unbacked warsteeds, albeit they have carried no heavier burden than their trappings, have nathless lost some deal of their morning's mettle, and judging from their sobered paces, methinks they would gladly exchange their day chamfronts for the more vulgar hempen-halters of some well-littered stable."

"Depardieux, but I have mine own sympathy with them," said Assueton. "Said'st thou not that we should lie at Norham to-night?"

"Methought to cast the time and the distance so," replied Hepborne; "and by those lights that twinkle from yonder dark mass, rising against that yellow streak in the sky, I should judge that I have not greatly missed in meting our day's journey to that of the sun. Look between those groups of trees—nay, more to the right, over that swelling bank;—that, if I mistake not, is the keep of Norham Castle, and those are doubtless the torches of the warders moving along the battlements. The watch must be setting ere this. Let us put on."

" Thou dost not mean to crave hospitality from the captain of the strength, dost thou?" demanded Assueton.

" Such was my purpose," replied Hepborne; " and the rather, that the good old knight, Sir Walter de Selby, hath a fair fame for being no churlish host."

" Nay, if thou lovest me, Hepborne, let us shun the Castle," said Assueton. " I have, 'tis true, heard of this same Sir Walter de Selby; and the world lies, if he be not, indeed, as thou say'st, a hospitable old knight. But they say he hath damsels about him; and thou knowest I love not to doff mine armour only to don the buckram of etiquette; and to have mine invention put upon the rack to minister to woman's vanity. Let us then to the village hostel, I entreat thee."

" This strange unknightly disease of thine doth grow on thee, Assueton," said Hepborne, laughing. " I have, indeed, heard that the widowed Sir Walter was left with one peerless daughter, who is doubtless the pride of her father's hall; nay, I confess to thee, my friend, that the much-bruited tale of her beauty hath had its own share in begetting my desire to lodge me in Norham; but since thou wilt have it so, I am content to pleasure thee, trusting that this my ready penance of self-denial may count against the heavy score of my sins. But stay; —What may this be that lies fluttering here among the gorse?"

" Meseems it a wounded hawk," said Assueton, stooping from his horse to look at it.

" In truth, 'tis indeed a fair falcon," said Hepborne's esquire, Mortimer Sang, as he dismounted to pick it up. " He gasps as if he were dying. Ha! by'r lady, but he hath nommed a plump partridge; see here, it is dead in his talons."

" He hath perchance come by some hurt in the swooping," said Hepborne; " Can'st thou discover any wound in him?"

" Nay, I can see nothing amiss in him," replied Sang.

" I'll warrant me, a well-reclaimed falcon," said Hepborne, taking him from his esquire; " ay, and the pet of some fair damsel too, if I may guess from his silken jesses. But hold —he reviveth. I will put him here in the bosom of my surcoat, and so foster the small spark of life that may yet remain in him."

At this moment their attention was arrested by the sound of voices; and by the meagre light that now remained, they could descry two ladies, mounted on palfreys, and followed by two or three male attendants, who came slowly from behind a wooded knoll, a little to the left of the path before them. Their eyes were thrown on the ground, and they seemed to be earnestly engaged in looking for something they had lost.

" Alas, my poor bird l" said one of the ladies, " I fear I shall never see thee more."

" Marry, 'tis vain to look for him by this lack of light," said an esquire.

" Do thou thy duty and seek for him, Master Turnberry," said the second lady, in a haughty tone.

" A murrain on't !" said the esquire again; " this comes of casting a hawk at a fowl at sundown."

" I tell thee he must be hereabouts," said the second lady again; " it was over these very trees that I saw him stoop."

" Stoop ! ay, I'll be sworn I saw him stoop," said the squire. " But an I saw him not dash his brains 'gainst one of those gnarled elms, my name is not Thomas, and I have no eyes for falconry. He's amortised, I promise thee."

" Silence, Master Turnberry," said the same

lady again; " thou givest thy tongue larger license than doth well beseem thee."

" By the Rood, but 'tis well to call silence," replied the esquire, sulkily, " and to me too who did verily steal these two hours' sport of hawking for thee at mine own proper peril."

" Ay, stolen indeed were they on thy part, Master Turnberry," replied the same lady; " but forget not that they were honestly bought of thee on ours."

" Nay, then, bought or not," said the esquire, " the last nail's breadth of thy merchandize hath been unrolled to thee. We must e'en clip short, and haste us to Norham, else will Sir Walter's grey beard become redder than a comet's tail with ire. Thou knowest this hath been but a testy day with him."

" Peace with thine impudence, sir knave," said the same lady, hotly. " Dost thou dare thus to speak in presence of the Lady Eleanore de Selby? A greybeard's ire shall never——"

" Nay, talk not so," said the first lady, mildly interrupting her. " The honest squire equerry hath reason. Though it grieveth me to lose my poor falcon thus, we must e'en give him up, and haste us to the Castle."

" Stay, stay, fair damsel," cried Hepborne, urging his steed forward from the hollow bushy

path where he and his party had hitherto remained concealed, from dread of alarming the
ladies, a precaution which he now entirely forgot in his eagerness to approach her, whose person and manners had already bewitched him.
" Stay, stay—fly not, lady—your hawk—your
falcon !"

But the sudden appearance of armed men
had so filled the ladies with alarm, that they
had fled at his first word ; and he now saw himself opposed by sturdy Squire Turnberry, who,
being too much taken by surprise to catch the
knight's meaning, and taking it for granted that
his purpose was hostile, wheeled his horse round,
and planting himself firmly in the midst of the
path, at the head of the grooms, couched his
hunting-spear, as if determined to prevent pursuit.

" What, ho ! sir stranger knight—what seek
ye, in the fiend's name ?" demanded the squire,
sternly.

" Credit me no evil," said Sir Patrick. " It
galleth me sore that mine intemperate rudeness
should have so frayed these beauteous damsels.
Mine intent was but to restore the fair lady's
lost falcon, the which we chanced to pick up in
this hollow way. He had ta'en some unseen

hurt in swooping at this partridge, which he had nommed."

" Nay, by the mass, but I thought as much," said the squire.

" Tell the lovely mistress of this fair bird, that Sir Patrick Hepborne willingly submits him to what penance she may enjoin for the alarm he caused her," said the knight; " and tell her too, that he gave life to her expiring falcon, by cherishing it in his bosom."

" I give thee thanks in mine own name, and that of the lady who owneth the hawk," said the esquire. " Trust me, thy sin will be forgotten in the signal service thou hast done her. The bird, methinks, rouseth him as if there were no longer evil in him."

" Yea, he proyneth and manteleth him as if rejoicing that he shall again embrace his lady's wrist with his sengles," said the knight. " Happy bird! depardieux, but he is to be envied. Tell his fair mistress, that if the small service it hath been my good fortune to render her may merit aught of boon at her hands, let my reward be mine enlistment in that host of gallant knights who may have vowed devotion to her will."

" Sir Knight," said the squire, " I will bear thy courteous message to her who owneth the falcon; and if I tarry not longer to give thee greater store of thanks, 'tis that the Lady Eleanore de Selby hath spurred away so fast, that I must have a fiend's flight if I can catch her." And turning his horse with these words, he tarried not for further parlance.

"'Tis a strange adventure, Assueton," said Hepborne to his friend, as they pursued their journey; "to meet thus with the peerless Eleanore de Selby at the very moment she formed the subject of our discourse."

"'Tis whimsical enow," said Assueton, drily, "yet it is nothing marvellous."

"Albeit that the growing darkness left me but to guess at the excellence of her features, from the elegance of her person," continued Hepborne, "yet do I confess myself more than half enamoured of her by very intuition. Did'st thou observe that her attendant who talked so forwardly, though not devoid of grace, showed in her superior presence but as a mere mortal beside a goddess?"

"Nay," replied Assueton, "though I do rarely measure or weigh the points of women, and am more versant in those of a battle-steed, yet methought that the attendant, as thou callest her, had the more noble port of the two."

"Fie on thy judgment, Assueton," cried

A 2

Hepborne; " to prefer the saucy pert demeanour of an over-indulged handmaid, to the dignified deportment of gentle birth. The Lady
Eleanore de Selby—she, I mean, in the reddish-
coloured mantle, she who wept for her hawk—
was as far above her companion in the elegance
of her air, as heaven is above earth."

" May be so," replied Assueton, with perfect
indifference, " 'tis a question not worth the
mooting."

" To thee, perhaps, it may be of little interest," said Hepborne; " but I could be well contented to be permitted to solve it in Norham
Castle. Why wert thou born with feelings so
much at war with what beseemeth a knight, as
to make thee eschew all converse with those fair
beings, the sun of whose beauty shineth but to
brace up the otherwise damp and flaccid nerves
of chivalrous adventure ?"

" Nay, thou mightest as well demand of me
why my raven locks are not as fair as thine,"
said Assueton, with a smile; " yea, or bid him
who is born blind to will to see."

" By Saint Baldrid, but I do pity thee as
much as if thou wert blind," said Hepborne.
" Nay, what is it but to be blind, yea, to want
every sense, to be thus unmoved with——"

" Ha ! see where the broad bosom of Tweed

at last glads our eyes, glistening yonder with the pale light that still lingers in the west," exclaimed Assueton, overjoyed to avail himself of so happy an opportunity of interrupting his friend's harangue.

" Yonder farther shadowy bank is Scotland —our country," cried Hepborne, with deep feeling.

" God's blessing on her hardy soil !" said Assueton, with enthusiasm.

"Amen !" said Hepborne. "To her shall we henceforth devote our arms, long enow wielded in foreign broils, where, in truth, heart did hardly go with hand."

" But where lieth the hamlet of Norham ?" inquired Assueton.

" Seest thou not where a few feeble rays are shed from its scattered tenements on the hither meadow below?" replied Hepborne. " Nay, thou mayest dimly descry the church yonder, sanctified by the shelter it did of erst yield to the blessed remains of the holy St Cuthbert, what time the impious Danes drove them from Lindisferne."

" But what, methinks, is most to thy present purpose, Sir Knight," observed Mortimer Sang, " yonder brighter glede proceedeth, if I rightly guess, from the blazing hearth of Master Syl-

vester Kyle, as thirsty a tapster as ever broached a barrel, and one who, if he be yet alive,
hath hardly, I wot, his make on either side the
Border, for knavery and sharp wit."

" Pray heaven his sharp wit may not have
soured his ale," muttered Roger Riddel, the
laconic esquire of Sir John Assueton.

They now hastened down the hollow way that
led to the village, and soon found themselves
in its simple street.

" Ay," exclaimed Sang, " by St Andrew,
but old Kyle's gate is right hospitably open.
I promise ye, 'tis a good omen for Border quiet
to find it so. So please thee, Sir Knight, shall
I advance and give note of thine approach ?"

" Do so," said Hepborne to the esquire, who
immediately cantered forward.

" Ho ! house there !" cried Sang, halting in
the gateway. " Come forth, Monsieur, mine
host of the hostel of the Norham Tower.—Where
art thou, Master Sylvester Kyle ?—Where be
thine hostlers, drawers, and underskinkers ?—
Why do not all appear to do themselves honour
by waiting on two most puissant knights, for I
talk not of their esquires, or of the other gentlemen soldiers of pregnant prowess, of the very
least of whom it were an honour to undo the
spur ?"

By the time that Sang had ended his summons, the party were at the gate, and had leisure to survey the premises. A rude wall of
considerable strength faced the irregular street
of the village, having the gateway in the centre.
The thatch-roofed buildings within formed the
other three sides of the quadrangular court.
Those to the right were occupied as stables, and
in those to the left were the kitchen, and various
other domestic offices; whilst the middle part
was entirely taken up by one large room, from
whence gleamed the light of a great fire, that
burned on a hearth in the midst, shedding
around a common comfort on the motley parties
of noisy ale-drinkers seated at different tables.

"What, ho! Sylvester, I say—what a murrain keeps thee?" cried Sang, although the port-
ly form of the vintner already appeared within
the aperture of the doorway, like a goodly por-
trait in a frame, his carbuncled face vying in
lustre with the red flare of the torch he held
high in his hand. "Gramercy, Master Kyle,
so thou hast come at last. By the mass, but
that paunch of thine is a right fair warrant for
the goodness of thine ale, yet will it be well that
it do come quicker when it be called for than
thou hast."

"Heyday, what a racket thou dost make,

gaffer horseman !" cried Kyle. " But the emp-
tiest vessel doth ever make the most din."

" Tut, man, thou hast hit it for once with
thy fool's-head," replied Sang. " I am, as thou
sayest, at this present, in very sober earnest, an
empty vessel ; yea, and for that matter, so are
we all. But never trust me an we make not a
din till we be filled. The sooner thou stoppest
our music, then, the better for thine ears, seeing that if we be forced to pipe thus, and that
thou dancest not more quickly to our call, thou
mayest perchance lose them."

" By the mass, but thy music is marvellously out of tune, good fellow," replied the publican. " Thy screeching is like that of a cracked
rebeck, the neck of which must be hard griped,
and most cruelly pinched, ere its tone be soft-
ened. But of what strength is thy company ?"
continued he, whirling his torch around so as to
obtain a general view of the group of horsemen. " By St Cuthbert, I wish there may be
stabling for ye all."

" Stabling for us all, Sir knave ?" cried Sang ;
" marry, thou dost speak as if we were a herd
of horses."

" Cry you mercy, noble esquire," rejoined
Kyle. " An thou beest an ass, indeed, a halter
and a hook at the gate-cheek may serve thy

turn, and so peraunter I may find room for the rest."

A smothered laugh among his comrades proclaimed Squire Sang's defeat. The triumphant host ran to hold Sir Patrick Hepborne's stirrup.

" By the Rood," cried the squire, as he dismounted, with a good-natured chuckle at his own discomfiture,—"by the Rood, but the rogue hath mastered me for this bout. But verily my wit is fasting, whilst his, I warrant, hath the full spirit of his potent ale in't. Never trust me but I shall be even with him anon."

" Master Kyle," said Assueton to their host, as he ushered his guests into the common room, " we should be glad to see some food. The rising sun looked upon our last meal; so bestir thyself, I prithee, goodman, and let us know as soon as may be how we are to fare."

" Room there, sirs, for two valiant knights," cried Kyle, getting rid of the question by addressing himself to a party seated at a table near the hearth; " room, I say, gentlemen.—What, are ye stocks, my masters ?"

" Nay, treat not the good people so rudely," said Hepborne, as some eight or ten persons were hastily vacating their places; " there is room enow for all. Go not thou, at least, old man," continued he, addressing a minstrel who

was following the rest, his snowy locks and
beard hanging luxuriantly around a countenance that showed all the freshness of a green
old age; "sit thee down, I do beseech thee, and
vouchsafe us thy winning discourse. Where is
the chevalier to whom a bard may not do·ho-
nour?"

The minstrel's heart was touched by Sir Patrick's kind words; his full hazel eye beamed
on him with gratitude; he put his hand to his
breast, and modestly bowed his head.

" My time is already spent, most gentle
knight," said he. " Ere this I am looked for at
the Castle; yet, ere I go hence, let me drink
this cup of thanks for thy courtesy. To thee I
wish tender love of fairest lady; and may thy
lance, and the lance of thy brave companion,
never be couched but to conquer." And so
draining the draught to the bottom, he again
bowed, and immediately retired.

" So, Master Kyle," said Assueton to the
host, who returned at this moment, after having
ascertained the country and quality of his new
guests, " what hast thou in thy buttery?"

" Of a truth, Sir Knight, we are now but ill
provided for sike guests," replied Kyle. " Had
it but been thy luck to have sojourned here yestere'en, indeed, I wot ye mought ha' been feast-

ed. But arrives me my Lord Bishop of Durham at the Castle this morning;—down comes
me the seneschal with his buttery-men, and
whips me off a whole beeve's carcase;—then in
pour me the people of my Lord Bishop, clerks,
lacqueys, and grooms;—bolt goes me a leg of
mutton here—crack goes me a venison pasty
there—gobble goes me a salmon in this corner,
whilst a whole flock of pullets are riven asunder
in that;—so that there has been nothing from
sunrise till sundown but wagging of jaws."

" Marry, these church-followers are wont to
be stout knights of the trencher," said Assueton, with a smile. " But let us have a supper
from what may be left thee, and that without
more ado."

" Anon, courteous Sir Knight," said Master
Kyle, with a grin. " But, as I was a-saying,
there hath been such stuffing; nay, ye may
know by the clinking of their cans that the
rogues drink not fasting. By the mass, 'tis easy
to guess from the seas of ale they are swallow-
ing, what mountains of good provender they
have to float in their stomachs. Why, yonder
lantern-jaws i' the corner, with a mouth that
opens as if he would swallow another Jonas,
and wangs like the famine-ground fangs of a
starving wolf—that same fellow devoured me a

couple of fat capons single-handed; and that
other churl——"

"Have done with thine impertinence, villain," said Assueton, interrupting him; "have
done with thine impertinence, I say, and let us
straightway have such fare as thou canst give,
or by St Andrew——"

"Nay, then, sweet sir," replied the host,
"there be yet reserved some delicate pig's liver
for myself and Mrs Kyle, but they shall be
forthwith cheerfully yielded to thy necessities."

"Pestilence take thee, knave," cried Assueton, "couldst thou not have set them down to
us at once, without stirring up our appetites to
greater keenness by thine enumeration of the
good things that are gone? Come, come, dispatch—our hunger is beyond nicety."

Sir John Assueton now sat down to put in
practice that patience of hunger, the exercise of
which was one of the chief virtues of knighthood. As for Sir Patrick Hepborne, his attention was so entirely absorbed by a conversation
that ensued at the adjoining table, to which the
Bishop's people had retired, that he altogether
forgot his wants.

"And was it thy luck to see the Lady
Eleanore de Selby, Master Barton?" demanded

one of the persons of the dialogue; "Fame speaketh largely of her perfections."

"Yea, Foster, I did indeed behold her," replied the other, who seemed to be a person of more consequence than the rest. "When I entered the Castle-hall this morning, to receive the commands of my lord the Bishop, she was seated between him and her father. They were alone, and the old knight was urging something to her in round soldier-like terms; but I gathered not the purport of his speech, for he broke off abruptly as I appeared."

"And is she so rare a beauty as folks do call her?" demanded Foster.

"Verily so much loveliness did never bless these eyes before," replied Barton. "Yet was the sunshine of her face disturbed by clouds. Tear-drops, too, had dimmed the lustre of her charms. But methought they were more the offspring of a haughty spirit than of an afflicted heart."

"Nay, of a truth they do say that she lacketh not haughtiness," observed Foster. "'Tis whispered that she hath already scorned some noble knights who would fain have wedded the heiress of the rich Sir Walter de Selby."

"Nay, I warrant me she hath had suitors enow, and those no mean ones," replied Barton. " What thinkest thou of Sir Rafe Piersie, brother to the gallant Hotspur? Marry, they say that he deigns to woo her with right serious intent."

" Sayest thou so?" exclaimed Foster; " then must the old knight's gold have glittered in the. young knight's eyes, that a proud-blooded Piersie should even him thus to the daughter of him who is but a soldier of fortune."

" Ay, and welcome, I ween, would the old knight's hard-won wealth be to the empty coffers of a younger brother who hath never spared expense," replied Barton.

" Yea, and high, I wot, mought Sir Walter's hoar head be held with such a gallant for his son-in-law,'" observed Foster again.

" Trust me," said Barton, " he would joyfully part with all the golden fruits he hath gleaned from Scottish fields, to see this solitary scion from his old stock grafted on the goodly and towering tree of Northumberland. But they say that the Lady Eleanore is so hard to win, that she even scorns this high alliance; and if I might guess at matters the which to know are beyond my reach, I should say, heark ye, that this visit of our Right Reverend Lord Bishop to Sir Walter de Selby, hath something in

it of the nature of an ambassage from the Piersie touching this same affair."

" I do well know our Right Reverend Lord's
affection for that house," said Foster.

" Nay, he doth stand related to the Piersie in
no very distant degree," replied Barton.

" Perchance this marriage treaty then had
something to do with the lady's tears," observed
Foster.

" Doubtless," said Barton. " But I mistake
if she carrieth not a high brow that will be ill
to bend. Her doting father hath been ever too
foolishly fond of her to thwart her will, till it
hath waxed too strong for his opposing. She
will never yield, I promise thee."

" Then hath our Bishop lost his travel," said
Foster. " But when returneth our Reverend
Lord homeward ?"

" His present orders are for to-morrow," replied Barton.

" How say'st thou, Assueton?" said Hepborne,
in a whisper to his friend, after the conversation
between the two strangers had dropped ; " how
sayest thou now ? Did I right, think ye, to yield
to thine importunity, to shun the hospitality of
Norham Castle, that we might hostel it so vilely
here i' the vale of the Norham Tower ? Dost
thou not grieve for thy folly ?"

" Why, faith," replied Assueton, " to thee it
may be cause of some regret; and I may grieve
for thee, seeing that thou, an idolater of woman's beauty, hast missed worshipping before the
footstool of this haughty damsel. Thou mightest
have caught a shred of ribbon from her fair hand,
perchance, to have been treasured and worn in
thy helmet; but, for mine own particular part,
I despise such toys. Rough, unribboned steel,
and the joyous neighing of my war-steed, are to
me more pleasing than the gaudy paraments and
puling parlance of love-sick maidens." .

" Nay, then, I do confess that my desire to
behold this rare beauty hath much grown by
what I have heard," replied Hepborne. " Would
that thou had'st been less indolently disposed,
my friend. We might have been even now in
the Castle; and ere we should have left it, who
knows but we might have rescued this distress-
ed damosel from an alliance she detesteth? Even
after all these protestations to the contrary, thine
icy heart mought have been thawed by the fire
of her eyes, and the adventure mought have been
thine own."

" St Andrew forbid!" replied Assueton. " I
covet no such emprise. I trust my heart is
love-proof. Have I not stood before the light-
ning-glances of the demoiselles of Paris, and

may I not hold my breastplate to be good armour against all else?"

"Nay, boast not of this unknightly duresse of thine, Assueton," replied Hepborne. "Trust me, thou wilt fall when thine hour cometh. But, by St Baldrid, I would give this golden chain from my neck—nay, I would give ten times its worth, to be blessed with but a sight of her."

"Ay," said Assueton, "thou art like the moth, and would'st hover round the lamp-fire till thy wings were singed."

"Pshaw, Sir Adamant," said Hepborne, "thou knowest I have skimmed through many a festal hall, blazing with bright eyes, and yet are my pinions as whole as thine. But I am not insensible to woman's charms as thou art; and to behold so bright a star, perdie, I should care little to risk being scorched by coming within the range of its rays."

"Nay, then, I do almost repent me that I hindered thee from thy design of quartering in the Castle," said Assueton. "Thou mightest have levied new war on our ancient and natural foeman, by snatching an affianced bride from the big house of Northumberland."

"Depardieux, but it were indeed a triumph, and worthy of a Scottish knight, to carry off the Lady Eleanore de Selby by her own consent from the proud Piersic," said Hepborne. " 'Tis well enow to jest of."

Whilst this dialogue was going on between the two friends, their esquires entered the place. Mortimer Sang, after reconnoitring the different tables, and perceiving that there were no convenient places vacant, except at that occupied by the attendants of the Bishop, went towards it, followed by his comrade Roger Riddel.

" By your good leave, courteous gentlemen," said Sang, with a bow, at the same time filling up an empty space with his person; " I hope no objection to our joining your good company? —Here, tapster," cried he, at the same time throwing money on the table, " bring in a flagon of Rhenish, that we may wash away the dryness of new acquaintance."

This cheering introduction of the two esquires was received with a smiling welcome on the part of those to whom it was addressed.

" Come ye from the south, Sir Squire?" demanded Barton, after the wine had silently circulated, to the great inward satisfaction of the partakers.

" Ay, truly, from the south, indeed," replied Sang, lifting the flagon to his head.

" Then was I right, Richard, after all," said

5

Barton, addressing one of his fellows. "Did I not tell thee that these strangers had none of the loutish Scot in their gait?"

"Loutish Scot!" cried Sang, taking the flagon from his lips, and starting up fiercely; "What mean ye by loutish Scot?"

Barton eyed the tall figure, broad chest, and sinewy arms of the Scottish esquire.

"Nay, I meant thee not offence, Sir Squire," replied he.

"Ha!" said Sang, regaining his good-humour; "then I take no offence where none is meant. Your Scot and your Southern are born foes to fight in fair field; yet I see no just cause against their drinking together in good fellowship when the times be fitting, albeit they may be called upon anon to crack each other's sconces in battle broil.—Thine hand," said he, stretching his right across the table to the Bishop's man, whilst he poised the flagon with his left. "Peraunter thou be'st a soldier, though of a truth that garb of thine would speak thee to be as much of a clerk as an esquire; but indeed, an thy trade be arms, I am bold to say, that Scotland doth not hold a man who will do thee the petites politesses of the skirmish more handsomely than I shall, should chance ever throw us against each other. Meanwhile my hearty service to thee."

" Spoke like a true man," said Roger Riddel, taking the flagon from his friend. " Here, tapster, we lack wine."

" Nay, Roger," said Sang, " but we cannot drink thus fasting. What a murrain keeps that knave with the——Ha! he comes. Why, holy St Andrew, what meanest thou, villain, by putting down this flinty skim-milk? Caitiff, dost take us for ostriches, to digest iron? Saw I not hogs' livers a-frying for our supper?"

" Nay, good master Sir Squire," said the flaxen-polled lad of a tapster, " sure mistress says, that the livers be meat for your masters."

" Meat for our masters, sirrah!" replied Sang; " and can the hostel of Master Sylvester Kyle, famed from the Borders to the Calais Straits—can this far-famed house, I say, afford nothing better for a brace of Scottish knights, whose renown hath filled the world from Cattiness to the land of Egypt, than a fried hog's liver? Avoid, sinner, avoid; out of my way, and let me go talk to this same hostess."

So saying, he strode over the bench, and kicking the rushes before him in his progress towards the door, made directly for the kitchen.

CHAPTER II.

On entering the kitchen, Master Mortimer Sang found the hostess, a buxom dame with rosy cheeks, raven hair, and jet black eyes, busily employed in cooking the food intended for the two knights. Having already had a glimpse of her, he remarked her to be of an age much too green for so wintry a husband as Sylvester Kyle; so checking his haste, he approached her with his best Parisian obeisance.

" Can it be," said he, assuming an astonished air—" can it possibly be, that the cruel Master Sylvester Kyle doth permit so much loveliness to be melted over the vile fire of a kitchen, an 'twere a piece of butter, and that to fry a paltry pig's liver withal?"

The dame turned round, looked pleased, smiled, flirted her head, and then went on frying. Sighing as if he were expiring his soul, Sang continued,—

" Ah, had it been my happy fate to have

owned thee, what would not I have done to pre-
serve the lustre of those charms unsullied!"

Mrs Sylvester Kyle again looked round,
again she smiled, again she flirted her head, and
leaving the frying-pan to fry in its own way,
she dropped a curtsey, and called Master Sang
a right civil and fair-spoken gentleman.

"Would that thou hadst been mine," continued Sang, throwing yet more tenderness into
his expression: "locked in these fond arms,
thy beauty should have been shielded from every
chance of injury." So saying, he suited the action to the word, and embracing Mrs Kyle, he
imprinted on her cheeks kisses, which, though
burning enough in themselves, were cold compared to the red heat of the face that received
them. Having thus paved the way to his purpose—

"What could possess thee, beauteous Mrs
Kyle," said he, "to marry that gorbellied glut-
ton of thine, a fellow who, to fill his own rapa-
cions bowke, and fatten his own scoundrel carcase, starveth thee to death? I see it in thy sweet
face, my fair hostess; 'tis vain to conceal it;
the wretch is miserably poor; he feedeth thee
not. The absolute famine that reigneth in his
beggarly buttery, nay, rather flintery, (for buttery it were sacrilege to call it,) cannot suffice

to afford one meal a-day to that insatiable maw of his, far less can it supply those cates and niceties befitting the stomach of an angel like thyself."

Mrs Kyle was whirled up to the skies by this rhapsody; Master Sylvester had never said anything half so fine. But her pride could not stand the hits the squire had given against the poverty of her larder.

" Nay thee now, but, kind sir," said she, " we be's not so bad off as all that; Master my goodman Kyle hath as fat a buttery, I warrant thee, as e'er a publican in all the Borders."

" Nay, nay, 'tis impossible, beautiful Mrs Kyle," said Mortimer again—" 'tis impossible; else why these wretched pigs' entrails for a couple of knights, of condition so high, that they may be emperors before they die, if God give them good luck ?"

" La, now there," exclaimed Mrs Kyle; " and did not Sylvester say that they were nought but two lousy Scots, and that any fare would do for sike loons. Well, who could ha' thought, after all, that they could be emperors ? An we had known that, indeed, we might ha' gi'en them emperors' fare. Come thee this way, kind sir, and I'll let thee see our spense."

This was the very point which the wily Mas-

ter Sang had been aiming at. Seizing up a
lamp, she led the way along a dark passage.
As they reached the end of it, their feet sounded hollow on a part of the floor. Mrs Kyle
stopped, set down her lamp, slipped a small
sliding plank into a groove in the side wall
made to receive it, and exposed a ring and bolt
attached to an iron lever. Applying her hand
to this, she lifted a trap-door, and disclosed a
flight of a dozen steps or more, down which
she immediately tripped, and Sang hesitated
not a moment to follow her. But what a sight
met his eyes when he reached the bottom! He
found himself in a pretty large vault, hung
round with juicy barons and sirloins of beef,
delicate carcases of mutton, venison, hams,
flitches, tongues, with all manner of fowls and
game, dangling in most inviting profusion from
the roof. It was here that Master Kyle pre-
served his stock in trade, in troublesome times,
from the rapacity of the Border depredators.
Mortimer Sang feasted his eyes for some moments in silence, but they were allowed small
time for their banquet.

A distant foot was heard at the farther extremity of the passage, and then the angry
voice of Kyle calling his wife. Mortimer Sang

sprang to the top of the steps, just as mine host had reached the trap-door.

" Eh! what l" exclaimed Kyle, with horror and surprise—" A man in the spense with my wife! Thieves! Murder!"

He had time to say no more, for Sang grappled him by the throat, as he was in the very act of stooping to shut the trap-door on him, and down he tugged the bulky host, like a huge sack; but overpowered by the descent of such a mountain upon his head, he rolled over the steps with his burden into the very middle of the vault. More afraid of her husband's wrath than anxious for his safety, Mrs Kyle put her lamp on the ground, jumped nimbly over the prostrate strugglers, and escaped. The active and herculean Sang, rising to his knees, with his left hand pressed down the half-stunned publican, who lay on his back gasping for breath; then seizing the lamp with his right, he rose suddenly to his legs, and regaining the trap-door in the twinkling of an eye, sat him down quietly on the floor to recover his own breath; and taking the end of the lever in his hand, and half closing the aperture, he waited patiently till his adversary had so far recovered himself as to be able to come to a parley.

"So, Master Sylvester Kyle," said the squire "thou art there, art thou—caught in thine own trap? So much for treating noble Scots, the flower of chivalry, with stinking hog's entrails. By'r lady, 'tis well for thee thou hast such good store of food there. Let me see;—methinks thou mayest hold out well some week or twain ere it may begin to putrify. Thou hadst better fall to, then, whiles it be fresh; time enow to begin starving when it groweth distasteful. So wishing thee some merry meals ere thou diest, I shall now shut down the trap-door—bolt it fast—nail up the sliding plank—and as no one knoweth on't but thy wife, who, kind soul, hath agreed to go off with me to Scotland to-night, thou mayest reckon on quiet slumbers for the next century."

"Oh, good Sir Squire," cried Kyle, wringing his hands like a maniac, "let me out, I beseech thee; leave me not to so dreadful a death. Thou and thy knights and all shall feast like princes; thou shalt float in sack and canary; thou shalt drink Rhinwyn in barrelfuls, and Malvoisy in hogsheads, to the very lowest lacquey of ye. No, merciful Sir Squire, thou canst not be so cruel—Oh, oh!"

"Hand me up," said Sang, with a stern voice, "hand me up, I say, that venison, and

·these pullets there, that neat's tongue, and a brace of the fattest of these ducks; I shall then consider whether thou art worthy of my most royal clemency."

Mine host had no alternative but to obey. One by one the various articles enumerated by ˙Sang were handed up to him, and deposited beside him on the floor of the passage.

, "Take these flagons, there," said he, " and draw from each of these buts, that I may taste. —Ha! excellent, i'faith, excellent.—Now, Sir knave, others of thy kidney mount up a ladder to finish their career of villainy, but thy fate lieth downwards; so down, descend, and mingle ·with thy kindred dirt."

He slapped down the trap-door with tremeudous force, bolted it firmly, and replaced the sliding plank, so that the wretch's shrieks of horrible despair came so deafened through the immense thickness of the solid oak, as to sound but as the moaning of some deep subterranean stream.

Master Sang had some difficulty in piling up the provender he had acquired, and carrying it with the flagons to the kitchen. There he found Mrs Kyle, who, in the apprehension of a terrible storm from her lord, was sitting in a corner drowned in tears.

" Cheer up, fair dame," said Sang to the disconsolate Mrs Kyle; " thou needest be under no fear of him to-night. I have left him in prison, and thou mayest relieve him thyself when thou mayest, and on thine own terms of capitulation. Meanwhile, hash up some of that venison, and dress these capons, and this neat's tongue, for the knights, our masters, and make out a supper for my comrade and me and the rest as fast as may be. I'll bear in the wine myself."

Mrs Kyle felt a small smack of disappointment to find that the so lately gallant esquire, after all he had said, should himself put such an office upon her; but she dried her eyes, and quickly begirding herself for her duty, went to work with alacrity.

CHAPTER III.

ON the return of Mortimer Sang to the common room, he found that a new event had taken place in his absence. An esquire had arrived from the Castle, bearing a courteous message from Sir Walter de Selby, its captain, setting forth, that it pained him to learn that Sir Patrick Hepborne and Sir John Assueton had not made experiment of his poor hospitality; that their names were already too renowned not to be well known to him; and that he trusted they would not refuse him the gratification of doing his best to entertain them, but would condescend to come and partake of such cheer and accommodation as Norham Castle could yield. An invitation so kind it was impossible to resist. Indeed, whatever Sir John Assueton might have felt, Sir Patrick Hepborne's curiosity to see the fair maid of the Castle was too great to be withstood. The distance was but short, and Sir Walter's messen-

ger was to be their guide. Leaving their esquires and the rest of their retinue, therefore,
to enjoy the feast so ingeniously provided for
them by Sang, their horses were ordered out,
and they departed.

The night was soft and tranquil. The moon
was up, and her silvery light poured itself on
the broad walls of the keep, and the extensive
fortifications of Norham Castle, rising on the
height before them, and was partially reflected
from the water of the farther side of the Tweed,
here sweeping widely under the rocky eminence,
that threw its shadow half way across it. They
climbed up the hollow way leading to the outer
ditch, and were immediately challenged by the
watch upon the walls. The pass-word was
given by their guide, the massive gate was un-
barred, the portcullis lifted, and the clanging
draw-bridge lowered at the signal, and they
passed under a dark archway to the door of the
outer court of guard. There they were surrounded by pikemen and billmen, and narrowly examined by the light of torches; but the
officer of the guard appeared, and the squire's
mission being known to him, they were formally saluted, and permitted to pass on. Crossing a broad area, they came to the inner gate,
where they underwent a similar scrutiny.

They had now reached that part of the fortress where stood the barracks, the stables, and various other buildings necessarily belonging to so important a place; while in the centre arose the keep, huge in bulk, and adamant in strength, defended by a broad ditch, where not naturally rendered inaccessible by the precipitous steep, and approachable from one point only by a narrow bridge. Lights appeared from some of its windows, and sounds of life came faintly from within; but all was still in the buildings around them, the measured step of the sentinel on the wall above them forming the only interruption to the silence that prevailed.

The esquire proceeded to try the door of a stable, but it was locked.

"A pestilence take the fellow," said he; "how shall I get the horses bestowed?—What, ho!—Turnberry—Tom Equerry, I say."

"Why, what art thou?" cried the gruff voice of the sentinel on the wall; "what art thou, I say, to look for Tom Turnberry at this hour? By'r lackins, his toes, I'll warrant me, are warm by the embers of Mother Rowlandson's suttling fire. He's at his ale, I promise thee."

"The plague ride him then," muttered the squire; "how the fiend shall I find him? I crave pardon, Sirs Knights, but I must go look

for this same varlet, or some of his grooms, for
horses may not pass to the keep; and who
knoweth but I may have to rummage half the
Castle over ere I find him?" So saying he left
the two knights to their meditations.

He was hardly gone when they heard the
sound of a harp, which came from a part of the
walls a little way to the left of where they were
then standing. The performer struck the chords,
as if in the act of tuning the instrument, and the
sound was interrupted from time to time. At
last, after a short prelude, a Scottish air was
played with great feeling.

" By the Rood of St Andrew," exclaimed
Assueton, after listening for some time, " these
notes grapple my heart, like the well-remem-
bered voice of some friend of boyhood. May
we not go nearer ?"

" Let us tie our horses to these palisadoes,
and approach silently, so as not to disturb the
musician," said Hepborne.

Having fastened the reins of their steeds, they
moved silently in the direction whence the music proceeded, and soon came in sight of the
performer.

On a part of the rampart, at some twenty
yards distance, where the wall on the outside
rose continuous with the rock overhanging the

stream of the Tweed, they beheld two figures; and creeping silently for two or three paces farther, they sheltered themselves from obser-vation under the shadow of a tower, where they took their stand, in the hope of the music being renewed. The moonlight was powerful, and they easily recognized the garb of the harper whom they had so lately seen at the hostel. He was seated on the horizontal ropes of one of those destructive implements of war, called an *onager* or *balista*, which were still in use at that period, when guns were but rare in Europe. His harp was between his knees, his large and expressive features were turned upwards, and his long white locks swept backwards over his shoulders, as he was in the act of speaking to a woman who stood by him. The lady, for her very mien indicated that she was no com-mon person, stood by the old man in a listen-ing posture. She was enveloped in a mantle, that flowed easily over her youthful person, giving to it roundness of outline, without ob-scuring its perfections.

" By St Dennis, Assueton," whispered Hepborne to his friend, " 'tis the Lady Elea-nore de Selby. The world lies not; she is beau-tiful."

" Nay, then thine eyes must be like those of

an owl, if thou canst tell that by this light," replied Assueton.

" I tell thee I caught one glance of her face but now, as the moonbeam fell on it," said Hepborne; " 'twas beauteous as that of an angel. But hold, they come this way."

The minstrel arose, and the lady and he came slowly along the wall in the direction where the two knights were standing.

" Tush, Adam of Gordon," said the lady, in a playful manner, as if in reply to something the harper had urged, " thou shalt never persuade me; I have not yet seen the knight,— nay I doubt me whether the knight has yet been born who can touch this heart. I would not lose its freedom for a world."

" So, so," whispered Assueton, " thou wert right, Master Barton; a haughty spirit enow, I'll warrant me."

" Hush," said Hepborne, somewhat peevishly; " the minstrel prepares to give us music."

The minstrel who had again seated himself, ran his fingers in wild prelude over his chords, and graduating into a soft and tender strain, he broke suddenly forth in the following verses, adapted to its measure.

" Oh think not, lady, to despise
The all-consuming fire of Love,
For she who most his power defies
Is sure his direst rage to prove.
Was never maid, who dared to scorn
The subtile god's tyrannic sway,
Whose heart was not more rudely torn
By his relentless archery.

Do what thou canst, that destined hour
Will come, when thou must feel Love's dart;
Then war not thus against his power,
His fire will melt thine icy heart.
Oh, let his glowing influence then
Within thy bosom gently steal;
For sooth, sweet maid, I say again,
That all are doom'd Love's power to feel."

" Why, Adam," exclaimed the lady, as the
minstrel concluded, " this is like a prophecy.
What, dost thou really say that I must one day
feel this fire thou talkest of? Trust me, old man,
I am in love with thy sweet music, and thy
sweet song; but for other love, I have never
thought of any such, and thou art naughty, old
man, to fill mine ears with that I would fain
keep from having entrance there."

" Nay, lady, say not so," cried Adam of Gordon, earnestly; " thou knowest that love and
war are my themes, and I cannot ope my lips,
or touch my harp, but one or other must have
way with me. How the subject came, I know
not; but the verses were the extemporaneous
effusion of my minstrel spirit."

" Come, Hepborne," whispered Assueton,
" let us away; we may hear more of the lady's
secrets than consists with the honour of knights
wilfully to listen to."

" Nay, I could stay here for ever, Assueton,"
replied Hepborne; " I am spell-bound. That
ethereal creature, that enchantress, has chain-
ed me to the spot: and would'st thou not wish
to have more of that old man's melody? Methought his verses might have gone home to
thee as well as to the lady."

" Pshaw," said Assueton, turning away,
" dost think that I may be affected by the dri-
velling song of an old dotard? Trust me, I laugh
at these silly matters."

" Laugh while thou may'st, then," replied
Hepborne; " thou may'st weep anon. Yet, as
thou say'st, we do but ill to stand listening here.
Let us away then."

When they had reached the spot where their
horses were tied, they found that the esquire
who guided them to the castle had but just returned with Master Turnberry, the equerry,
whose state sufficiently betrayed the manner in
which he had been spending his evening, and
showed that the sentinel had not guessed amiss
regarding him. He came staggering and grum-
bling along.

" Is't not hard, think ye, that an honest man cannot be left to enjoy his evening's ease undisturbed? I was but drinking a draught of ale, Master Harbuttle."

" A draught of ale," replied Harbuttle; " ay, something more than one draught, I take it, Master Thomas. But what makest thou with a torch in such a moonshiny night as this?"

" Moonshiny," cried Turnberry, hiccuping; " moonshiny, indeed, why, 'tis as dark as a pit well. Fye, fye, Master Harbuttle, thou must have been drinking—thou must have been drinking, I say, since thou hast so much fire in thine eyes; for, to a sober, quiet, cool-headed man like myself, Master Harbuttle, the moon is not yet up. Fye, fye, thou hast been taking a cup of Master Sylvester Kyle's tipple. 'Tis an abominable vice that thou hast fallen into; drink will be the ruin of thee."

" Thou drunken sot thou," exclaimed Harbuttle, laughing, " dost not see the moon there, over the top of the keep?"

" That the moon!" cried Turnberry, holding up his torch, as if to look for it; " well, well, to see now what drink will do—what an ass it will make of a sensible man; for, to give the devil his due, thou art no gnoffe when thou art sober, Master Harbuttle. That the moon! Why, that's the lamp burning in Ancient Fenwick's loophole window. Thou knowest he is always at his books—always at the black art. St Cuthbert defend us from his incantations !"

"Amen !" said the squire usher, fervently crossing himself.

"But what a fiend's this ?" cried Turnberry; "here are two horses, one black and t'other white. I see that well enow, though thou mayn't, yet thou wouldst persuade me I don't know the Wizzard Ancient's lamp from the moon. Give me hold of the reins."

But as he stretched forth his hand to take them, he toppled over, and fell sprawling among the horses' feet, whence he was opportunely relieved by two of his own grooms, who arrived at that moment.

"Where hast thou been idling, varlets ?" demanded Turnberry, as he endeavoured to steady himself, and assume the proper importance of authority; "drinking, varlets, drinking, I'll be sworn—John Barleycorn will be the overthrow of Norham Castle. See, villains, that ye bestow these steeds in good litters, and that oats are not awanting. I'll e'en return to my evening's repose."

At this moment the lady, followed by Adam of Gordon, came suddenly upon the group from a narrow gateway, at the bottom of a flight of steps, that led from the rampart, and were close upon Hepborne and his friend before they perceived the two knights. The lady drew back at first from surprise, and seemed to hesitate for an instant whether she should advance or not. She pulled her hood so far over her face as to render it only partially visible; but the flame of Master Turnberry's torch had flashed on it ere she did so, and Hepborne was ravished by the momentary glance he had of her beauty. The lady, on the other hand, had a full view of Sir Patrick's features, for his vizor was up. The minstrel immediately recognized him.

" Lady," said the old man, " these are the courteous stranger knights who come hither as the guests of Sir Walter de Selby."

" In the name of Sir Walter de Selby, do I welcome them then," said the lady, with a modest air: " welcome, brave knights, to the Castle. But," added she, hesitatingly, " in especial am I bound to greet with mine own guerdon of good thanks him who is called Sir Patrick Hepborne, to whose gentle care I am so much beholden for the safety of my favourite hawk."

" Proudly do I claim these precious thanks as mine own rich treasure, most peerless lady," exclaimed Sir Patrick, stepping forward with ardour. " Blessed be my good stars, which have thus so felicitously brought me, when least expecting such bliss, into the very presence of a demoiselle whose perfections have already been so largely rung in mine ears, short as hath yet been my time in Norham."

" Methinks, Sir Knight," replied the lady, in some confusion, " methinks that thy time, albeit short, might have been better spent in Norham than in listening to idle tales of me. Will it please thee to take this way ? Sir Walter, ere this, doth look for thee in the banquet-hall."

" Lady, the tale of thy charms was music to me," said Sir Patrick; " yet hath it been but as some few notes of symphony to lure me to a richer banquet. Would that the gentle zephyrs, which do now chase the fleecy cloud from yonder moon, might unveil that face. Yet, alas, I have already seen but too much of its charms for my future peace."

" Nay, Sir Knight," replied the lady, " this fustian is but thrown away on me. Thy friend, perhaps, may talk more soberly—Shall I be thy guide, chevalier ?" added she, addressing Assueton.

" No, no, no," interrupted Hepborne, springing to her side, " I'll go with thee, lady, though thou should'st condemn me to eternal silence."

" Here, then, lieth thy way," said the lady,
hurrying towards the bridge communicating
with the entrance to the keep; " and there
come the lacqueys with lights."

The squire, who had gone in before, now appeared at the door with attendants and torches.
Hepborne anxiously hoped to be blessed with
a more satisfactory view of the lady's face than
accident had before given him ; but as she approached the lights, she shrouded up her head
more closely in her hood, yet not so entirely as
to prevent her eyes from enjoying some stolen
glances at the noble figure of Sir Patrick. She
had no sooner got within the archway of the
great door, however, than she took a lamp from
an attendant, and making a graceful obeisance
to the two friends, disappeared in a moment,
leaving Sir Patrick petrified with vexation and
disappointment.

CHAPTER IV.

Sir Patrick Hepborne was roused from the astonishment the sudden disappearance of the lady had thrown him into, by the voice of the Squire Usher, who now came to receive them.

" This way, Sirs Knights," cried he, showing them forwards, and up a staircase that led them at once into a large vaulted hall, lighted by three brazen lamps, hanging by massive chains from the dark wainscot roof, and heated by one great projecting chimney. A long oaken-table, covered with pewter and wooden trenchers, with innumerable flagons and drinking vessels of the same materials, occupied the centre of the floor. About a third of its length, at the upper end, was covered with a piece of tapestry or carpet, and there the utensils were of silver. The upper portion of the table had massive high-backed carved chairs set around it, and these were furnished with cushions of red cloth, whilst long benches were set against it in other parts. The rest of the movables in the hall consisted of various kinds of arms, such as helmets, burgonets, and bacinets—breast-plates and back pieces—pouldrons, vambraces, cuisses, and greaves—gauntlets, iron-shoes, and spurs—cross-bows and long-bows, hanging in irregular profusion on the walls,—whilst spears, pikes, battle-axes, truncheons, and maces, rest-ed everywhere in numbers against them. The floor was strewed with clean rushes; and a dozen or twenty people, some of whom were warlike, and some clerical in their garb, were divided into conversational groups of two or three together.

Sir Walter de Selby, an elderly man, with a rosy countenance, and a person rather approach-ing to corpulency, clad in a vest and cloak of scarlet cloth, sat in *tête-à-tête* with a sedate and dignified personage, whose dress at once decla-red him to be of the religious profession and episcopal rank.

" Welcome, brave knights," said Sir Walter, rising to meet them as the Squire Usher an-nounced them; " welcome, brave knights. But, by St George," added he, with a jocular air, as he shook each of them cordially by the hand, " I should have weened that ye looked not to

be welcomed here, seeing ye could prefer bestowing yourselves in the paltry hostelry of the
village, rather than demanding from old Sir
Walter de Selby that hospitality never refused
by him to knights of good fame, such as thine.
But ye do see I can welcome, ay, and welcome
heartily too.—My Lord Bishop of Durham,
this is Sir Patrick Hepborne, and this, Sir
John Assueton, Scottish knights, of no mean
degree or renown." Sir Walter then made
them acquainted with the chief personages of
the company, some of whom were knights, and
some churchmen of high rank.

After the usual compliments had passed, the
Scottish knights were shown to apartments,
where they unarmed, and were supplied with
fitting robes and vestments. Sir Patrick Hepborne was happy in the expectation of being
speedily introduced to the Lady Eleanore; but
on returning to the hall, he found that she had
not yet appeared, and he was mortified to hear
Sir Walter de Selby give immediate orders for
the banquet.

." These gallant knights," said he, " would,
if I mistake not, rather eat than talk, after a
long day's fast. We shall have enow of converse anon. Bring in,—bring in, I say." And
seating himself at the head of the table, he pla-

ced the Lord Bishop on his right hand, and the two stranger knights on his left, while the other personages took their places of themselves, according to their acknowledged rank. Immediately after them came a crowd of guests of lesser note, who filled up the table to the farther extremity.

The entertainment consisted of enormous joints of meat, and trenchers full of game and poultry, borne in by numerous lacqueys, who panted under the loads they carried; and the dishes were arranged by the sewer, whose office it was to do so.

When the solid part of the feast had been discussed, and the mutilated fragments removed, Sir Walter called for a mazer of malvoisie. The wine was brought him in a silver cup of no despicable manufacture, and he drank a health to the stranger knights; which was passed round successively to the Bishop and others, who sat at the upper end, and echoed from the lower part of the table by those who drank it in deep draughts of ale. Numerous pledges succeeded, with hearty carouse.

"Sir Walter," said Hepborne, taking advantage of a pause in the conversation, "the fame of thy peerless daughter the Lady Eleanore de Selby hath reached our ears: Shall our eyes not be blessed with the sight of so much beauty? May we not look to see thy board graced with her presence ere the night passeth away?"

"Nay, Sir Knight," replied Sir Walter, his countenance undergoing a remarkable change from gay to grave, "my daughter appeareth not to-night. But why is not the minstrel here?" exclaimed he aloud, as if wishing to get rid of Hepborne's farther questioning; "why is not Adam of Gordon introduced? Let him come in; I love the old man's music too well to leave him neglected. Yea, and of a truth, he doth to-night merit a double share of our regard, seeing that it is to him we do owe the honour of these distinguished Scottish guests. A chair for the minstrel, I say."

A chair was accordingly set in a conspicuous place near the end of the hall. Adam entered, with his harp hanging on his arm, and making an obeisance to the company, advanced towards the top of the table.

"Ay, ay, come away, old man; no music without wine; generous wine will breed new inspiration in thee: Here, drink," said Sir Walter, presenting him with the mantling cup.

The minstrel bowed, and drinking health to the good company, he quaffed it off. His tardy blood seemed quickened by the draught; he hastened to seat himself in the place appointed for him; and striking two or three chords to ascertain the state of his instrument, he proceeded to play several airs of a martial character.

"Come, come, good Adam, that is very well," said Sir Walter, as the harper paused to rest his fingers awhile—"so far thou hast done well; but my good wine must not all ooze out at the points of thy fingers in unmeaning sounds. Come, we must have it mount to thy brain, and fill thee with inspiration. Allons. Come, drink again, and let the contents of this cup evaporate from thee in verse. Here, bear this brimming goblet to him: And then, dost thou hear, some tale of hardy dints of arms; 'tis that we look for. Nay, fear not for my Lord Bishop; I wot he hath worn the cuirass ere now."

"Thou sayest truly, Sir Walter," said the Bishop, rearing himself up to his full height, as if gratified by the remark; "on these our Eastern Marches there are few who have not tasted of war, however peaceful may have been their profession; and I cannot say but I have done my part, thanks be to Him who hath given me strength and courage."

Adam quaffed off the contents of the cup that had been given him, and seizing his harp

again, he flourished a prelude, during which he
kept his eyes thrown upwards as if wrapt in
consideration of his subject, and then dashed
the chords from his fingers in a powerful ac-
companiment to the following verses :—

The Tourney of Noyon.

PROUD was the bearing of fair Noyon's chivalry,
Brave in the lists did her gallants appear;
Gay were their damosels, deck'd out in rivalry,
Breathing soft sighs from the balconies near.
       Each to her knight,
       His bright helm to dight,
Flung her love-knot, with vows for his prowess and might;
       And warm were the words
       Of their love-sick young lords,
Mingling sweet with the tender harp's heart-thrilling chords.

But long ere the trumpet's shrill clamour alarming
Told each stark chevalier to horse for the strife;
Ere yet their hot steeds, in their panoply arming,
Were led forth, their nostrils wide breathing with life;
       Ere the lists had been clear'd,
       The barve Knollis appear'd
With his heroes, the standards of England who rear'd :
       But nor billman nor bowman
       Came there as a foeman,
For peace had made friends of these stout English yeomen.

As afar o'er the meadows, with soldiers' gear laden,
They merrily march'd for their dear native land;
Their banners took sighs from full many a maiden,
And trembled, as love-lorn each waved her white hand.
       But see from the troops
       Where a warrior swoops,
From the speed of his courser his plume backward droops;
       'Tis a bold Scottish Knight,
       Whose JOY and delight
Is to joust it in sport—or at outrance to fight.

His steed at the barrier's limit he halted,
And toss'd to his Squire the rich gold-emboss'd rein;
Cased in steel as he was, o'er the high pales he vaulted,
And, bowing, cried, " Messieurs Chevaliers, pray deign
   To lend me an ear—
   Lo, I'm singly come here,
Since none of you dared against me to appear.
   One and all I defy,
   Nor fear I shall fly,
Win me then, if you can—for my knighthood I try."

Then a huge massive mace round his head quickly whirling,
He charged their bright phalanx with furious haste,
And some he laid prostrate, with heads sorely dirling,
And some round the barrier swiftly he chased.
   Where'er he attacked,
   The French knighthood backed,
Preux Chevalier le brave Jean de Roy he thwacked,
   Till his helmet rang well,
   Like the couvre-feu bell,—
By the Rood, but 'twas nearly his last passing knell.

Then Picardy's pride, Le Chevalier de Lorris,
He soon stretch'd on the sand in most pitiful case,
And he rain'd on the rest, till they all danced a morris
To the music he played on their mails with his mace.
   Till tired with his toil,
   He breathed him a while,
And bowing again, with a most courteous smile,
   " Adieu, Messieurs!" said he,
   " Je vous rend graces, Perdie!
For the noble diversion you've yielded to me."

Then some kind parting-blows round him willingly dealing,
That on breastplates, and corslets, and helmets clang'd loud,
Sending some ten or dozen to right and left reeling,
He soon clear'd his way through the terrified crowd.
   O'er the pales then he bounded
   As all stood confounded,
To the saddle he leap'd—and his horse's heels sounded
   As he spurr'd out of sight,
   Leaving proofs of his might,
That had marr'd the bold jousting of many a knight.

Loud applauses followed the minstrel's merry performance, and Sir Walter de Selby called Adam towards him, to reward him with another cup of wine.

" But thou hast not told us the name of thy mettlesome knight, old bard," said he.

Adam looked over his shoulder with a waggish smile, towards Sir John Assueton.

" 'Twas a certain Scottish knight," said he, " one whose heart was as easily wounded as his frame was invulnerable—one who was as remarkable for his devotion to the fair as for his prowess in the field. It was whispered at Noyon, that the feat was done to give jovisaunce to a pair of bright eyes which looked that day from the balcony."

" By St Andrew, but thou art out there, goodman harper," cried Assueton, caught in the trap so cunningly laid for him by the minstrel; " trust me thou wert never more out in thy life. My heart was then, as it is now, as sound, entire, firm, and hard as my cuirass. By'r Lady, I am not the man to be moved by a pair of eyes. No pair of eyes that ever lighted up a face could touch me; and as to that matter, a—a—" But observing a smile playing over the countenances of the guests, he recollccted that he had betrayed himself, and stopped in some confusion. The harper turned round to the host,—

"Sir Walter," said he, "there never sat within this hall two more doughty or puissant knights than these. Both did feats of valour abroad that made Europe ring again. Sir John Assueton was indeed the true hero of my verses. As to his love I did but jest, for I wot 'tis well known that he hath steeled himself against the passion, and hath never owned it. I but feigned, to draw him into a confession of the truth of my tale, the which his consummate modesty would else have never permitted him to avow."

Sir Walter called for a goblet of wine—

"To the health of the brave knight of Noyon!" cried he. "Well did we all know to whom the merry minstrel alluded."

The health was received with loud applause, and compliments came so thick upon Assueton, that he blushed to receive them.

"Load me not thus, courteous knights, load me not thus, I beseech you, with your applause for a silly frolic. Here sits one," said he, wishing to turn the tide from himself, and tapping Hepborne on the shoulder,—"here sits one, I say, who hath done feats of arms, compared to which, my boyish pranks are but as idle pastime. This is the Scottish knight, who, at the fight of Rosebarque, did twice recover the flag of France from the Flemings, and of whom the whole army admitted, that the success of that day belonged to the prowess of his single arm."

This speech of Assueton's had all the effect he desired. Sir Walter was well aware of the renown acquired by Hepborne upon that occasion, and there were even some at table who had witnessed his glorious feats of arms on that day. His modesty was now put to a severe trial in its turn, and goblets were quaffed in honour of him. He looked with a reproachful eye at his friend for having thus saved himself at his expense; and at last, to get rid of praises he felt to be oppressive, he signified to his host a wish to retire for the night. Accordingly the Squire Usher was called, and the two knights were shown to their apartments; soon after which the banquet broke up, leaving the Lord Bishop and Sir Walter in deep conference.

As Hepborne and Assueton passed up the narrow stair that led to the apartments appropriated to them, they were interrupted in their progress by a pair of limbs of unusual length, that were slowly descending. The confined and spiral nature of the stair kept the head and body belonging to them entirely out of view; and the

huge feet were almost in Hepborne's stomach
before he was aware. He called out, and the
limbs halting for an instant, seemed to receive
tardy instructions to retire from the invisible
head they were commanded by, which, judging
of the extent of the whole person by the parts
they saw, must have been, at that moment at
least, in the second story above them. The way
being at last cleared, the two friends climbed to
the passage leading to their apartments. Irresistible curiosity, however, induced them to lin-
ger for a moment on the landing-place to watch
the descent of a figure so extraordinary. It came
as if measured out by yards at a time. In the
right hand was a lamp, carried as high as the
roof of the stair would permit, to enable the
bearer to steer his head under it without injury,
and the light being thus thrown strongly upon
the face, displayed a set of features hardly human.

The complexion was deadly pale, the forehead
unusually low and broad, and the head was hung
round with lank tangles of black hair. A pair
of small fiery eyes smouldered, each within the
profound of a deep cavity on either side of the
nose, that, projecting a good inch or two nearly
in a right angle from the forehead, dropped a
perpendicular over the mouth almost conceal-

ing the central part of that orifice, in which it was assisted by the enormous length of chin thrust out in a curve from below. The cheek-bones were peculiarly enlarged, and the cheeks drawn lankly in; but the corners of the mouth, stretching far backwards, were preternaturally expanded, and, by a convulsive kind of twist, each was alternately opened wide, so that, in turn, they partially exhibited the tremendous grinders that filled the jaws. It is not to be supposed that Hepborne and Assueton could exactly note these particulars so circumstantially as we have done; but the uncouth figure moved with so much difficulty downwards, in a serpentine sort of course, that they had leisure to remark quite enough to fill them with amazement.

The apparition, clad in a close black jerkin and culottes, had no sooner wormed itself down, than both knights eagerly demanded of the Squire Usher who and what it was.

"'Tis Master Haggerstone Fenwick, the Ancient," replied he, with a mysterious air.

"Nay," said Assueton, " he surely is fitter for hoisting the broad banner of the Castle upon, than for carrying the colours in the field."

" Why, as to that, Sir Knight," said the Usher, " he might i'faith do well enough for the banner; and he would be always at hand too when wanted, seeing that he rarely or ever quitteth the top of the keep. He liveth in the small cap-room, where he must lig from corner to corner, to be able to stretch himself; yet there he sitteth night and day, reading books of the black art, and never leaveth it, except when he cometh down as now, driven by hunger, the which he will sometimes defy for a day or two, and then he descendeth upon the buttery, like a wolf from the mountains, and at one meal will devour theè as much provender as would victual the garrison for a day, and then mounteth he again to his den. He is thought to possess terrible powers; and strange sights and horrible spectres have been seen to dance about the battlements near his dwelling."

" Holy Virgin! and is all this believed by Sir Walter de Selby?" inquired Hepborne.

" Ay, truly," said the Usher gravely; " most seriously believed (as why should it not?) by him, and all in the Castle. But I beseech thee, Sir Knight, let us not talk so freely of him. Holy St Mary defend us! I wish he may not take offence at our stopping him in his way to his meal. Let us not talk more of him. I bid thee good night."

" But tell me ere thou goest why we saw not

that star of female beauty, the Lady Eleanore de Selby at the banquet this evening?" demanded Hepborne.

"'Tis a fancy of her father's, Sir Knight," replied the Squire Usher, smiling; "and if it may not offend thee, 'tis because he willeth not that the lady may marry her with a Scottish chevalier, that he ever doth forbid her entrance when any of thy nation are feasted in his hall."

"It irketh me to think that we should have caused her banishment," said Hepborne. "What, is she always wont to keep her chamber on like occasions?"

"Yea," replied the Squire Usher, "ever save when the evening air is so bland as to suffer her to breathe it upon the rampart. She is often wont to listen to the minstrel's notes there.— But there are your chambers, Sirs Knights. The squires of your own bodies will be with you in the morning. Sir Walter hath issued orders for the admission of your retinue into the Castle, and he hopes you will sojourn with him as long as your affairs may give you sufferance. Good night, and may St Andrew be with you."

The two friends separated, and quickly laid themselves down to repose. The hardy and heart-whole Assueton slept soundly under the

protection of his national saint, to whom he
failed not to recommend himself, as a security
against the incantations of the wizard. Nor
did Sir Patrick Hepborne neglect to do the
same; for these were times when the strongest
minds were subject to such superstitions. But
his thoughts soon wandered to a more agreeable subject. He recalled the lovely face he
had seen, and he sighed to think that he had
not been blessed with a somewhat less transi-
tory glance of features, which he would have
wished to imprint for ever upon his mind.

" Why should her father thus banish her from
the eyes of all Scotchmen? By the Rood, but
it can and must be only from the paltry fear of
his wealth going to fatten our northern soil.
But I can tell him, that there be Scots who
would cheerfully take her for her individual
merit alone, and leave her dross to those sordid
minds who covet it."

Such was Sir Patrick's soliloquy, and imper-
fect as his view of the lady had been, it was
sufficient to conjure up a vision that hovered
over his pillow, and disturbed his rest, in defiance of the good St Andrew. Having lain
some time awake, he heard the laborious ascent
of the Ancient Fenwick to his dwelling in the

clouds; but fatigue at length vanquished his restlessness, and he had been for some hours ·in a deep sleep, ere another and a much lighter· footstep passed up in the same direction.

CHAPTER V.

THE Ancient Fenwick was sitting drawn together into a farther corner of his den. His
everlasting lamp was raised on a pile of manu-
script volumes near him, that it might throw
more light on a large parchment roll that lay
unfolded on the floor before him. His right
elbow rested on the ground, and the enormous
fingers of his hand embraced and supported his
head; while his eyes, burning without meaning,
like two small red fragments of ignited charcoal, could have been supposed to be occupied
with the characters before them, only from the
position of his face, which was so much turned
down that the tangled hair, usually drooping
from behind, was thrown forwards over his
ears. He was so absorbed, that he heard not
the soft barefooted tread of the step on the stair,
or as it approached his den along the vaulted
roof of the keep. .

The person who came thus to have midnight
converse with him, stooped his head and body

to enter the low and narrow doorway, and
halted with his head thrust forward within it
to contemplate the object he was about to address.

" Ancient Fenwick," said he, after a pause
of some moments.

Fenwick started at the sound of the voice, and
looked towards the little doorway. A pair of
keen eyes glared upon him from beneath a dark
cowl; and, plunged as he had been in the mys-
teries of conjuration, it is not wonderful that he
should have believed that the Devil himself had
appeared to further his studies.

" Avaunt thee, Sathanas !" exclaimed he,
speaking with the alternate sides of his mouth,
and drawing himself yet more up into the corner—" I say unto thee, Sathanas, avaunt !"

" What !" said the figure, creeping into the
place, and seating himself on the floor opposite
to him, " what ! Master Ancient Fenwick, dost
thou wish to conjure up the Devil, and yet art
afraid to look on him ? I weened that thou had'st
been a man of more courage than to be afraid of
a friar coming to thee at midnight."

Fenwick made an exertion to compose himself, seeing his visitor bore all the externals of a
mortal about him.

" And what dost thou see in me," said he, in

his usual harsh, discordant, and sepulchral ut_
terance, " that may lead thee to think different_
ly ?"

" Umph, why, nothing—nothing now," said
the monk, bending his brows, and throwing a
penetrating glance from under them into the
Ancient's face ; " nothing now, but methought,
for a conjuror, thou wert rather taken unawares."

" And who art thou, who thus darest to disturb my privacy ?" demanded Fenwick, somewhat sternly, and advancing his body at the
same time, from the more than ordinarily con-
strained attitude he had assumed.

The monk drew up his lips so as to display a
set of long, white teeth, and raising his eyelids so
as to show the white of his eye-balls, he glared
at the Ancient for some time, and then slowly
pronounced in a deep voice, " The Devil ! what
wouldst thou with me now ?"

In a paroxysm of terror, Fenwick again drew
himself up in his corner, with a force as if he
would have pressed himself through the very
wall ; his teeth chattered in his head, and he
sputtered so vehemently with the alternate corners of his mouth, that his words were unintelligible, except that of " Sathanas," frequently
repeated.   The monk relaxed his features, and

with a laugh, and a look of the most sovereign contempt—

"So," said he, "thou must confess now that I proved thy courage to be in my power. I banished it with a look and a word. But 'tis not with thy courage I have to do at present; 'tis thy cunning I want."

"Art thou then verily no devil?" demanded the Ancient, doubtingly.

"Tush, fool, I am a poor monk of the order of St Francis; so calm thy craven fears and listen to me." He paused for some moments, to give Fenwick time to recollect himself, and when he saw that the latter had in some degree regained his composure: "Now listen to me, I say. Thou knowest doubtless that the Bishop of Durham came to Norham Castle this morning?" He waited for a reply.

"I did hear so," answered the Ancient, "when I went down to take food."

"Knowest thou what he came about?" demanded the Franciscan.

"I know not, I inquired not," replied the Ancient.

"Then I will tell thee," proceeded the Franciscan.—"Sir Rafe Piersic, brother to the noble Hotspur, has stooped to fix his affection on the Lady Eleanore de Selby; he has deigned to

court her for his bride, and has met with ready
acceptance from her father. Not sufficiently sensible of this his great condescension, the lady
has treated his high offer with neglect,—with
indifference. Her father, a weak man, though
eager for so splendid an alliance, hath allowed
himself to be trifled with by the silly girl, who
hath done all she could to oppose it, though to
the sacrifice of her own happiness. But Sir
Rafe Piersic, being too much love-stricken,
abandoneth not the demoiselle so easily. He
therefore availeth himself of his ally the Bishop of Durham, to urge, through him, his suit
with the lady, and to endeavour to stir up Sir
Walter to a more determined bearing with his
daughter, should she continue in her obstinacy. I shall not tell how I know, yet I do
know, that the lady treated the proposals of the
Bishop, as well as the name and person of the
renowned Piersie, with contempt. His efforts
to rouse Sir Walter de Selby to the assertion
of his rights as a father, have, however, been
more successful. The old man, who passionate-
ly desireth great connexion, even became irri-
tated against her obstinacy. But Sir Rafe Piersie, wisely considering that a peaceful religious
pastor was not the fittest instrument for his purpose, judgeth it right to put other hotter and
more efficient irons in the work. Unknown to

the Bishop, and unknown to every one, therefore, he hath deputed me to seek thee and to
urge thee to aid his plans.   Now, Master Ancient Fenwick, thou hast the whole intricacies
of the affair; thou understandest me, dost thou
not?"

The Franciscan paused for a reply, and tried
to read the face of him he was addressing; but
it was in vain he tried it, for, except when very
strongly excited by the passion of fear, or something equally forcible, the features of the Ancient were at all times illegible. After twisting
and smacking the alternate corners of his mouth,
which was always his prelude to speaking, and
which even his actual utterance did not always
go much beyond,—

" Well," said he, " and what can I do in this
matter?—What can magic do in it?"

" Magic!" exclaimed the Franciscan; " pshaw,
fool that thou art, thinkest thou that thou can'st
impose upon me as thou dost on the common
herd of mankind?—on one who hath dived into
the arcana of nature as I have done?—Thinkest thou that an active mind like mine hath not
searched through all the books of these divinals,
—hath not toiled by the midnight lamp, and
worked with their uncouth and horrible charms
and incantations?—Thinkest thou——"

- " Hast thou so, brother ?" exclaimed the Ancient, eagerly interrupting . him ; " hast thou in truth studied so deeply?" Then throwing his body earnestly forward,. " Perhaps thou wilt clear up some small difficulties that have arisen in my path towards perfection in the invaluable art."

The Franciscan paused. He saw at once that he had so far mistaken his man. The Ancient, whilst engaged in deceiving others, had also succeeded in deceiving himself, and was in truth a believer in the art he professed. To undertake the barren task of convincing him of his error, was foreign to the Franciscan's present purpose; and seeing that Fenwick, in his eagerness for an accession to his knowledge of magic, had mistaken the contemptuous expressions he had thrown out against it for the approbation and eulogy of an adept, he deemed it best to permit him to continue in his mistake, nay rather to foster it. He therefore commenced a long and very mystical disquisition on necromancy, answering all his questions, and solving all his doubts, but in such a manner, that although Fenwick, at the moment, firmly believed they were solved, yet, when he afterwards came to look back into his mind, he could find nothing there but a vast chaos of smoke and ashes, from which he in vain tried to extract anything tangible or systematic.

But this is not to our point. The Franciscan gained all he wanted, in acquiring a certain ascendancy over his mind by pretended superiority of knowledge,—an ascendency which he afterwards hoped to bring to bear towards the object of his mission; and to this object he gradually led the Ancient back from the wide waste of enchantment he had been wandering over.

" Thou art indeed much more learned in the sublime art than I did at first suppose thee," said the Franciscan at length, gravely; " thy study hath been well directed; and now that I have poured the mere drop of knowledge I possessed into the vast ocean flowing in thy capacions head, thou art well fit to be my master. Some of those ingredients I talked of are of high price; thou must buy them with gold."

" Ah!" exclaimed Fenwick, " but where shall I find gold to buy them withal?"

The Franciscan groped in the canvass pouch that hung at his girdle of ropes, and drawing forth a leathern bag, with a weight of broad gold pieces in it, he threw it down on the floor between the Ancient's knees.

" There !" said he; " Sir Rafe Piersic sends thee that; 'tis to secure thee as his friend. Use

thine art magic in his favour, to incline the
haughty damosel to his wishes. Thou may'st
do much with her father. 'Tis well known that
the old Knight looketh with awe upon thy
powers. Thou art thyself aware, that thou
canst bend him as thou wilt; he doth hold thee
as his oracle. Work upon his fears, then; work
upon him, I say, to compel this marriage,—
a marriage, the which is so well calculated to
gratify his desire of high family alliance. He
is ignorant that thou knowest of the negotia-
tion; to find that thou dost, when he supposes
that it is only known to the chief parties, will
increase his veneration for thy skill. Exert
thy power over him; he is weak, and thou
may'st easily make him thy slave. Stimulate
him to firmness, to severity, nay, if necessary,
to harshness, with his daughter. Thou knowest 'tis for his happiness, as well as for the
happiness of the silly damosel, that she should
be coarcted. Then do thy best to screw him
up to that pitch of determination that may secure her yielding. I leave it to thyself to find
out what schemes and arguments thou must
employ. The world lies if thou canst not in-
vent enow to make him do as thou would'st
have. Remember, the Piersie is thy friend, as
thou may'st do him proper service. There are

more bags of broad pieces in the same treasury that came from. And now I leave thee to the hatching of thy plans. Let them be quickly concerted and speedily put in execution, for your Piersie never was famous for patience. Farewell, and may powerful spirits aid thee!"

The Franciscan gathered up his grey gown, drew his cowl over his face, and creeping on hands and knees to the door, disappeared in a moment.

The Ancient remained for some minutes in a state of stupid astonishment, with his back against his corner, and his vast length of limbs stretched across the floor. He almost doubted the reality of the vision that had appeared to him. He drew up his knees to his mouth, and the leathern bag appeared. He thought of the Devil as he seized it; and as he poured the glittering gold into his broad palm, he almost expected to see the pieces change into dried leaves, cinders, slates, or some such rubbish. Twice or thrice the thought recurred that it might have been the Great Tempter himself who had visited him. The hour—the place—the difficulty of anything mortal reaching him there, through all the intricacies of a well-watched garrison—the great knowledge displayed by the unknown —all contributed to support the idea that his

visitor was something more than man. Then,
on the other hand, he remembered the friar's
bare feet, that were certainly human. He again
looked at the broad pieces of gold; they were
bright, and fresh, and heavy as he poised them.
His confidence that they were genuine became
stronger, and he slipped them into the bag, and
the bag into an inner pocket of his black jerkin,
resolving that they should be the test of the reality of the seeming friar.

The Ancient had been for many years plunged
in the study of necromancy. His uncouth appearance, and awkward ungainly port, rendered
him so unfit for the gay parade of war, that Sir
Walter de Selby had more than once refused
him that promotion to which he was entitled in
the natural course of things, and of which he
had been very ambitious. This rankled at his
heart, and made him shun his fellows, slight the
profession of arms, and take to those studies
that, in so superstitious a period, met with the
readiest belief and reverence, and from which he
hoped to discover the means of gratifying both
his ambition and his avarice. His necromantic
fame, increased by tales hatched or embellished
by the fertile imaginations of weak and superstitious minds, rapidly grew among all ranks;
and Sir Walter de Selby was as firm a believer

in his powers as the meanest soldier under his command. He readily excused the Ancient from all duty; so that, being thus left to the full and undisturbed possession of the solitary cap-house he had himself selected for his habitation, he became so immersed in his work that he rarely left it, except when driven by hunger to seek food. Living so entirely secluded as he did, it is not to be wondered at that he had hardly seen a female face. As for the Lady Eleanore, he had never beheld her since her childhood, until a few days previous to the time we are now speaking of, when, having been led by some extraordinary accident beyond the walls of the keep, he had met her by chance in the court-yard; and the young lady was so alarmed by the appearance of the strange monster, who blocked up her way to the bridge, and stood surveying her with his horrible eyes, that she fled from him precipitately. It must be admitted, then, that he was but little calculated to produce any favourable change on her mind in behalf of Sir Rafe Piersie, unless indeed it were by the art magic. With that brave old soldier of fortune, Sir Walter de Selby, he was much more likely to be successful, since the chief wish of his heart was, that his daughter and his wealth should be the means of allying him with some family eminent for the grandeur of its name, as well as for its power and influence. It was a grievous disappointment to him that he had had no son; but as he had been denied this blessing, he now looked forward to having a grandson, who might give him good cause to be proud, from the high rank he would be entitled to hold in the splendid galaxy of English chivalry. He was far from being without affection for his daughter; yet his affection was in a great measure bottomed upon these his most earnest wishes and hopes; and of all this the Ancient Mr Haggerstone Fenwick was very sufficiently aware.

CHAPTER VI.

WHEN Sir Patrick Hepborne and Sir John Assueton arose in the morning, they found their own squires and lacqueys in attendance. The busy note of preparation was in the Castle-yard, and they were told that the Bishop of Durham was just taking his departure.

The mitred ecclesiastic went off on an ambling jennet, accompanied by the knights and churchmen who had come with him, and followed by a long cavalcade of richly-attired attendants; and he was saluted by the garrison drawn up in array, and by the guards, as he passed outwards. He was, moreover, attended by Sir Walter and his principal officers, who rode half a day's journey with him. The two friends were thus left to entertain themselves until the evening. Assuetou occupied himself in studying the defences of the place, whilst Hepborne loitered about the exterior of the keep, and the walls commanding a view of its

various sides, in the hope of being again blessed
with a sight of the Lady Eleanore.

As he was surveying the huge mass of masonry, so intently that a bystander might have
supposed he was taking account of the number
of stones it was composed of, the lady appeared
at one of the high windows on the side facing
the Tweed. The knight had his eyes turned in
a different direction at the moment, so that she
had a full and undisturbed view of him, as he
stood nearly opposite to her on the rampart, for
some time ere he perceived her. He turned suddenly round, and she instantly withdrew; but
not before he had enjoyed another transient
glimpse of that face, which had already created
so strong a sensation in his breast.

" Provoking !" thought Hepborne; " yet
doth the very modesty of this angelic lady lead
me the more to admire her.—Unbending spirit, said that knave at the hostel? She is as
gentle as the dove. Would I could behold her
again."

Sir Patrick stepped back upon the rampart
so as to have a better view inwards, and he was
gratified by observing that her figure was still
within the deep window, though her face was
obscured by its shade. He recognized the rose-
coloured mantle she had formerly appeared in.

He kissed his hand, and bowed. He saw her alabaster arm relieve itself from the mantle, and beheld the falcon he had rescued seated on her glove. She stepped forward in such a manner to return his salute, that he enjoyed a sufficient view of her face to make him certain that he was not mistaken in the person. The lady pointed with a smile to her falcon, kissed it, waived an acknowledgment of his courtesy, and again retreating, disappeared.

As Sir Patrick was standing vainly hoping for her reappearance, the old minstrel, Adam of Gordon, chanced to come by. Hepborne saluted him courteously.

" Canst thou tell me whose be those apartments that do look so cheerily over the Tweed into Scotland?" demanded he.

" Ay," said the old man, " 'tis, as thou sayest, a cheering prospect; 'tis the country of my birth, and the country of my heart; I love it as lover never loved mistress."

" But whose apartments be those ?" demanded Hepborne, bringing him back to the question.

" Those are the apartments of the Lady Eleanore de Selby," replied the minstrel.

" Is it thy custom to play thy minstrelsy under the moonlight on the rampart, as thou didst yestere'en?" demanded Hepborne.

"Yea, I have pleasure in it," said Adam, with a shrewd look.

"And art thou always so attended?" demanded Hepborne; "is thy music always wont to call that angel to thy side whom I last night beheld there?"

"So thou dost think her an angel, Sir Knight?" cried Adam, with pleasure glancing in his eyes.

"I do," said Sir Patrick. "Already hath my heart been wounded by the mere momentary glances to which chance hath subjected me, and eagerly do I look for a cure from those eyes whence my hurt hath come. She is beautiful."

"Yea," said old Adam, "and she is an angel in soul as well as in form.—But St Andrew keep thee, Sir Knight, I must be gone;" and he hurried away without giving Hepborne time to reply.

Assuetou now came up, and Sir Patrick detailed to him the occurrences we have just narrated, after which he walked about, looking every now and then impatiently towards the window.

"Would I could have but one more sight of the Lady Eleanore," cried he; "her features

D 2

have alréady become faint in my mind's eye;
would I might refresh the picture by one other
gaze." But the lady appeared not; and he became vexed, and even fretful, notwithstanding
all his resolution to the contrary.

"Hepborne, my friend," said Sir John Assueton, "why should'st thou afflict thyself, and
peak and pine for a silly girl? A knight of thy
prowess in the field may have a thousand baubles as fair for the mere picking up; let it not
irk thee that this trifle is beyond thy reach.
Trust me, women are dangerous flowers to
pluck, and have less of the rose about them
than of the thorn."

"Pshaw!" replied Hepborne, "thou knowest not what it is to love."

"No, thank my good stars," answered Assueton, "I do not, and I hope I shall never be
so besotted; it makes a very fool of a man.
There, for instance, thou art raving about a
damosel, of whose face thou hast seen so little
that wert thou to meet her elsewhere thou
could'st never tell her from another."

"It is indeed true, Assueton," replied Hepborne, "that I have seen but too little of her
face; but I have seen enough of it to know that
it is the face of an angel."

In such converse as this did they spend the

day until the evening's banquet. Then Sir Walter exhibited the same hospitality towards his guests that had characterized him the night before; but he seemed to be less in spirits, nay, he was sometimes peevish. Hepborne, too, being restless and unhappy, mirth and hilarity were altogether less prevalent at the upper end of the festal board than they had been the previous evening. The minstrel, however, was not forgotten, and was treated with the same personal attention as formerly; but he sang and played without eliciting more than an ordinary meed of applause. At last he struck some peculiarly powerful chords on the instrument, and as Hepborne turned his head towards him, in common with others, at the sound, old Adam caught his eye, and looking significantly, began to pour forth the following irregular and unpremeditated verse :

'Twas thus that a minstrel address'd a young knight,
Who was love-lorn, despairing, and wan with despite,
What, Sir Knight, canst thou gain by these heart-rending sighs ?
The hero ne'er pines, but his destiny tries,
And pushes his fate with his lance in the rest,
Whether love or renown be his glorious quest.
    Let not those who droop for Love,
    Fly in grief to wild Despair,
    She, wither'd witch, can ne'er remove
    The cruel unkindness of the fair.
        Then with the gladd'ning ray
        Of Hope's bright star to cheer thee,

Do thou still press thy way,
Nor let obstructions fear thee.
True Love will even bear
A hasty moment's slighting,
And boldly will it dare,
Nor ever fear benighting.
'Twill often and again
Return, though ill entreated ;
'Twill blaze beneath the rain ;
Though frozen, 'twill be heated.
When least thy thoughts are turn'd on joy,
The smiling bliss is nigh ;
No happiness without alloy
Beneath the radiant sky.
But haste to-night, to meet thy love
Upon the Castle-wall ;
Thou know'st not what thy heart may prove,
What joy may thee befall.

These seemingly unmeaning verses passed
unnoticed by all at table except by Hepborne,
on whom they made a strong impression. He
was particularly struck by the concluding stan-
za, containing an invitation which he could not
help believing was meant to apply to himself.
He resolved to visit the ramparts as soon as he
could escape from the banquet. This he found
it no very difficult matter to accomplish, for Sir
Walter was abstracted, and evidently depressed
with something that weighed on his spirits; so,
taking advantage of this circumstance, Hepborne rose to retire at an early hour. His
friend followed him, and when left to the se-
cresy of their own apartments,—

"Assueton," said Sir Patrick, "didst thou remark the glance, full of meaning, which the minstrel threw on me to-night? or didst thou note the purport of his ditty?"

"As for his glances," replied Sir John, "I noticed nothing particular in them; your bards are in use to throw such around them, to collect their barren harvest of paltry praise; and as for his verses, or rather his rhymes, I thought them silly enow in conscience. But thou knowest I do rarely listen when love or its follies are the theme."

"But I saw, and I listened," replied Hepborne. "By St Denis, they carried hints to me that I shall not neglect. I go to take the air on the ramparts, and hope to meet the angelic Eleanore de Selby there."

"Art thou mad?" said Assueton: "What can old Adam have looked or said that can induce thee to go on such a fool's errand? Thou hast but fancied; thy blind passion hath deceived thee."

"I shall at least put his fancied hints to the proof," said Hepborne, "though I should watch all night."

"Then I wish thee a pleasant moonlight promenade," said Assueton. "I'll to my couch. To-morrow, I presume, we shall cross the Tweed;

and yede us into Scotland. By St Andrew, I would gladly meet again with those well-known faces whose smiles once reflected the happiness of my boyhood!"

" Go to-morrow!" exclaimed Hepborne, as if their so speedy departure was far from being agreeable in the contemplation; " surely thou wilt stay, Assueton, if thou seest that thy so doing may further my happiness ?"

" Nay," replied Assueton, " thou need'st hardly fear that I will scruple to sacrifice my own wishes to thy happiness, Hepborne; but I confess I would that thy happiness depended on some more stirring cause, and one in which we both could join."

Here the friends parted. Hepborne, wrapped up in a cloak, stole gently down stairs, and slipping unperceived from the keep, bent his steps towards that part of the ramparts where he had formerly seen the lady. To his inexpressible joy, he saw the minstrel already on the spot. There were two ladies in company with the old man. As Sir Patrick passed near the base of the tower under which he and his friend had concealed themselves the night before, a huge figure began to rear itself from under it, throwing a shadow half-way across the court-yard. It looked as if the tower itself were in motion.

He stood undaunted to observe it, as it gradually arose story over story.   It was the Ancient Fenwick. His enormous face looked downwards upon Hepborne, and his red cinder-like
eyes glared upon him as he sputtered out some
unintelligible sounds from the corners of his
mouth, and then moved away like a walking
monument.

Whilst Hepborne's attention was occupied in
observing the retreat of the monster, who seemed to have secreted himself there for no good
purpose, the minstrel, and the two ladies who
were with him, had already walked down the
rampart until they were lost within the shade of
a projecting building. He began to fear that they
were gone, but he soon saw one of them, whom
he believed to be the attendant, emerge from the
shadow and retire by a short way to the keep,
whilst the other returned along the wall with
the minstrel. As they stopped to converse, the
lady leaned on one of the engines of war.   A
breeze from the Tweed threw back the hood
of her mantle, and Hepborne could no longer
doubt it was the Lady Eleanore de Selby he
saw: Her long and beautiful hair streamed
down, but she hastily arranged it with her fingers, and then came onwards with Adam of
Gordon.   Sir Patrick flew to the rampart and

sprung on the wall. The lady was alarmed at
first by his sudden appearance, but perceiving
immediately that it was Sir Patrick Hepborne,
she received him graciously yet modestly.

"The soft and perfumed air of this beauteous
night," said Hepburne, "and yonder lovely
moon, lady, tempted me forth awhile; but what
bliss is mine that I should thus meet with her,
who in softness, sweetness, and beauty, doth
excel the Queen of Night herself!"

"Sir Patrick Hepborne, thou art at thy fustian again," replied the lady seriously. "This
high-flown phrase of thine, palatable though
it might be to the pampered ears of Parisian
dames, sorteth ill with plainness such as mine.
Meseems," continued she somewhat more play-
fully, "meseems as if the moon were thy favourite theme. Pray Heaven that head may
be right furnished, the which hath the unstable
planet so often at work within it."

"And if I am mad, as thy words would im-
ply," said Hepborne, smiling, "'tis thou, lady,
who must answer for my frenzy; for since I
first saw thee last night, I have thought and
dreamt of thee alone."

"Sir Knight," said the lady, blushing, "methinks it savours of a more constitutional mad-

ness to be so affected by so short a meeting. We were but some few minutes together, if I err not."

" Ay, lady," said Adam of Gordon, significantly; " but love will work miracles like this."

" 'Tis indeed true," said the lady, with a sigh; and then, as if recollecting herself, she added, " I have indeed heard of such sudden affections."

" Ay," said Sir Patrick, " and that fair falcon of thine! Depardieux, I begin to believe that he was Cupid himself in disguise, for ever sith I gave the traitor lodgment in my bosom, it hath been affected with the sweet torment the urchin Love is wont to inflict. My heart's disease began with thy hawk's ensayning."

" Nay, then, much as I love him," said the lady, " yet should I hardly have purchased his health, I ween, at the price of that of the gallant knight who did so feelingly redeem it."

" Heaven's blessings on thee for thy charity, lady," exclaimed Hepborne; " yet should I rejoice in my disease were it to awaken thy sympathy, so that thou mightest yield me the healing leechcraft that beameth from those eyes."

" Verily, my youth doth lack experience in all such healing skill," said the lady.

" Nay, 'tis a mystery most easily learned by

the young," replied Hepborne. "Thou dost possess the power to assuage, if not to heal, my wound," added he tenderly. "Let me but be enlisted among the humblest of the captives whom thine eyes hath made subject to thy will; and albeit thy heart may be already given to another, spurn not the adoration of one whose sole wish is to live within the sphere of thy cheering influence, and to die in thy defence."

"In truth, Sir Knight, these eyes have been guiltless of any such tyranny as thou would'st charge them withal," replied the lady artlessly; "at least they have never wilfully so tyrannized. As for my heart, it hath never known warmer feeling than that which doth bind me to him to whom I owe the duty of a daughter."

"Then is thy heart unenthralled," cried Hepborne in an ecstasy, in the transport of which he threw himself on one knee before her who had produced it. "Refuse not, then, to accept my services as thy true and faithful knight. All I ask is, but to be allowed to devote my lance to thy service. Reject not these my vows. Cheer me with but one ray of hope, to nerve this arm to the doing of deeds worthy of the knight who calleth himself thy slave. I swear——"

"Swear not too rashly, Sir Knight," said

the lady, with a deep sigh, and with more of seriousness than she had yet displayed, " to one such as me, to one so obscure——"

" Obscure, lady !" cried Hepborne, interrupting her : " Hath not high Heaven stamped thee with that celestial face and form to place thee far above all reckonings of paltry pedigree ? What, then, is that obscurity which may have dimmed the birth of so fair a star ?   What—"

" Nay," said the lady, interrupting him with an air of uncommon dignity and animation, " obscure though mine origin may be, Sir Patrick, yet do I feel within me that which doth tell me that I might match with princes."

" Lady, I well know thy high and justly-grounded pretensions," said Hepborne, in a subdued tone ; " yet scorn not mine humble devotion."

" I scorn thee not, Sir Knight," said the lady, with combined modesty and feeling, and again sighing deeply ; " it would indeed ill become me to scorn any one, far less such as thee ; nor is my heart insensible to the courtesy thou hast been pleased to show to one who——"

" Thanks, thanks, most peerless of thy sex," cried Hepburne, gazing with ecstasy in her face, that burned with blushes even under the cold light of the moon.

" But in truth it beseemeth me not to stand talking idly with thee thus, Sir Knight," said the lady, suddenly breaking off; " I must hie me to my chamber."

" Oh, stay, sweet lady, stay—one moment stay!" cried Hepborne; " rob me not of thy presence until thou hast left me the cheering prospect of meeting thee to-morrow."

" I hope Sir Walter hath induced thee and thy friend to tarry some longer space in Norham; if so, it will pleasure me to meet thee again," said the lady, with a trembling voice.

" Then trust me I go not from Norham, betide me what may," cried Sir Patrick, energetically. " But tell me, lady, I entreat thee, when these eyes may be again blest with thy presence; give me hope, the which is now the food I feed on."

" Nay, in sooth, I can enter into no arrangements," said the lady, with yet greater agitation; " but," said she, starting away, " I have tarried here too long; in truth, Sir Patrick Hepborne, I must be gone; may the Holy Virgin be with thee, Sir Knight!"

" And may thou be guarded by kindred spirits like thyself!" cried Sir Patrick, earnestly clasping his hands, and following her with his eyes as she hastily retreated with old Adam.

Sir Patrick took several turns on the walls, giving way to the rapture which this meeting had occasioned him, and then hastened to regain his apartment, where he laid himself down, not to repose, but to muse on the events of the evening.

"The minstrel was right," thought he; "the good Adam's prophecy did not deceive me. She admitted that her heart was free, and she confessed, as far as maiden modesty might permit her, that she is not altogether without an interest in me. She was pleased with the idea of our farther stay at Norham; and in her confusion she betrayed, that to meet me again would give her pleasure. And she shall meet me again —ay, and again; mine excellent Assueton's patience must e'en bear some days' longer trial, for go, at least, I shall not. Days, did I say? ha! but let events determine." With such happy reflections, and yielding to a train of the most pleasing anticipation, he amused himself till he fell asleep.

CHAPTER VII.

It was past the hour of midnight, when all in the Castle had been for some time still, save when the sentinels on the ramparts repeated their prolonged call, that a footstep was again heard upon the stair leading to the top of the keep. It was the heavy slow step of Sir Walter de Selby. He carried a lamp in his hand, and often stopped to breathe; but at last he made his way to the roof, and sought the aerial den of the monstrous Ancient. He went thither, deluded man, imagining that he went of his own free will; but the crafty Ancient had taken secret measures to insure his coming.

When the good old knight had sought the little private oratory within his chamber, immediately after his attendants had retired, he was fearfully dismayed by observing a blue lambent light flitting over the surface of an ancient shield that hung above a small altar within a dark Gothic recess. In that age of igno-

rance, a circumstance so unaccountable might
have shaken the firmest nerves; but it had been
the shield of his father, a bold moss-trooper,
and from him he had learned, that this was the
ill-omened warning sign that was always said
to appear to foretell some dire calamity affecting him or his issue. With extreme agitation
of mind, he at once recurred to recent events
for an explanation of it. During his ride with
the Bishop of Durham, that prelate had repeated the arguments he had employed the day before, particularly in the long conference they
had held after the banquet, to fortify him in
the resolution of pressing the Lady Eleanore
into a marriage with Sir Rafe Piersic; and, indeed, Sir Walter's heart was so eagerly set on
the accomplishment of a union, in every respect equal to his most sanguine wishes, that
little eloquence was necessary to convince him
of the propriety of urging his daughter to it
by every means in his power. Nay, although
she was his only child, and that he so doted on
her as to have got into a habit of yielding to
every wish she expressed, yet this was a point
on which he was very easily brought to adopt a
determined line of conduct with her. She had
somewhat provoked him, too, by the licence she
had given her tongue in presence of the Bishop,

when she indulged herself in ridiculing the very
august person he was proposing to her as a husband; and the knight's passion at the moment
had so far got the better of his affection, that
he spoke to her with a degree of harshness he
had never used before. His after conversations
with the Bishop had now brought him to the
determination of compelling the Lady Eleanor
to a marriage, so much to her advantage, and
so flattering to his own hopes of high alliance.
So firmly was he fixed in this resolution, that
in a meeting he had with his daughter, after
his return from accompanying the Bishop, he
withstood all her entreaties, and steeled himself against all her grief, and all her spirited
remonstrances. After such an interview, it is
not surprising that Sir Walter should have immediately supposed, that the menacing prodigy
which now appeared before his eyes, had some
reference to the purposed marriage of the Lady
Eleanore. On all similar occasions of threatened misfortune, he had been for some years accustomed to apply for counsel to the cunning
Ancient Fenwick, whom he believed to possess
supernatural powers of foretelling and avert-
ing the greatest calamities; nay, he had more
than once been convinced of the happy effects
of his interference in his behalf. His impa-

tience to seek him at present, therefore, was
such, that he could hardly restrain himself until he had reason to think that all eyes in the
Castle were closed but his own. He paced his
chamber in a state bordering on distraction,
stopping from time to time at the door of the
oratory to regard the terrific warning, and
wringing his hands as he beheld it still flitting
and playing over the surface of the shield.

He was no sooner certain, however, that he
might move from his apartment without risk of
observation, than he seized his lamp, and, as we
have seen, sought the lonely cap-house of the
Ancient. The small door of the place was closed. So strongly were men's minds bound by
the thraldom of superstition in those days, that
the gallant Sir Walter de Selby, who had so
often faced the foe like a lion in the field, and
who would even now have defended the Castle
of Norham to the uttermost extremity, yea, so
long as one stone of its walls remained upon
another,—this brave old warrior, I say, absolutely trembled as he tapped at the door of
the wretched Ancient Haggerstone Fenwick,
who once formed his most common subject of
jest. He tapped, but no answer was returned;
he listened, but not a sound was heard. He
tapped again—and again he tapped louder. He

called the Ancient by his name; but still all was profound silence. He hesitated for some moments, in doubt what to do. At last he brought himself to the determination of pushing the door up. He bent down on his knees to force it, and it yielded before his exertions; but the sight which met his eyes so appalled him, that he was unable at first to advance.

The Ancient Fenwick, to all appearance dead, lay stretched, with his arms and legs extended on the floor. His face had the leaden hue of death on it; and a small orb, composed of a number of points of bluish lambent flame, like that so ominously illuminating the shield, flitted on his forehead—a book of necromancy lay open on the floor—his lamp burned on the usual pile of volumes—and on a temporary altar, composed of several folios, raised one above the other against the wall, were placed a human skull, and thigh bones, and an hour-glass. Immediately over these, a number of cabalistical figures were described with charcoal on the plaster; and a white rod seemed, from the position it lay in, to have been pointed towards them, and to have fallen from his hand, as if he had been suddenly struck down in the very act of conjuration.

Sir Walter was so overpowered with horror

and superstitious fear, that some moments elapsed ere he could summon up resolution to creep into the place and examine the body more narrowly. He looked down on the hideous ghastly face, over which the magical flame still flitted. The small fiery eye-balls glared—but they were still; not a feature moved, nor was there the slightest sound or appearance of respiration. Scarcely bearing to behold such a spectacle, the old knight looked. timorously around him, afraid that the demon, who had done this fearful work upon his disciple, might appear to annihilate him also. In truth, his terrors so far overcame him, that he was just about to retreat hastily, when he observed a certain spasmodic twitch about the mouth, which soon afterwards became powerfully convulsed, writhing from side to side, and throwing the whole features of the countenance into the most fearful contortions. By degrees, the convulsion seemed to extend itself along the muscles of the body, arms, and limbs, until the whole frame was thrown into violent agitation; unintelligible sputtering sounds came from the alternate corners of the mouth; and Sir Walter quaked to hear the name of "Sathanas" often repeated energetically. At last, by a convulsion stronger than the rest, the head and body were erected, and, after a little time, the Ancient seemed to recover the use of his senses, and the command over his muscles, as well as of his powers of utterance.

" What, Master Ancient Fenwick, hath befallen thee?" exclaimed Sir Walter, in a voice almost indistinct from trepidation; " tell me, I beseech thee, what hath happened?"

" My brain burneth," cried the Ancient, with a hideous yell, and striking his forehead with the palms of both hands, after which the flame no longer appeared. Then, after a pause, " Where am I?" said he, staring wildly around; —" where am I? Ha! I see I am again in the world of men. What!" exclaimed he, with surprise, on beholding Sir Walter—" art thou here? —How camest thou to this place?"

" My friend," replied the old knight, " my excellent friend, I came to consult thee; I came to take counsel from thy superhuman knowledge —thy knowledge gathered from converse with the spirits of another world."

" Another world!" exclaimed the Ancient, in a sepulchral voice—" in another world, didst thou say? Ay, I have indeed long had converse here, face to face, with some of its blackest inmates; but never, till this night," added he, shuddering, " did I visit its fiery realms."

" Where hast thou been, then?" asked the knight, in a tone of alarm.

" In Hell!" cried the Ancient, with a horrible voice that chilled the very blood in Sir Walter's veins: " Yes," continued he, " I have visited those dreadful abodes; but I may not tell their awful secrets. Some, it is true, I am permitted to disclose, if I can bring myself to speak of them—of things on which depend the fate of thyself and thy daughter, and deeply affecting thy country's weal."

" What, good Ancient, hast thou learned, that may affect me or my daughter? I do beseech thee let me straightway be informed. The blue fire burns on my father's shield to-night; some dreadful calamity impends."

" Ha! said'st thou so?" cried the Ancient, with a sudden start—" The blue fire, said'st thou?—Signs meet then; prodigies combine to overwhelm thee."

" They do indeed, most terribly," said the knight, shuddering with alarm.

" Their portent is direful," said the Ancient, groaning deeply.

" In mercy tell me by what means they may be averted," anxiously inquired Sir Walter.

" Nay," said the Ancient, with a desponding air, " 'tis thyself who art bringing them on thine own head." Then, after a long pause—" Thou art about to marry thy daughter to the brother of the Piersie ?"

" By what miracle knowest thou this ?" demanded Sir Walter, in amazement.

" Ask me not by what miracle I know this," replied the Ancient, " after what thou hast thyself witnessed. Have I not been in the world below ?—Do I not know all things ?—Do I not know that Sir Rafe Piersie hath sought the hand of the Lady Eleanore ?—that he hath been scorned by her ?—that even the Lord Bishop of Durham's influence hath been employed by him to incline thee to the match; and that, overcome by his counsels, thou art about to compel thy daughter to accept of his hand ? Yea, all this do I know, to the veriest item of the conversation held between thee : And now, can'st thou doubt whence I have had this knowledge ?" .

Sir Walter replied not, but groaned deeply.

" Sit down by me," said the Ancient, " and listen to me. 'Tis registered in the dread Book of Fate," continued he solemnly, " that if this marriage be concluded, consequences the most direful will result from it. First, thy daughter shall produce a son, of countenance so inhuman, that it shall be liker that of a wild boar than a man; and the monstrous birth will

produce the death of the mother. Then the
child shall grow up, and wax exceeding strong,
so that his might shall overmatch that of the
most powerful men. But though his mind shall
not ripen in proportion, yet shall his passions
terribly expand themselves; and after murder-
ing thee, from whom he shall have sprung, he
shall gather unto himself a host of demons of
his own stamp, and lay waste the fair face of
England, cruelly slaying and oppressing its innocent people for the space of ten years, when
he shall be at last overthrown by a Scottish
army, which, being brought against him, shall
subdue and enslave our nation."

The white hairs of the aged Sir Walter bristled
on his head as he listened to this dreadful prophecy. The scourge with which his country was,
menaced was worse, in his eyes, than even his
own unhappy fate.

"Tell me, oh tell me, most excellent Ancient," said he, in the agony of despair, "tell
me, I entreat thee, how this awful mass of approaching misery may be averted."

"There is only one way to shield yourself
and mankind from the threatened curse," replied the Ancient tardily, and rather as if he
felt difficulty in bringing it out; "there is only
one course to pursue, but it is such that, slave

as thou art to the prejudices of the world, it is vain to hope, that even the dread of these impending calamities will induce thee to adopt it."

" Talk not so, good Ancient, talk not so," cried the old knight impatiently. " There is nothing I would not do—Holy Virgin, forgive me !—there is nothing I would not do honestly, to prevent this threatened curse from arising, to the destruction of my family and my country."

" Sayest thou so ?" said the Ancient, calmly shaking his head, as if in doubt : " I will put thee to the proof then. It is written, as I have already declared, in the book of the fates of men, that this marriage shall take place, and that from it shall proceed this two-edged sword, to smite both thee and England, unless thou shalt bestow thy daughter on one whom—But thou wilt never condescend——"

" Nay," impatiently interrupted the knight, " better she should marry any honest man of good family, than that she should be suffered to match so proudly, only to be the mother of destruction to herself, to me, and to her country."

" Thou sayest well," calmly replied the Ancient; " but the Fates have not left the choice of her mate to thee or to her. Yet hear me patiently; and thou shalt know all. Thou art not ignorant that I have long abjured the pitiful affairs of men. 'Tis now more than fifteen years since, quitting their society, I have devoted myself to those studies by which thou hast more than once benefited. I have sacrificed all earthly prospects and enjoyments for the sake of that sublime knowledge, which doth enable me to foresee and control coming events; and it is to me a reward in itself so great, as to make every other appear despicable in comparison with it. But though I have forsworn the world, yet cannot I rid myself of attachment to thee; my early feelings must tie me to thee and thine for ever. Thou hast had proofs of this devotion too often, to require me to repeat that it doth exist; but I am now prepared to give thee a demonstration of it yet stronger than any thou hast hitherto received from me."

"Kind, excellent Ancient," exclaimed the grateful Sir Walter, "I well know the care with which thou hast watched over the welfare of my house; I feel the magnitude of the debt I owe thee, and 'tis with gratitude I acknowledge it. What is it, I beseech thee, thou canst do?"

"Yes," exclaimed the Ancient, with a show of much feeling, "yes, I will sacrifice myself. I will come forth again into the haunts of deceitful and cold-blooded man. I will give up all I prize, my quiet, my solitude, to save thee and thine from ruin. On my part there shall be no failure, however at war with my habits and inclinations the sacrifice may be. 'Tis upon thyself, therefore, upon thine own decision, that thine own fate, and the fate of thy daughter, and of thy country, must depend."

" Name—name, I entreat thee, the terms," cried the anxious old knight ; " name the conditions that I must fulfil—tell me what I must do, and no time shall be lost in carrying it into effect."

The Ancient paused for some moments, during which he looked into the face of the knight with his fiery inexpressive eyes, and then, with slow and solemn, though harsh utterance—

" I must espouse thy daughter, the Lady Eleanore !" said he. " The Fates have willed it so ; no other remedy doth now remain against the overwhelming destruction thou art doomed to behold."

This fatal declaration—this dreadful contrast to all those hopes of splendid alliance which had filled Sir Walter's thoughts, came upon him like a thunderbolt, and was perfectly annihilating. He could not stand the bitter alternative that was thus presented to him. Overcome by his feelings, he threw himself back among the straw composing the lair of the monster he had been listening to, and covering his eyes with the palms of his hands, he, hardy soldier as he was, burst into a flood of tears.

A grim meteor smile of inward satisfaction shot over the pallid face of the impostor.

" Ay," said he, " no one can expect thee to match thy daughter with such as me. Better that she should give birth to ten thousand such demons, as her fated marriage with the brother of the Piersic is infallibly destined to produce— better that she should die, and thou be cruelly murdered by the parricidal hand of thine inhuman grandchild, than that thou should'st call such a wretch as me son. Thy determination hath been well taken; 'tis like a good soldier, as thou art, to brave the Fates. I thank thee, too, for mine emancipation from the vow I had resolved to subject myself to for thy sake. My time, and my quiet, and my solitude, shall be again mine own, and my darling studies shall receive no interruption."

" Is there no other alternative?" cried the distracted father, rising with energy from the position he had thrown himself into.

" None !" replied the Ancient : " But that thou mayest be ignorant of no tittle of what it

so deeply concerns thee to know," continued he,
after a pause, " it is destined that if ever I do
so espouse me, my son shall be the most perfect
model of bravery and of virtue that ever England saw; and that, taking the proud name of
de Selby, he shall wax exceeding mighty, and
leading a small band of gallant youths, march
into Scotland as a conqueror, until at last, de-
throning the monarch of the North, he shall
himself be proclaimed king of that country, and
uniting himself by marriage with the King of
England, he and his posterity shall reign for
twelve centuries.   To look farther into futu-
rity is denied; but enow hath been told thee
to point out the way that doth lie before thee.
The space of three days and three hours is given
thee to choose thy daughter's destiny.   And
now," continued the Ancient, putting out his
hand to the hour-glass, and solemnly inverting
it; " and now the stream of thy time beginneth
to run ; see how the sand floweth down :—a portion of it hath already glided away ;—so will the
rest, till the period assigned thee be irrecoverably gone. 'Twere better that thou should'st retire to thy chamber, to weigh well the fates of
thy daughter, for the balance of her destinies is
in thine hand."

The impostor paused.   The agitated mind of

Sir Walter de Selby had eagerly grasped at the flattering picture which the Ancient had so cunningly reserved to the last, and which was so perfectly in harmony with every wish of the old man's heart. In his contemplation of it, he had almost forgotten the uncouth son-in-law destined to make him the grandfather of a hero, who was to raise the glory of his country's arms so high, and who was at last to become a King of Scotland. His pride was peculiarly flattered by the notion of the name of de Selby being retained to become eventually royal; and he began to reason with himself as he sat, that it was but stooping to present humiliation, in order to rise to the summit of human ambition. The crafty Ancient saw the working of his mind, from its operation on his honest countenance, as well as if he had been thinking audibly.

" Such proud prospects of an issue so glorious tempt not me," said he. " These dark volumes, and the retirement of this unseemly chamber, whence the stars can be most easily conversed with, are to me worth a world of such. But for thee, if thou demandest it of me, the sacrifice shall be made; and should'st thou make me the humble instrument of the salvation and exaltation of thyself and thy issue, it would," said he, with an affectation of extreme

humility, " be no more, after all, than burying
good seed in the soil of a dunghill, to see it
buxion with the more vigour, shoot the more
aloft, and rear its proud head far above the
meagre plants on higher but more sterile spots.
But it is matter worthy of grave thought. Yet
judge me not as I seem ; as the poor, the wretched inmate of this howlet's nest. Why am I so ?
Even because I despise all those gewgaws men
esteem most valuable, and covet only that most
precious of all jewels—the perfection of knowledge. Thinkest thou that it would not help me
to all the rest, were it my pleasure to command
them ? Thinkest thou that I could not command
worldly wealth and honours, were I to fancy
such baubles ? Would'st thou have me conjure
up gold ? Lo!—there !" said he, plucking the
leathern bag from his jerkin, and emptying the
shining contents of it on the ground, to the astonishment of Sir Walter ; " a little midnight
labour would raise me up a hoard that might
purchase the earth itself. But what is the vile
dross to me?—Nay, I would not inundate the
wretched world with that which hath already
caused sufficient human misery. To pour out
more, would be to breed a more accursed scourge
than e'en thy grandson Piersie will prove."

" Talk not of him," exclaimed the knight in terror; " the very thought of his existence is racking to me. I want not time for consideration on a point so plain. I do now resolve me on the alliance with thee. Sir Rafe Piersic comes to-morrow morning;—I shall break with him abruptly—and then, my resolution being taken, my daughter must yield to the irresistible decrees of Fate."

With these words Sir Walter rose to his knees, and, snatching up his lamp, scrambled hastily to the door, and stole softly down to his apartment. He looked with fear and trembling into the oratory, when, to his extreme relief, he saw that the ominous flame had left the fatal shield, and he retired to his couch in a state of comparative composure.

" So," said the Ancient, in grim soliloquy, after Sir Walter's footsteps had died away on the stairs,—" so, the hook is in thy nose, and thou shalt feel the power, as well as the vengeance, of him thou didst despise and make thy mock of. Thou didst thwart mine ambition; but my helm ere long shall tower amid the proudest crests of chivalry, and wealth and honours, yea, and the haughty smile of beauty too, shall be at my will. This is indeed to rise by mine abasement, even beyond the highest soaring of those early hopes which this man did so cruelly level with the earth. The thought is ecstasy."

CHAPTER VIII.

Sir John Assueton was early astir next
morning, for his head was so filled with the remembrance of those friends, and scenes of his
youth, he now hoped to revisit after a long absence, that he was impatient to depart from
Norham Castle. He had already given orders
to the squires to hold themselves in readiness,
and he had visited the stable, where Blanche-
etoile neighed a recognition to his master, and
was spoken to with the kindness of a friend.
The knight then ascended the ramparts to enjoy a short promenade; and there he was soon
afterwards joined by Hepborne, who came
springing towards him, urged by an unusual
flow of spirits.

" Good morrow, Hepborne," said Assueton;
" I am glad to see thee so alert this morning.
I have looked at our steeds; they are courageous as lions, and gamesome as kids. They will
carry us into Scotland with as much spirit as
we shall ride them thither. After breaking our

fast, and bestowing our meed of thanks on the good old Knight for his hospitality, we may yet make our way o'er many a good mile of Scottish ground, ere yonder new-born sun shall sink in the west."

" Nay, my dear Assueton," said Hepborne, " what need hast thou for so much haste? Hadst thou some fair damosel in Scotland—some lady bright, who, with her swan-like neck stretched towards the mid-day sun, looketh day after day from her lofty towernet, with anxious eyes, in the hope of descrying thee her true and constant Knight—hadst thou such a fair one as this, I say, impatience might indeed become thee; but what reason hast thou, despiser of the lovely sex as thou art, to long for a change of position? By the Rood of St Andrew, I begin to believe that thou art no such woman-hater as thou would'st pretend, and that all this seeming coldness of thine is nothing but thy laudable constancy to some Scottish maid, who hath thine early-pledged vows of love in keeping."

" Thou art welcome to rally me as it may please thee, Hepborne," replied Assueton, with a smile; " but, on the faith and honour of my knighthood, I have not seen the maiden for whom I would go three ells from my intended path, except for common knightly courtesy, or to redress some grievous wrong. Nay, nay, thou knowest my natural duresse—that my heart is adamant to all such weak impressions. Perdie, I cannot understand how any such can affect the good, hardy, soldier-like bosom, though I do observe the melancholy truth exampled forth, in daily occurrence, with those around me.—But I perceive thy drift, my politic friend. To assail is the best tactique against being assailed. Thou camest forth conscience-stricken, and being well aware that thy foolish fondness for this masquing damosel of the Castle here would come under my gentle lash, to divert the attack against thyself, thou dost begin to skirmish against me. But I see well enow that 'tis the Lady Eleanore's attraction that would keep thee here."

" It is e'en so, I candidly confess it," replied Hepborne. " I candidly confess it, dost mark me? so, throwing myself at thy feet, I cry for quarter."

" Nay, an thou dost disarm me thus," replied Assueton, " I can say no more."

" Oh, Assueton, Assueton, my bel ami," said Hepborne enthusiastically, " I was the happiest of human beings last night. I did indeed meet her on the ramparts. Old Adam of Gordon was a good seer; nay, perchance, though as to that I

know not, he may have been Cupid's messenger.
Yet, hold! Depardieux, I do her most foul
wrong in so supposing; for she hath too much
maiden modesty to have been guilty of so much
boldness. But, be that as it may, her words—
her looks—were kind and most encouraging.
She did blushingly confess that her heart had
known no other affection than that which she
bears towards her venerable father. She half
admitted that I was not altogether indifferent
to her;—she did utter a hope that we should
remain her father's guests for some longer
space;—yea, and she even admitted, that to
see me again would give her pleasure. Then
her accents were so sweet, and her demeanour
so gentle—Oh, Assueton, she is in very truth
an angel!—But what is all this to thee, thou
Knight of Adamant? I forgot that I might as
well speak to the stones of these walls of amo-
rets and love passages, as to Sir John Assueton."

"Thou art right, i'faith, Hepborne," replied
Assueton; "they say walls have ears, whilst I,
in good earnest, may with truth enow be said
to have none for such matters, since they do
irk whenever the theme of love is handled in
their hearing. Yet my friendship for thee bids
me listen to thy ravings, and compassion for
thy disease makes me watch the progress of its

symptoms, as I should do those of any other fever. From all thou hast said, then, I would gather that thou would'st fain loiter off another day or two, to catch fresh smiles and deeper wounds from the Lady Eleanore.—Is't not so, Hepborne?"

" In truth, Assueton," replied Sir Patrick, " her whole deportment towards me last night hath buoyed me up with hope, yea, and hath even led me to flatter myself that I am not in-different to her, Scot though I be. At so cri-tical a period, then, I cannot go, my dear As-sueton; and I am sure thy good nature will never allow thee to abandon thy friend in the crisis of his distemper."

" No, Hepborne," said Assueton, laughing, " I shall certainly not be so little of a Christian knight as to abandon thee when thine estate is so dangerous.—Well, then, I must wait thy time, I suppose: But parfoy I must have some rounds of the tiltyard, were it but to joust at the quintaine, or Blanche-etoile and I too will lose our occupation. Wilt thou not take a turn with me for exercise?—But soft—I need not talk to thee now of any such thing, for yonder comes the cause of thy malady."

" By St Denis, it is she indeed!" exclaimed Hepborne; " that is the very mantle she wore.

But who is that cavalier on whose arm she hangs so freely ?" added he, with a jealous tone and air.

" St Genevieve, but he is a tall, proper, handsome knight," said Assueton.

" Phsaw !" said Hepborne pettishly; " I see nothing handsome about him : meseems he hath the air of a sturdy swineherd."

" Is not that the Lady Eleanóre de Selby ?" inquired Assueton of a sentinel who walked on the rampart at some little distance from where the knights then stood.

" Ay, in truth, it is she," replied the man, stopping to look at her.

" And who may yonder knight be with whom she holds converse ?" demanded Hepborne eagerly.

" By the mass, I know not, Sir Knight," replied the man, as he turned to tread back his measured pace; " I never saw him before, that I knows on."

But notwithstanding the unfavourable remark which jealousy had made Hepborne cast on the stranger's appearance, he could not help secretly confessing that the knight with whom the lady Eleanore had come forth from the keep, and on whose arm she was now leaning with so little reserve, was indeed very handsome, even noble-looking. An esquire waited for him at the end of the bridge, with two magnificently-caparisoned black horses. The lady seemed to be a drag on his steps, and to keep him back, as it were, with a thousand last words, as if with a desire of prolonging the few remaining minutes of their converse. On his part, he displayed signs of the tenderest affection for her; and after they had crossed the bridge tardily together, she threw herself upon his mailed neck, and he enfolded her in his arms, both remaining locked together for some moments in a last embrace. The warrior then tore himself from her, and vaulting on his steed, struck the pointed steel into his sides, and galloped off at a desperate pace. The lady, leaning on the balustrades of the bridge, rested there a little space, and then turning slowly towards the door of the keep, disappeared.

The two knights commanded a full though distant view of this scene of dumb show, from the part of the rampart where they then stood. Assueton turned his eyes with compassion upon his friend to observe its effect upon him. He was standing like a marble statue, still gazing on the spot where it had been acted; his eyes fixed in his head as if with apathetical stupor. At length, after remaining in the same attitude

for several minutes, he struck his forehead violently with the palms of his hands, and addressing his friend in hurried accents,—

· "Assueton, Assueton," said he, " did'st thou
see? did'st thou mark? Oh, woman, woman,
woman! But it mattereth not. Assueton, let
our horses be ordered; I will forth with thee for
Scotland even now; ay, even now. Thou wert
indeed right, my friend; there is more of thorns
than roses about them all. Thou wert wise,
Assueton; but I am cured now—nay, I am as
sane as thyself. Our horses, Assueton—our
squires and cortege. Let us not lose a moment;
—we may yet dispatch good store of Scottish
miles ere we sleep."

" Nay, let us not be guilty of doing violence
to the courtesy of knighthood," replied Assueton; " Sir Walter de Selby hath used much
fair hospitality towards us. It beseems us not
to leave Norham Castle without giving thanks
to the good old governor in person, and bidding
him adieu. Besides, 'twere as well, methinks,
to go with less suspicious haste, lest we may be
misjudged; and, indeed, Sir Walter can have
hardly left his couch as yet."

" Ay, ay, true—thou sayest true, my friend,"
said Hepborne, interrupting him keenly. " I
had forgotten. Her father not yet astir, and

she taking leave of her lover so tenderly at such an hour. Oh, damnable! He came, doubt-, less, last night, and has been i' the keep without the old man's knowledge. So, all her deep and long-drawn suspires were but the offspring of her fears lest her leman should break faith."

" Come, come, Hepborne, my bel ami, compose thyself," said Sir John; " thou must not let this appear within; 'tis but a short hour sacrificed to common civility, and then let us boune us for Scotland."

" Thou sayest well, Assueton," said Hepborne, recollecting himself after a short pause, during which he sighed deeply; " I must endeavour to command myself—my passion too much enchafeth me. The good old man hath indeed been to us kindness itself. How cruel that he should be so deceived in his daughter! I pity him from the bottom of my soul. My wounds will soon be healed—war-toil must be their confecture; but his, alas! are yet to be opened, for now they do fester all unwist to him, and when they do burst forth, I fear me they may well out his life's blood. But come," added he, rousing himself, " let's in."

They turned their steps towards the keep, but before they had descended from the ramparts, their ears were struck with the sound of

a bugle, and as they looked over the walls they
descried a long cavalcade of knights, esquires,
grooms, lacqueys, and spearmen, advancing
with lances and pennons up the hollow way
leading towards the outer gate of the Castle.
The party soon came thundering over the draw-
bridge, and were saluted by the guards as they
passed. At the head of the troop rode the proud
Sir Rafe Piersie. The array of the very meanest of his people was magnificent; but his armour and his horse-gear shone like the sun, and
glittered with the splendour of its embossments.
They passed into the inner court-yard; loud
rang the bugle of announcement, and the ear
was assailed by the neighing of hot steeds, the
clattering and pawing of impatient hoofs, the
champing of foam-covered bits, the jingling of
chains, and the clinking of spurs; whilst a rout
of soldiers and grooms, with Master Thomas
Turnberry at their head, ran clustering around
them. The squires of the Castle, with the hoary
seneschal and a host of lacqueys, came forth
from the keep, and ushered in Sir Rafe Piersie
and his suite.

Hepborne and Assueton soon afterwards followed, and on reaching the banquet-hall they
found Sir Walter de Selby in the act of receiving and welcoming his newly-arrived guest,

whose supercilious air, when addressing the
plain honest old soldier, by no means prepos-
sessed the two Scottish knights in his favour.
Sir Walter introduced them to Piersic, and he
received them with the same offensive hauteur.
There is something in such a deportment that
provokes even the humble man to put on haughtiness. Hepborne, from late events, was not
prepared to be in the most condescending humour, so that he failed not to carry his head
fully three inches higher than he had done since
he became an inmate of the Castle of Norham.
Nor was Assueton at all behind him in state-
liness.

The table was covered with the morning's
meal, and but little conversation passed during
the time it was going on. Sir Walter de Selby
seemed to be more reserved, and even less disposed to risk his words than he had been the
previous night.

"I marvel much, Sir Governor," said Sir
Rafe Piersie with a haughty sneer—"I say, methinks, that 'tis marvellously strange that thou
hast as yet said nothing touching the object of
the visit I have thus paid thee. Am I, or am
I not, to have this girl of thine? Depardieux,
there hath been more ambassage about this affair than might have brought home and wedded

a queen of England. The damsel, I am informed, knew not her own mind, and thou wert weak
enough to suffer thyself to be blown about by
her wayward whimsies; but my kinsman, the
Bishop of Durham, tells me, that having at last
brought thine own determination up to the proper point, thou art finally resolved she shall be
mine. Marry, a matter of great exertion, truly,
to accept of Sir Rafe Piercie as a husband for
Eleanore de Selby !"

" My mind has indeed been made up, Sir
Rafe Piersie," said the old knight, " and would
to Heaven, beausir, that it could have been
made up differently, for, certes, it doleth me
sorely to be driven to answer thee, as I must of
needscost do. I should not have broached this
matter till privacy had put the seal on our converse; but since thou hast opened it, I am forced to tell thee, that since I saw the Bishop of
Durham, obstacles have appeared which render
it impossible for me to give thee my daughter,
the Lady Eleanore, to wife. She is affianced
to another."

" So," thought Hepborne, the ideas passing
rapidly through his mind, " her father knows
of the attachment between her and the knight
who left her this morning. Then, perhaps, she
has been less to blame than I thought; yet why

were her words and manner such, last night, towards me, as to mislead me into the idea that I had reason to hope? Oh, deceitful woman, never satisfied with the success of thy springes as long as there is a foolish bird to catch. So! thou must have me limed too? But, gramercy, I have escaped thy toils."

Such were Hepborne's thoughts;—but what Sir Rafe Piersie's were during the pause of astonishment he was thrown into, may be best gathered from the utterance he gave them.

" What is this I hear? has a limb of the noble Piersie been brought here to be insulted? Thou art a false old papelarde; and were it not for those hoary hairs of thine, by the beard of St Barnabas, I would brain thee with this gauntlet;" and saying so, he dashed it down on the board, making it ring again.

Hepborne and Assueton both started up, and stretched out their hands eagerly to seize it.

" Ah, thou art always the lucky man, Hepborne," said Assueton, much disappointed to see that his friend had snatched it before him.

" Sir Rafe Piersic," said Hepborne, " in behalf of this good old knight, whom thou hast so grossly insulted at his own board, I defy thee to instant and mortal debate; and in thy teeth I return the opprobrious epithets thou didst dare to throw in his face; and here, I say, thou liest!" and with these words he threw down his gauntlet.

"And who art thou?" said his antagonist, taking it up; "who art thou, young cockerel, who crowest so loud? By St George, but thou showest small share of wisdom to pit thyself thus against Sir Rafe Piersie. But fear not, thou shalt have thy will. Was thy darreigne for instant fight, saidst thou? In God's name, let us to horse then without farther parley. Let Sir Richard de Lacy here, and thine eager friend there, be the judges of the field; and as for the place, the Norham meadow below will do as well for thine overthrow as any other: thou wilt have easy galloping ere thou dost meet it. What, defy Sir Rafe Piersic to combat of outrance, and give him the lie too! Thou art doomed, young man, thou art doomed; thine insolence hath put thee beyond the pale of my mercy. By the holy Rood, thou must be the young cock-sparrow the old dotard hath chosen as a mate for his pretty popelot, else thou never could'st have been so bold."

"I am not so fortunate," replied Hepborne, with calm and courteous manner.

"And what may thy name and title be, then?" demanded Piersic, with yet greater hauteur.

" My name," replied he, with a dignified bow, " is Sir Patrick Hepborne."

" Ha! then, by my faith, thou hast some good Northern blood in thee," replied Piersie; " thou art less unworthy of my lance than I did ween thou wert. Thy father is a right doughty Scot; and, if I mistake not, I have heard of some deeds of thine done in France, which have made thine honours and renomie to bud and buxion rathely. But 'tis a warm climate they have sprouted in, and such early and unnatural shoots are wont to be air-drawn and unhealthy; and albeit they may vegetate under the more southern sun, they are often withered by the blasts of the North, as soon as they appear amongst us. But come, come, my horse, Delaval—my horse and gear, I say;" and leaving the hall hastily, he sought a chamber where he might prepare himself for single combat.

CHAPTER IX.

HEPBORNE was not slow on his part, and in a very short time the Castle-yard was again in commotion, and grooms and esquires were seen running in all directions, bringing out steeds and buckling on trappings. Hepborne's gallant steed Beaufront was led proudly forth from his stall by Mortimer Sang, and was no sooner backed by his master, than he pranced, neighed, and spurned the ground, as if he had guessed at the nature of the work he had to do. Attended by Assueton and their small party of followers, Sir Patrick rode slowly down to the mead of Norham, extending from under the elevated ground on which the Castle stood, for a considerable way to the westward, between the village and the bank of the Tweed. Here he halted, and patiently awaited the arrival of his opponent. Piersie came in all his pomp, mounted on a dapple-grey horse, of remarkable strength, figure, and action. Both horse and rider were splendidly arrayed, and his friends and people came crowding after him, boasting loudly of the probable issue of the combat. Sir Walter de Selby came last, attended by some few officers, esquires, and meaner people, and joined Hepborne's party, stationed towards one end of the field, Sir Rafe Piersie's having filed off and taken post towards the other extremity of it. Little time was lost in preparation. The two judges placed themselves opposite to the middle of the space, and there the combatants met and measured lances.

The bugle-mot gave them warning, so turning their steeds round, they each rode back about a furlong towards their respective parties, and suddenly wheeling at the second sound of the bugle, they ran their furious course against each other with lance in rest. The shock was tremendous. The clash of their armour echoed from the very walls of the neighbouring castle; nor had the oldest and most experienced men-at-arms who were there present ever seen anything like it. Sir Patrick Hepborne had received his adversary's lance, with great adroitness, on his shield, at such an angle that it glanced off broken in shivers; yet the force was so great that it had almost turned him in his saddle. But he on his part had borne his point so stoutly, so steadily, and so truly, that taking his adversary in the centre of the body,

he tossed him entirely over the croupe of his
horse. Piersie lay stunned by the fall; and
Sir Patrick checking Beaufront in his career,
made a circuit around his prostrate adversary,
and speedily dismounting, went up to him, and
kneeling on the ground beside him, lifted up his
head, and opened his vizor and beaver to give
him freer air. Sir Richard de Lacy and Assueton came up.

" Sir Richard," said Hepborne, " thou seest
his life is in mine hands; and after the bragging
and insolent threats he used towards me, perhaps I might be deemed well entitled to use the
privileges of my victory, and take it. But I
engaged in this affair only to wipe off the disgrace thrown on this good old knight Sir Walter de Selby, in whose hospitality I and my
brother-in-arms have so liberally shared; and
the blot having been thus removed, by God's
blessing on mine arm, I leave Piersie his life,
that he may use it against me when next we
meet in fair fight in bloody field, should the
jarring rights of our two countries summon us
against each other. But through thee, his friend,
I do most solemnly enjoin him, that on the honour of a knight, he shall henceforth hold Sir
Walter de Selby as acquitted of all intention of
doing him any injury or insult in the matter of

the marriage he contemplated with the Lady Eleanore, and that he think not of doing Sir Walter violence upon that account."

For all this Sir Richard de Lacy immediately pledged himself in name of Sir Rafe Piersic; and the discomfited knight, who was still insensible, having been lifted up by his esquires, was straightway borne towards the Castle. As they were carrying him away, Mortimer Sang, who had by chance caught the dapple-grey steed, as he scoured past him on the field after his rider's overthrow, trotted up to the group leading him by the bridle. The worthy esquire had heard and treasured up the taunts and boasting of Piersie's people, as they were approaching the field.

"Hath any of ye lost perchance a pomely grise-coloured horse, my masters?" exclaimed he; "here is a proper powerful destrier, if he had been but well backed. Hast thou no varlet of a pricksoure squire who can ride him? Here take him, some of ye; and, hark ye, let his saddle be better filled the next time ye do come afield."

Piersie's men were too much crest-fallen to return his jibes, so he rode back to the group that surrounded the conqueror, chuckling over his triumph. The good old Sir Walter de Selby, his eyes running over with gratitude, approached Sir Patrick Hepborne, and embraced him cordially.

"The time hath been," said he, "the time hath been, Sir Patrick, when it pleased Heaven to permit me to reap the same guerdon of inward satisfaction thou art now feeling, and could the weight of a few years have been lifted from off this hoar head, by God's blessing, thou should'st not have had this noble chance of gathering fame at the cost of Sir Rafe Piersic. As it is, I thank thee heartily for thy gallant defence of an old man, as well as for the generous use thou hast made of thy victory. Come, let us to the Castle, that by my treatment of thee, and Sir Rafe Piersie, I may forthwith prove my gratitude to the one, and my forgiveness of the other."

"Thanks, most hospitable knight," said Sir Patrick, "I beseech thee in mine own name, and that of my friend, to receive our poor thanks for thy kind reception of us at Norham. But now our affairs demand our return to our own country; nay, had it not been for this unlooked-for deed of arms, we had been ere now some miles beyond that broad stream. We boune us now for Scotland. Farewell, and may the holy St Cuthbert keep thee in health and safety. We may yet haply meet again."

Sir Walter de Selby was grieved to find that all his efforts to detain the two knights were ineffectual.

" Since it is thy will, then, to pleasure me no longer with thy good company and presence, Sirs Knights, may the blessed Virgin and the holy St Andrew guide you in safety to your friends; and may you find those ye love in the good plight you would wish them to be." And saying so, he again cordially embraced both the knights, and slowly returned towards the Castle with his attendants.

The bustle and commotion occasioned by the appearance of the knights and their followers on the mead of Norham, the sound of the bugle, and the clash of the shock, had brought out many of the inhabitants of the village to see what was a-doing. Amongst these was the black-eyed Mrs Kyle, who came up to Master Mortimer Sang, and laying hold of his bridle-rein,—

" When goest thou for Scotland ?" said she anxiously.

" " Even now, fair dame," said he calmly.

" Then go I with thee, Sir Squire," returned she. " Let me have a seat on that butt-horse ; I can ride right merrily there."

"Nay, my most beautiful Mrs Kyle," replied Sang, "that may in no wise be, seeing I am an honest-virtuous esquire, not one of those false faitors who basely run away with other men's wives. Thou canst not with me, I promise thee."

"Yea, but thou didst promise to take me," cried Mrs Kyle, a flood of tears bursting from her eyes, as she began to reproach Sang, with a voice half-choked by the violence of her sobbing; "So, false foiterer that thou art, I—I—I—I must be fordone by thee, must I, after all thy losengery and flattery? Here have I kept goodman Kyle all this time i' the vault, ygraven, as a body may say, that I mought the more sickerly follow thee when thou wentest. Oh, what will become of me? I am but as one dead."

"Why, thou cruel giglet thou," cried Sang, "didst thou in very truth mean to go off to Scotland with me, and leave thy poor husband ygraven i' the vault to die the most horrible of deaths? Did not I tell thee to let him out at thy leisure and on thine own good terms? By the mass, a pretty leisure hast thou taken, and pretty terms hast thou resolved to yield him."

"Nay, judge not so hastily, good Sir Squire," replied Mrs Kyle. "That I would boune me to

Scotland with thee, is sure enow; but as to leaving Sylvester Kyle to die a cruel death, Thomas
Tapster here knows that I taught him the use
of the sliding plank and the clicket of the trap-
door, and that Master Sylvester was to receive
his franchise as soon as Tweed should be atween
us. But what shall I do? I can never go back
to the Norham Tower again; goodman Sylvester will surely amortise me attenes when he doth
get freedom."

"Squire," said Hepborne, "thou must e'en
get thee back to the village, and make her peace
with the bear her husband; we shall wait for
thee at the ferry-boat."

"Nay, as for that matter," said Sang, "I
must go back at any rate, for I have yet to pay
the rascal for the excellent supper we had of
him, and for the herborow of our party for the
night we spent there. Come along then, Dame
Kyle, I see thou wert not quite so savage as I
took thee to be."

They soon reached the hostel, and Master
Mortimer Sang, dismounting from his horse in
the yard, entered and strode along the passage to
the place where he knew the trap-door to be,
and, sliding aside the plank that covered its
fastenings, he hoisted up the lever.

"Sylvester Kyle, miserable lossel wight,"

cried he, "art thou yet alive? Sinner that thou
art, I have compassion on thee, and albeit thou
hast been there but some short space—small
guerdon for thy wicked coulpe, seeing thou art
in the midst of so great a mountance of good
provender and drink, with which to fill thine
enormous bowke—I now condescend to let thee
come forth. Come up, come up, I say, and
show thy face, that we may hold parley as to
the terms of thine enlargement."

A groaning was heard from the farther end
of the place, and by and by Sylvester's head
appeared above the steps, his countenance wearing the most miserable expression. Horrible
fear of the agonizing death he had thought
himself doomed to die, had prevented him from
touching food; but the anxious workings of his
mind had done even more mortification upon
him than a starvation of a fortnight could have
accomplished. The red in his face was con-
verted into a deadly pale copper hue, for even
death itself could never have altogether extinguished the flame in his nose; his teeth projected beyond his lips, and chattered against
each other from the cold he had undergone;
and his eyes stared in their sockets, from the
united effects of want and terror.

" Should it please me to give thee the franchise, thou agroted lorrel, thou," said the Squire, " wilt thou give me thy promise to comport thyself more honestly in time to come, to have done with all knavery and chinchery, and to give thy very best to all Scots who may, in time to come, chance to honour thy hostelry with their presence ?"

" Oh, good Sir Squire," replied the host, " anything—I will promise anything that thou mayest please."

" Nay, nay, Sir Knave," cried Sang, " horrow tallowcatch that thou art—no generals—swear me in particulars—item by item, dost thou hear, as thou framest thy reckonings. If thou dost not, down goeth the trap-door again, and I leave thee here to meditate and ypend my proposal, until my return from the Holy Wars, whither I am boune. By that time thou wilt be more humble, and more coming to my terms. Swear."

" I swear, by the holy St Cuthbert," replied the host, " that all Scots shall henceforth be entertained with the best meats and drinks the nale of the Norham Tower can afford, yea, alswa the best herborow it can yield them."

" 'Tis well," said Sang; " swear me next,

then, and let the oath be strong, that thou wilt never again score double."

" Nay, Master Squire, that is a hard oath for a tapster to take; 'tis warring against the very nicest mystery of my vocation," said Kyle.

" No matter, Sir Knave," said Sang, " I shall not have my terms agrutched by thee. An thou swearest not this, down thou goest, and I leave thee to settle scores with a friend of thine below, with whom thou wilt find the single reckoning of thy sins a hard enough matter for thee to pay."

" Oh, for mercy's sake, touch not the trap-door, Sir Squire, and I will swear anything," cried Kyle, much alarmed at seeing Sang's brawny arm preparing to turn it over upon his head.

" Well, thou horrow lossel," cried Sang, " dost thou swear thou wilt never more cheat, or score double?"

" I do, I do," said the host; " by the holy Rood, I swear that I will never cheat or score double again. God help me," cried he, after a pause, " how shall I eschew it, and what shall I do without it?"

" Now, thou prince of knaves," cried Sang, " thou hast yet one more serment to swallow. Swear by the blessed Virgin, that thou

wilt receive thy wife back into thy bosom, and
abandoning thy former harshness towards her,
that thou wilt kindly cherish her, and do thy
possible to comfort and pleasure her, forgetting
all that may have hitherto happened amiss between ye. I restore her to thee pure. She was
not to blame for my being in the vault with
her. The coulpe was all thine own. Thou
madest me ravenous with hunger by thy villainous chinchery. My nose, through very
want, became as sharp in scent as that of a
sleuth-hound. I winded the steam that came
from the trap-door, yea, from the very common
room where I sat. I ran it up hot foot, and
descending the stair, I had but just begun to
feast mine eyes with that thou hadst denied to
my stomach, when thy pestiferous voice was
heard. Thy wife is as virtuous and innocent as
the child unborn. So swear, I say. "

Master Sylvester Kyle shook his head wo-
fully, and looked very far from satisfied; but
he had no alternative; he swore as the squire
wished him to do, and then was permitted to
issue from his subterranean prison.

" And now, Sir Knave," said Sang, " do but
note my extreme clemency. Thou would'st
have starved me, the knights, and our good
company, because we were Scots, for the which

grievous sin I did put thee in a prison full of goodly provender and rich drinks; whence I now let thee forth, with thy greedy carcase crammed to bursting, and thy whole person plump and fair as a capon. Do but behold him, I beseech ye, how round he looks. Now get thee to thine augrim-stones, and cast up thine account withal. Thou knowest pretty well what we have had, for thou didst give me the victuals and wine with thine own hand."

" Nay, good Sir Squire," said Kyle, glad to escape, " take it all, in God's name, as a free gift, and let us part good friends."

" Nay, nay," said Master Sang, " we take no such beggarly treats, we Scottish knights and squires. Come, come—thy reckoning, thy reckoning, dost hear? No more words; my master doth wait, and I must haste to join him."

Kyle, with his wife's assistance, and that of the pebbles or augrim-stones, by which accounts were usually made out in those days, scored up the first fair reckoning he had ever made in his life, and Sang paid it without a word.

" And now," said he, " let us, as thou said'st, Master Kyle, let us e'en part good friends. Bring me a stirrup-cup of thy best."

The host hastened to fetch a cup of excellent Rhenish. They drank to each other, and shook hands with perfect cordiality; and the squire, smacking the pouting lips of Mrs Kyle, mounted his horse, and rode away to join his party.

As the knights and their small retinue were crossing the Tweed in the ferry-boat, Hepborne cast his eyes up to the keep of the Castle, towering high above them, and frowning defiance upon Scotland. A white hand appeared from a narrow window, and waved a handkerchief; and by a sort of natural impulse, he was about to have waved and kissed his fervently in return.

" Pshaw !" said he, pettishly checking himself, for being so ready to yield to the impulse of his heart. The white hand and handkerchief waved again—and again it waved ere he reached the Scottish shore; but he manfully resisted all temptation, and gave no sign of recognition.

As he mounted, however, he looked once more. The hand was still there, streaming the little speck of white. His resolution gave way —he waved his hand, and his eyes filling with tears, he dashed the rowels of his spurs against the sides of his steed, sprung off at full gallop, and was immediately lost amongst the oak copse through which lay their destined way.

CHAPTER X.

AFTER tarrying for a while at the small town
of Dunse, the two knights pursued their journey over the high ridge of Lammermoor, and
early on the second day they reached Hailes
Castle, the seat of the Hepbornes, a strong fortress, standing on the southern banks of the
river Tyne, in the heart of the ˈfertile county
of East Lothian. At the period we are now
speaking of, the varied surface of the district
surrounding the place was richly though irregularly wooded; and even the singular isolated
hill of Dunpender, rising to the southward of
it, had gigantic oaks growing about its base,
and towering upon its sides, amidst thick hazel
and other brushwood, wherever they could find
soil enough to nourish them.

Sir Patrick Hepborne had been particularly
silent during their march. The events which
took place at Norham, and the conviction he
felt that the Lady Eleanore de Selby had indi-

rectly endeavoured to draw him into an attachment for her, when her heart either was or
ought to have been engaged to another, made
him unhappy. It is needless to inquire why it
should have done so, since he was always con-
gratulating himself on having escaped uninjured from the toils of one so unworthy of him.
But the truth was, he had not escaped uninjured; he had " tane a hurt" from her, of a
nature so serious as not to be very easy of cure.
Assueton, who had never felt the tender passion, and who had consequently very little sympathy for it, had more than once complained of
the unwonted dulness of his companion, who
used to be so full of life and cheerfulness, and
had made several vain attempts to rouse him,
until at last, despairing of success, he amused
himself in jesting with Master Mortimer Sang,
who possessed a never-failing spring of good-
humour.

As they drew near the domains of Sir Patrick Hepborne the elder, however, a thousand
spots, and things, and circumstances, began to
present themselves in succession, and to force
themselves on the attention of the love-sick
knight, awakening warm associations with the
events of his youthful days, and overpowering,
for a time, his melancholy. To these he began

to give utterance in a language his friend could not only comprehend, but participate in the feelings they naturally gave rise to.

"Assueton," said he, "it was here, in this very wood, that I took my first lessons in the merry art of woodcraft; in yonder hollow were the rethes and paukers spread to toyle the deer; and, see there, under yonder ancient tree, was I first planted with my little cross-bow, as a lymer, to have my vantage of the game. It was old Gabriel Lindsay, then a jolly forester, who put me there, and taught me how to behave me. He is now my father's seneschal, if, as I hope, he be yet alive. He was a hale man then, and though twenty years older than my father, he had a boy somewhat younger than myself, who took up his father's trade of forester, just before I went to France. Alas, the old tree has had a fearful skathe of firelevin since last I saw it. See what a large limb hath been rent from its side. Dost see the river glancing yonder below, through the green-wood? Ay, now we see it better. In yonder shallow used I to wade when a child, with my little hauselines tucked up above my knees. I do remember well, I was so engaged one hot summer's day, when, swelled by some sudden water-spout or upland flood, I saw the liquid wall come sweeping on-

wards, ready to overwhelm me. I ran in child-
ish fear, but ere I reached the strand it came,
and overtaking my tottering steps, hurried me
with it into yonder pool. I sank, and rose,
and sank again. I remember e'en now how
quickly the ideas passed through my infant
mind, as I was whirling furiously round and
round by the force of the eddy, vainly struggling and gasping for life, now below, and now
on the surface of the water. I thought of the
dreadful death I was dying; I thought of the
misery about to befall my father and mother;
nay, strange as it may seem, I saw them in my
mind's eye weeping in distraction over my pale
and dripping corpse, and all this was intermixed
with flitting hopes of rescue, that were but as
the flash amidst the darkness of the storm. The
recollections of the five or six years I could remember of my past childhood, were all conden-
sed into the short period of as many minutes;
for that was all the time my lucky stars permitted me to remain in jeopardy, till Gabriel
Lindsay came, and plunging into the foaming
current, dragged me half dead to the shore.
Full many a time have I sithence chosen that
very pool as a pleasure bayne wherein to exercise my limbs in swimming, when hardier boyhood bid me defy the flood."

" My dear friend," said Assuetou, " trust
me, I do envy thee thine indulgence in those
remembrances excited by the scenes of thy childhood ;—they make me more eager than ever to
revel in those that await me around my paternal boure. I shall be thy father's guest to-night;
but I can no longer delay returning to my widowed mother, who doubtless longs to embrace
me, and to my paternal possessions. I must
leave thee to-morrow."

" Nay, Assueton, thou didst promise to bestow upon me three or four days at least," said
Hepborne : " let me not then have thy promise
amenused. To rob me of so large a portion of
thy behote were, methinks, but unkind."

" I did promise thee indeed," said Assueton ;
" but then I wist not of the time we should
waste at Norham. I must e'en go to-morrow,
Hepborne ; but, trust me, I shall boune me
back again some short space hence."

Hepborne was not lacking in argument to
overcome his friend's intentions, but he could
gain no more than a promise, reluctantly granted, that his departure should be postponed until the morning after the following day.

" But see, Assueton," said Hepborne, " there
are the outer towers and gateway of the Castle,
and behold how its proud barbicans rise beyond

them. As I live, there is Flo, my faithful old wolf-dog, lying sunning himself against the wall. He is the fleetest allounde in all these parts for taking down the deer at a view. What ho, boy, Flo, Flo! What means the brute, he minds me not," continued Hepborne, riding up to him; " I wot, he was never wont to be so litherly : he used to fly at my voice with all the swiftness of the arrow, which he is named after. Ah! now I see he is half-blind; and peraunter he is deaf too, for he seems as if he heard me not. But, fool that I am, I forget that some years have passed away sith I saw him last, and that old age must ere this have come upon him. 'Twas but a week before I left home, Assueton, that he killed a wolf. But let us hasten in, I am impatient to embrace my father, and my dear mother, and my sister Isabelle."

Loud rang the bugle blast in the court-yard of the Castle. Throwing his reins to his esquire, Hepborne sprang from his horse, and running towards the doorway, whence issued a crowd of domestics, alarmed by the summons, he grasped the hand of an old white-headed man, who presented the feeble remains of having been once tall and powerful, but who was now bent and tottering with age.

· · " My worthy Gabriel," said he, in an affectionate tone and manner, and with a tear trembling in his eye, " dost thou not know me? How fares my father, my mother, and my sister, the Lady Isabelle ?"

The old man looked at him for some moments, with his hand held up as a pent-house to his dim eyes.

" Holy St Giles," exclaimed he at last, " art thou indeed my young master? Art thou then alive and sound? Well, who would ha'e thought, they that saw me last winter, when I was so ill, that I should ha'e lived to ha'e seen this blessed day !"

" But, tell me, Gabriel,'" cried Hepborne, interrupting him, " tell me where are they all; I suppose I shall find them in the banquet-hall above?"

" Stop thee, stop thee, Sir Patrick," said the old seneschal; " thy father and the Lady Isabelle rode to the greenwood this morning. There was a great cry about a rout of wolves that have been wrecking doleful damage on the shepens; they do say, that some of the flocks ha'e been sorely herried by them; so my master and the Lady Isabelle rode forth with the sleuth-hounds, and the alloundes, and the foresters; and this morning, ere the sun saw the

welkin, my boy yode away to lay out the rethes
and the pankers. I wot, thou remembers thee
of my son Robert? He is head forester now.
Thy noble father, Heaven's blessing and the
Virgin's be about him, did that for him; may
long life and eternal joy be his guerdon for all
his good deeds to me and mine! And Ralpho
Proudfoot was but ill content to see my Rob
get the place aboon him; so Ralpho yode his
ways, and hath oft sithes threatened some malure to Rob; but as to that——"

"Nay, my good Gabriel," said Hepborne,
impatiently interrupting him, " but where, I
entreat thee, is my mother?"

A cloud instantly overcast the face of the
venerable domestic; he hesitated and stam-
mered—

" Nay, then, my dear young master, thou
hast not heard the doleful tidings?"

" What doleful tidings? Quick, speak, old
man. My mother!—is she ill? Good God,
thou art pale. Oh, thy face doth speak too
intelligibly;—my mother—my beloved mother,
is no more!"

The old man burst into tears. He could not
command a single word; but the grief and agitation he could not hide was enough, for Sir

Patrick Hepborne.   In a choked and hollow voice—

" Assueton," said he, " walk up this way, so please thee; there is the banquet-hall; I must retire into this apartment for some moments. If thou hadst but known my mother—my excellent, my tenderly affectionate mother—my mother, by whose benignant and joy-beaming eyes I looked to be now greeted withal—thou would'st pardon me for being thus unmanned. But I shall be more composed anon."

And with these words, and with an agitation he could not hide, he burst away into an adjacent chamber, where he shut himself in, that he might give way to his emotions without interruption.

It was his mother's private room.   In the little oratory opening from the farther end of it was her prie-dieu and crucifix, and on the floor opposite to it was the very velvet cushion on which he found her kneeling, and offering up her fervent orisons to Heaven in his behalf, as he entered her apartment to embrace her for the last time, the morning he left Hailes for France.   He remembered that his heart was then bounding with delight at the prospect of breaking into the world, and figuring among knights and warriors, amidst all the gay splen-

dour of the French court. Alas! he little thought
then that he was embracing her for the last
time. He now looked round the chamber, and
her missal-books, with a thousand trifles he had
seen her use, called up her graceful figure and
gentle expression fresh before his eyes. He
wept bitterly, and seating himself in the chair
she used, wasted nearly an hour in giving way
to past recollections, and indulging in the grief
they occasioned. At last his sorrow began to
exhaust itself, and he became more composed.
The cushion and the little altar again caught
his eye, and, rising from the chair, he prostrated himself before the emblem of the Sa-
viour's sufferings and the Christian's faith and
hope, pouring out his soul in devotional exercise. As his head was buried in the velvet drapery of the prie-dieu, and his eyes covered, his
imagination pictured the figure of his mother
floating over him in seraphic glory. He started up, almost expecting to see his waking vision
realized; but it was no more than the offspring
of his fancy, and he again seated himself on his
mother's chair, to dry his eyes and to compose
his agitated bosom.

Though still deeply afflicted, he now felt himself able to command his feelings, and he left
his mother's apartment to rejoin Assueton. At

the door he met old Gabriel Lindsay, and he being now able to ask, and the hoary seneschal to tell, the date and circumstances of his mother's death, he learned that she had been carried off by a sudden illness about three months previous to his arrival. The firmness of the warrior now returned upon him, and, with a staid but steady countenance, he rejoined his friend.

" Assueton," said he, " if thou art disposed to ramble with me, it would give me ease to go forth a little. Let us doff our mail, and put on less cumbrous hunting-garbs and gippons, and go out into the woods. We may chance to hear their hunting-horns, and so fall in with them; else we may loiter idling it here till nightfall ere they return.

Assueton readily agreed; and both having trimmed themselves for active exercise, and armed themselves with hunting-spears, and with the anelace, a kind of wood-knife or falchion, usually worn, together with the pouch, hanging from the girdle-stead of the body, they left the Castle, with the intent of taking the direction they were informed the hunting-party had gone in. As they passed from the outer gateway, the great rough old wolf-hound again attracted his master's attention.

" Alas! poor old Flo," said Hepborne, going up to him, and stooping to caress him,—

" thou canst no more follow me as thou wert wont to do. Thou art now but as a withered and decayed log of oak—thou who used, whenever I appeared, to dart hither and thither around me like the fire-levin."

The old dog began to lick his master's hand, and to whine a dull recognition.

" I believe he doth hardly remember me," said Hepborne, moving away ; " he seems now to be little better than a clod of earth."

The old dog, however, though he had scarcely stirred for many months before, began to whimper, and rearing up his huge body with great pain, as if in stretching each limb he required to break the bonds that age had rivetted every joint withal, and getting at last on his legs, he began to follow Sir Patrick, whining and wagging his tail. Hepborne, seeing his feeble state, did what he could to drive him back ; but the dog persisted in following him.

" Poor old affectionate fellow," said Hepborne, " go with me, then, thou shalt, though I should have to carry thee back.—Assueton," continued he, " let us climb the lofty height of Dunpender, whence we shall have such a view around us as may enable us to descry the hunting-party, if they be anywhere within the range of our ken."

CHAPTER XI.

THEY accordingly made their way through the intervening woods, lawns, and alleys, and ascended the steep side of the hill. From the summit, the beautiful vale of the Tyne was fully commanded, and the extent and variety of the prospect was such as to occupy them for some time in admiration of it. Hepborne discovered a thousand spots and points in it connected with old stories of his youth. He touched on all these in succession to Assueton, his heart overflowing with his feelings, and his eyes with the remembrance of his beloved mother, whose image was continually recurring to him. He made his friend observe the distant eminences in parts of Scotland afar off; and Assueton, amongst others, was overjoyed to descry the blue top of that hill, at the base of which he had been born, and whither his heart bounded to return.

" Hark," said Hepborne, suddenly interrupting the enthusiastic greeting his friend was waft-

ing towards his distant home—" hark! methinks I hear the sound of distant bugles echo-
ing through the woods below; dost thou not
hear?"

" I do," said Assueton, " and methinks I
also hear the yelling note of the sleuth-hounds."

" That bugle-mot was my father's," said
Hepborne; " I know it full well; I could swear
to it anywhere. Nay, yonder they ride. Dost
not see them afar off yonder, sweeping across
the green alunes and avenues, where the woodshaws are thinnest? Now they cross the wide
lawnde yonder—and now they are lost amid the
shade of these oakshaws. They come this way;
let us hasten downward; we shall have ill luck
an we meet them not at the bottom of the hill."

Hepborne was so eager to embrace his father,
that, forgetting his friend was a stranger to the
perplexities of the way, he darted off, and descended through the brushwood, leaving Assueton to follow him as he best might. Assueton,
in his turn, eager to overtake Hepborne, put
down the point of his hunting-spear to aid him
in vaulting over an opposing bush. There was
a knot in the ashen shaft, and it snapt asunder
with his weight. He threw it away, and, guided
by the distant sounds of the bugle-blasts and
the yells of the hounds, he pressed precipitate-

ly down the steep, but in a direction different
from that taken by Hepborne.

, As he was within a few yards of the bottom
of the hill, he saw an enormous wolf making towards him, the oblique and sinister eyes of the
animal flashing fire, his jaws extended, and his
tongue lolling out. Assueton regretted the loss
of his hunting-spear, but resolving to attack him,
squatted, to hide himself, behind a bush directly
in the animal's path, and springing at him as he
passed, he grappled him by the throat with both
hands, and held him with the grasp of fate.
The furious wolf struggled with all his tremendous strength, and before Assueton could venture to let go one hand to draw out his anelace,
he was overbalanced by the weight of the creature, and they rolled over and over each other
down the remainder of the grassy declivity, the
knight still keeping his hold, conscious that the
moment he should lose it he must inevitably be
torn in pieces. There they lay tumbling and
writhing on the ground, the exertions of the
wolf being so violent, as frequently to lift Assueton and drag him on his back along the green
sward. Now he gained his knees, and pressing down his savage foe, he at last ventured
to loose his right hand to grope for his anelace; but it was gone—it had dropped from the

sheath; and, casting a glance around him, he saw it glittering on the grass, at some yards distance. There was no other mode of recovering it, but by dragging the furious beast towards it, and this he now put forth all his strength to endeavour to effect. He tugged and toiled, and even succeeded so far as to gain a yard or two; but his grim foe was only rendered more ferocious in his resistance, by the additional force he employed. The wolf made repeated efforts to twist his neck round to bite, and more than once succeeded in wounding Assueton severely in the left arm, the sleeve of which was entirely torn off. As the beast lay on his back too, pinned firmly down towards his head, he threw up his body, and thrust his hind feet against Assueton's face, so as completely to blind his eyes, and by a struggle more violent than any he had made before, he threw him down backwards.

The situation of the bold and hardy knight was now most perilous, for, though he still kept his grasp, he lay stretched on the ground; and whilst the wolf, standing over him, was now able to bring all his sinews to bear against him, from having his feet planted firmly on the ground, Assueton, from his position, was unable to use his muscles with much effect. The

panting and frothy jaws, and long sharp tusks
of the infuriated beast, were almost at his throat,
and the only salvation that remained for him,
was to prevent his fastening on it, by keeping the head of the brute at a distance by the
strength of his arms. The muscles of the neck
of a wolf are well known to be so powerful,
that they enable the animal to carry off a sheep
with ease; so that, with all his vigour of nerve,
Assueton had but a hopeless chance for it. Still
he held, and still they struggled, when the tramp
of a horse was heard, and a lady came galloping
by under the trees. She no sooner observed the
dreadful strife between the savage wolf and the
knight, than, alighting nimbly from her palfrey,
she couched the light hunting-spear she carried,
and ran it through the heart of the half-choked
animal. The blood spurted over the prostrate
cavalier, and the huge carcase fell on him, with
the eyes glaring in the head, and the teeth
grinding together in the agony of death.

The bold Assueton, sore toil-spent with the
length of the contest, threw the now unresist-
ing body of the creature away from him, and
instantly recovered his legs. All bloody and
covered with foam as he was, he bowed grace-
fully to his preserver, and gazed at her for some
time ere he could find breath to give his grati-

tude utterance. She was lovely as the morning.
Her fair hair, broken loose from the thraldom
of its braiding bodkins by the agitation of riding, streamed from beneath a hunting hat she
wore, and fell in flowing ringlets over the black
mantle that hung from her shoulder. Her mild
and angelic soul spoke in expressive language
through her blue eyes, though they were more
than half veiled by her modest eyelids. Her
full fresh lips were half open, and her bosom
heaved with her high breathing from the exercise she had been undergoing, and the unwonted exertion she had so lately made, and her
cheek was gently flushed by the consciousness
of the glorious deed she had achieved.

" Sir Knight," inquired she, timidly though
anxiously, " I hope thou hast tane no hurt
from the caitiff salvage? Thou dost bleed, meseems?"

" Nay, lady," said Assueton, at last able to
speak, " I bleed not; 'tis the blood of the brute
yonder. Perdie, thy bold and timely aid did
rid me of a strife that mought have ended sorely to my mischaunce. Verily, thou camest, like
an angel, to my rescue, and my poor thanks are
but meagre guerdon for the heroic deed thou
didst adventure to effect. Do I not speak to

the sister of my friend, Sir Patrick Hepborne?
—do I not address the fair Lady Isabelle?"
.; "Patrick Hepborne?" inquired she eagerly;
" art thou, indeed, the friend of my brother?
Welcome, Sir Knight; thou art welcome to me,
as thou wilt be to my father. What tidings
hast thou of my gallant brother?"

" Even those, I ween, beauteous lady, which
shall give thee belchier," said Assueton; " my
friend is well, as thou would'st wish him; nay,
more, he is here with me. We parted but now
above yonder at the crop of the hill. I lost
him in the thickets on its side, just before I en-
countered with gaffer wolf yonder." .

" Pray Heaven, " said Isabelle, with alarm
in her countenance, " that he may not meet
with some of the wolves we drove hither before
us. Thou seemest to be altogether without
weapon, Sir Knight; perhaps he is equally de-
fenceless."

" Nay, lady," replied Assueton, " I broke a
faithless rotten-shafted hunting-spear ere I came
down, and I lost my anelace from my girdle-
stead as I was struggling with the wolf. Sir
Patrick has both, I warrant thee, and will make
a better use of them than I did. Shall we seek
him?"

" Oh, yes," cried the Lady Isabelle joyfully;
" how I long to clasp my dear brother in these
arms. But hold, Sir Knight," said she, her
face again assuming an air of anxiety, " thou
dost bleed, maugre all thou didst say. Truly
thy left arm is most grievously torn by the mis-
creant wolf; let me bind it up with this rag
here." And notwithstanding all Assueton's
protestations to the contrary, she took off a
silken scarf, and bound up his wounds with it
very tenderly, exposing her own lovely neck to
the sun, that she might effect her charitable
purpose.

" And now," said she, " let's on in the direction my father took; he and my brother may
have probably met ere this.—Hey, Robert,"
cried she to a forester who appeared at the moment, " whither went my father?"

" This way, lady," said he, pointing in a particular direction; " I heard his bugle-mot but
now."

" Charge thyself with the spoils of this wolf,
Robert," said the Lady Isabelle; " I do mean
to have his felt hanged up in the hall, in remembrance of the bold and desperate conflict,
waged without aid of steel against him, by dint
of thewes and sinews alone, by this valiant

knight; 'tis a monster for size, the make of which is, I trow, rarely seen."

" Nay, lady," cried Assueton, " rather hang up his spoils in commemoration of thine own brave deed; for it was thou who killed him. And had it not been for thee, gaffer wolf might, ere now, have made a dinner of me."

" In truth, Sir Knight," replied Isabelle, " hadst thou not held him by the throat so starkly, I trow I should have had little courage to have faced him."

The lady vaulted on her palfrey, and Assueton, his left arm decorated with her scarf, and holding her bridle with his right, walked by the side of her palfrey, like a true lady's knight, unwittingly engaged, for the first time in his life, in pleasing dialogue with a beautiful woman.

Sir Patrick Hepborne, who thought only of seeing his father, had rushed down the steep side of Dunpender in the hope of meeting him somewhere near the base of the hill, for the sound of the chase evidently came that way. His old dog Flo had difficulty in following him; and stumbling over the stumps of trees, and the stones that lay in his way, he was at last completely left behind. As Sir Patrick had nearly reached the bottom of the steep, he too observed a large wolf making up the hill. The animal came at a lagging pace, and was evidently much blown. Hepborne hurled his hunting-spear at him without a moment's delay, wounding him desperately in the neck; and eager to make sure of him with his anelace, rushed forward, without perceiving a sudden declivity, where there was a little precipitous face of rock, over which he fell headlong, and rolling downwards, his head came in contact with the trunk of an oak, at the foot of which he lay stunned and senseless. The wolf, writhing for some time with the agony of the wound he had received, succeeded at last in extricating himself from the spear-head, and then observing the man from whose hand he had received it, lying at his mercy on the ground near him, he was about to take instant vengeance on him, when he was suddenly called on to defend himself against a new assailant.

This was no other than poor Flo, who, having followed his master's track as fast as his old legs could carry him, came up at the very moment the gaunt animal was about to fasten his jaws on him. His ancient spirit grew young within him as he beheld his master's danger; he sprang on the wolf with an energy and fury which no one who had seen him that morning

could have believed him capable of, and seizing
his ferocious adversary by the throat, a bloody
combat ensued between them.

Hepborne having gradually recovered from
his swoon, and hearing the noise of the fight,
roused himself, and getting upon his legs, beheld with astonishment the miraculous exertions his faithful dog was making in his defence,
and the deadly strife that was waging between
him and the wolf. The fierce and powerful
animal was much an overmatch for the good
allounde, who had already received some dreadful bites, but still fought with unabated resolution. Hepborne ran to his rescue, and burying his anelace in the wolf's body, killed him
outright. But his help came too late for poor
old Flo, who licked the kind hand that was
stretched out to succour and caress him, and
turning upon his side, raised his dim eyes towards his master's face, and slowly closed them
in death.

Hepborne lifted him up, all streaming with
blood, and carrying him to a fountain a few
paces off, bathed his head and his gaping wounds,
with the vain hope that the water might revive
him; but life was extinct. Sir Patrick laid him
on the ground, and wept over him as if he had
been a friend.

The sound of the horns now came nearer, the yell of the dogs approached, and by and by some of the hounds appeared, and ran in upon their already inanimate prey. Immediately behind them came Sir Patrick Hepborne the elder, a powerful, noble-looking man, in full vigour of life, mounted on a gallant grey, and with a crowd of foresters at his back. He took off his hunting-hat to wipe his brow as he halted, and though he displayed a bald forehead, the hinder part of his head was covered with luxuriant black hair, on which age's winter had not yet shed a single particle of snow. His beard and moustaches were of the same raven hue; and his eyes, though mild, were lofty and penetrating in their expression.

"How now, young man," said he to his son, as he reined up his steed, "what, hast thou killed the wolf?"

"My father!" cried the younger Sir Patrick, starting up, and running to his stirrup.

"My son!" exclaimed the astonished and delighted Sir Patrick the elder, and vaulting from his horse, they were immediately locked in each other's arms.

It was some minutes before either father or son could articulate anything but broken sentences. The minds of both reverted to the overwhelming loss they had sustained since they last saw each other, and both wept bitterly.

"My dear boy, forgive me," said the father; "but these tears are—we have lost—but yet I see thou hast already gathered the sad intelligence.—'Tis now three months—Good Heavens!—but she is a saint above, my dear Patrick."

Again they enclasped each other, and giving way to their feelings, the two warriors wept on each other's bosoms till the rude group of foresters around them were melted into tears at the spectacle. Sir Patrick the elder was the first to regain command of himself, and the first use he made of the power of speech was to put a thousand questions to his son. The younger knight satisfied him as to everything, and concluded by giving him the history of his accident, and the noble but afflicting death of his faithful old allounde.

"Poor fellow," said the elder Sir Patrick, going up to the spot where he lay, and dropping a tear of gratitude over him—"poor fellow, he has died as a hero ought to do—nobly, in stark stoure in the field. Let him be forthwith yirded, dost hear me, on the spot where he fell; I shall have a stone erected over him, in grateful memorial of his having died for his master."

Some of the foresters, who had spades for

digging out the vermin of the chase, instantly executed this command, and the two knights tarried until they had themselves laid his body in the grave dug for him.

"And now let us go look for Isabelle, and thy friend Sir John Assueton," said the elder Sir Patrick; "sound thy bugles, my merry men, and let us down to the broad lawnde, where we shall have best chance of meeting."

They had no sooner entered the beautiful glade among the woods that the elder knight had alluded to, than the younger Sir Patrick descried his sister the Lady Isabelle coming riding on her palfrey, and his friend Assueton leading her bridle-rein. He ran forward to embrace her, and she, instantly recognizing him, sprang from the saddle into his arms. The meeting between the brother and sister was rendered as affecting, by the remembrance of the loss of their mother, as that of the father and son had been. But the elder Sir Patrick having mastered his feelings, soon contributed to soothe theirs. The younger Sir Patrick introduced his friend Assueton to his father, and after their compliments of courtesy were made, the adventures of both parties detailed, and mutual congratulations had taken place between them,—

"Come," said the elder Sir Patrick, "come, Isabelle, get thee to horse again, and let us straightway to the Castle. The welkin reddens i' the west, and the sun is about to hide his head among yonder amber clouds; let us to the Castle, I say. I trow we shall have enow of food for talk for the rest of the evening. We shall have the spoils of these wolves hung up in the hall, in memorial of the strange events of this day—of the gallantry of the Lady Isabelle, who so nobly rescued Sir John Assueton, and of the courage and fidelity of the attached old allounde Flo, who so nobly died in defence of his master."

The bugles sounded a mot, and the elder Sir Patrick, with his son walking by his side, moved forward at the head of the troop. The Lady Isabelle sprang into her saddle, and Sir John Assueton, never choosing to resign the rein he had grasped, led her palfrey as before, and again glided into the same train of conversation with her which he had formerly found so fascinating. The foresters, grooms, and churls, who formed the hunting-suite, some on foot and others on horseback, armed with every variety of hunting-gear, followed in the rear of march, and in this order they returned to the Castle.

2

CHAPTER XII.

THE affliction which had so lately visited the elder Sir Patrick Hepborne had made him avoid company, and Hailes Castle had consequently been entirely without guests ever since his lady's death. But it must not be imagined that the evening of the hunting-day passed dully, because the board was not filled. The sweet and soothing sorrow awakened by tender and melancholy recollections soon gave way before the joy arising from the return of Sir Patrick the younger. In those days letters could not pass as they do now, with the velocity of the winds, by posts and carriers, from one part of Europe to another; and during Hepborne's absence his father had had no tidings of his son, except occasionally through the medium of those warriors or pilgrims, who, having fought in foreign fields, or visited foreign shrines, had chanced during their travels to see or to hear of him, and who came to Hailes Castle to receive the liberal guerdon of his hospitality for the good news they brought. The elder Sir Patrick, therefore had much to ask, and his son much to answer; so that the ball of conversation was unremittingly kept up between them.

The Lady Isabelle was seated between her brother and his friend Sir John Assueton, in the most provoking position; for she was thus placed, as it were, betwixt two magnets, so as to be equally attracted by both. Her affection for Sir Patrick made her anxious to catch all he said, and to gather all his adventures; whilst, on the other hand, Sir John Assueton's conversation, made up, as it in a great measure was, of the praises of his friend, intermixed with many interesting notes on the accounts of battles and passages of arms her brother was narrating to her father, proved so seducing, that she found it difficult to turn away her ear from him. Nor were Assueton's illustrations the less gratifying, that they often brought out the whole truth, where her brother's modesty induced him to sink such parts of the tale as were the most glorious to himself. As for Assueton himself, he seemed to have become a new man in her company. He was naturally shrewd, excessively good-humoured, and often witty in his conversation, but he never in his life before bestowed more of it on a lady than barely what the courtesy of chivalry required. This night, however, he was animated and eloquent; and the result was, that the Lady Isabelle retired to her couch at an unusually late hour, and declared to her handmaiden, Mary Hay, as she was undressing her, that Sir John Assueton was certainly the most gallant, witty, and agreeable knight she had ever had the good fortune to meet with.

" But thou dost not think him so handsome as thy brother Sir Patrick, Lady ?" said the sly Miss Mary Hay.

" Nay, as to that, Mary," replied the Lady Isabelle, " they are both handsome, yet both very diverse in their beauty. Thou knowest that one is fair, and the other dark. My brother Sir Patrick and I do take our fair tint from our poor mother. Is it not common for fair to affect dark, and dark fair ? My father, thou seest, is dark, yet was my dear departed mother fair as the light of day. Is it unnatural, then, that I should esteem Sir John Assueton's olive tint of countenance, his speaking black eyes, his nobly-arched jet eyebrows, and the raven curls of his finely-formed head, more than the pure red and white complexion, the blue eyes, and the fair hair of my dear brother ? Nay, nay, my brother is very handsome; but algate he be my brother, and though I love him, as sure never sister loved brother before, yet must I tell the truth, thou knowest, Mary; and in good foy I do think Sir John Assueton by much the properer man."

Hepborne had been by no means blind to that, of which neither his sister nor Sir John Assueton were as yet themselves aware. He saw the change on Assueton with extreme delight. He enjoyed the idea of this woman-hater being at last himself enslaved, and above all, he rejoiced that the enslaver should be his sister the Lady Isabelle. He longed to attack him on the subject; but lest he might scare him away from the toils, before he was fairly and irrecoverably meshed, he resolved to appear to shut his eyes to his friend's incipient disease. As he went with Sir John, therefore, to see him comfortably accommodated for the night, he only indulged himself in a remark, natural enough in itself, upon his wounded arm.

" Assueton," said he, " wilt thou not have thine arm dressed by some cunning leech ere thou goest to rest? Our chaplain is no mean proficient in leechcraft; better take that rag of a kerchief away, and have it properly bound up."

" Nay, nay," cried Assueton, hastily, " I thank thee, my good friend; but 'tis very well

as it is.   Thy sister, the Lady Isabelle, bound
it up with exceeding care; and in these cases,
I have remarked, that there is no salve equal in
virtue to the bloody goutes of the wound itself.
Good night, and St Andrew be with thee."

" And may St Baldrid, our tutelary Saint, be
with you," replied Hepborne, as he shut the
door.   " Poor Assueton, said he then to himself, with a smile, " my sister has cured one
wound for him, only to inflict another, which he
will find it more difficult to salve."

The next day being devoted to the gay amuse-
ment of hawking, was yet more decisive of the
fate of poor Sir John Assueton.   He rode by
the side of the Lady Isabelle; and as the nature
of the sport precluded the possibility of her using
that attention necessary to make her palfrey
avoid the obstacles lying in its way, or to keep
it up when it stumbled, Sir John found a ready
excuse for again acting the part of her knight;
and one-armed as he had been rendered by the
bites of the wolf, he ran all manner of risks for
his own neck, to save hers.   Hepborne was
more occupied in regarding them, than in the
sport they were following.   He rode after the
pair, enjoying all he saw; for in the malicious
pleasure he took in perceiving Assueton getting
deeper and deeper entangled in the snares of

love, and its fever mounting higher and higher into his brain, he almost forgot the toils he had himself been caught in, and found a palliative for his own heart's disease, producing a temporary relaxation of its intensity. Thus then they rode. When the game was on wing, the fair Isabelle galloped fearlessly on, with her eyes sometimes following the flight of the falcon after its quarry, but much oftener with her head turned towards Sir John Assueton, whilst Sir John's looks were fixed now with anxiety on the ground, to ensure safe riding to the lady, and now thrown with love-sick gaze of tenderness into the heaven of her eyes, for his had no wish to soar higher.

In the evening, the Lady Isabelle and her knight were again left to themselves by the father and son. Her brother's tales were less interesting to her than they had been the previous night, and though Assueton talked less of his friend, yet she by no means found his conversation the duller on that account; nay, she even listened much more intensely to it than before. The younger Sir Patrick, towards the close of the night, begged of his sister to sit down to her harp, and when she did so, Assueton hung over her with a rapture sufficiently marking the

strength of his new-born passion, and the little
art he had in concealing it.

Having been asked by her brother to sing,
she accompanied her voice in the following can-
zonette :—

> Why was celestial Music given,
>   But of enchanting Love to sing!
> Ethereal flame—that first from Heaven
>   Angels to this earth did bring.
>
> What state was man's, till he received
>   The genial blessing from the sky ?
> What though in Paradise he lived ?
>   Yet still he pined, and knew not why.
>
> But when his beauteous partner came,
>   The scene, that dreary was and wild,
> Grew lovely as he felt the flame,
>   And the luxuriant garden smiled.
>
> Oh, Love !—of man thou second soul,
>   What but a clod of earth is he,
> Who never yet thy flame did thole,
>   Who never felt thy witchery !

Assueton's applauses were more energetic,
and his approbation more eloquently expressed
at the conclusion of this song, than Hepborne
had ever heard them on any former occasion.
Though the theme was wont to be so very
unpalatable to him, yet he besought the Lady
Isabelle again and again to repeat it, and it seemed to give him new and increased pleasure every
time he heard it. At last the hour for retiring

came, and Hepborne inwardly rejoiced to observe a certain trembling in the voices of both Assueton and his sister, as they touched each other's hands to say good night.

Sir Patrick Hepborne the younger had no sooner accompanied his friend to his apartment, than Assueton seated himself near the hearth, and put up his feet against the wall, where he fell into a kind of listless dream. Hepborne took a seat on the opposite side of the fire-place, and after he had sat silently watching him for some time, in secret enjoyment of the state he beheld him reduced to, the following conversation took place between them.

" Well, Assueton," said Hepborne, first breaking silence, and assuming as melancholy a tone as the humour he was in would permit him to use, " well, mon bel ami, so we must part to-morrow? The thought is most distressing. My heart would have urged me to press thee to a farther sojournance with us at Hailes; but thou wert too determined, and urged too many and too strong reasons for thy return home, when we last talked of the matter, to leave room for hope that I might succeed in shaking thy purpose. I see that of very needscost thou must go; nay, in good sooth, thy motives for departure are of a nature, that, feeling as I

have myself felt, I should inwardly blame thee
were thy good nature to lead thee to yield to
my importunate entreaty. Yea, albeit thou
should'st consent to stay with me, I should verily tine half the jovisaunce that mought otherwise spring from thy good company; since,
from the all-perfect being I now hold thee to
be, thou would'st dwindle in my esteem, and be
agrutched of half the attraction thou dost possess in mine eyes, by appearing to lose some deal
of those strong feelings of attachment for thy
home, and for the scenes and friends of thy boyhood, which thou hast hitherto so eminently
displayed, and in which, I am led to think, we
do so much resemble each other. Having now
had mine somewhat satisfied, perdie, I could
almost wish to boune me with thee, were it
only to participate in thine,—were it only to see
thee approach the wide domains and the ancient
castle of thine ancestors—to see thee meet thy
beloved mother, now so long widowed, and
panting to press her only child, her long absent
son, to her bosom—to watch how thou mayest
encounter with old friends—to behold the hearty
shakes of loving souvenaunce, given by thy
hand to those with whom thou hast wrestled,
or held mimic tournay when thou wert yet but
a stripling.—Oh, 'twould be as a prolonging of

mine own feelings of like sort, to witness those
that might arise to thee. But the journey is too
long for me to take as yet; and besides, I cannot yet so soon leave my father and Isabelle.
Moreover, thou knowest that my heart yet ach-
eth severely from the wounds which it took at
Norham. Heigh ho! But, gramercy, forgive me,
I entreat thee, for touching unwittingly on the,
by thee, hated subject of love, the which, I well
know, is ever wont to erke thee."

During this long address, Assueton remained
with his heels up against the wall, his toes all
the time beating that species of march, that in
more modern times has been denominated the
devil's tattoo, and with his eyes firmly fixed on
the embers consuming on the hearth.

" I hope, however, my dearest friend," con-
tinned Hepborne, " that thou mayest yet be
able to return to me at Hailes. Thine affairs,
(though, perdie, thou must have much to settle
after such a succession, and so long an absence,)
thine affairs, I say, cannot at the worst detain
thee at home longer than a matter of twelve
months or so; after which, (that is, when thou
shalt have visited thy friends in divers other
parts,) I may hope perchance to see thee again
return hither."

Assueton shifted his position two or three

times during this second speech of Hepborne's, always again commencing his devil's tattoo on the wall; but when his friend ceased, he made no other reply than—

"Umph! Ay, ay, my dear Hepborne, thou shalt see me."

"My dear Assueton," continued Hepborne, "that is but a loose and vague reply, I ween. But, by St Genevieve, I guess how it is. Thou hast thoughts (though as yet thou would'st fain not effunde them to me) of returning to France in short space; and thou would'st keep them sicker in thy breast for a time, lest peradventure I should grieve too deeply at thy so speedy abandonment of thy country."

"Nay, nay," said Assueton, hastily, "trust me I have no such emprize in head."

"What then can make thee so little satisfactory in thy reply?" said Hepborne; "surely 'tis but a small matter to grant me; 'tis but a small boon to ask of thee to return to Hailes Castle some twelve months or year and half hence? I doubt me sore that thou hast been but half pleased with thy visit here; and truly, when I think on't, it has been but a dull one."

"Nay," replied Assueton, eagerly interrupting him, "I do assure thee, Hepborne, thou art grievously mistaken in so supposing. On the contrary, my hours never passed so happily as they have done here; nor," added he, with a deep sigh, " so swiftly, so very swiftly."

" 'Tis all well in thee, Assueton," said Hepborne, " 'tis all well in thee to use thy courtesy to say so; yet, I wot well, 'tis but to please thy friend. Thou knowest that my father hath been so voracious in his inquiries into the history of my life during my stay in France, that he hath never suffered me to leave him, so that thou hadst neither his good company, nor my poor converse to cheer thee, but, much to my distress, thou hast been left to be erked by the silly prattle and trifling speech of that foolish pusel my sister Isabelle, worn out by the which, 'tis no marvel thou should'st now be thus moody, as I see thou art; and to rid thyself of this dreriment of thine, it is natural enow that thou should'st be right glad to escape hence, yea, and sore afraid ever to return here. But fear thee not, my friend; she shall not stand long in thy way. She hath had many offers of espousal, on the which my father and I are to sit in counsel anon, that is, when other weightier matters are dispatched; and as soon as we shall have time to choose a fitting match for the maid, she shall forthwith be tochered off. She cannot, then, remain much longer at Hailes than some

three or four weeks at farthest, to frighten from
its hall my best and dearest friend. So that if
she be the hinderance to thy return hither, make
no account of her, and promise me at once that
thou wilt come. By St Baldrid, we shall have a
houseful of jolly stalwart knights to meet thee
here; and our talk shall be of deeds of arms,
and tourneys, till thy heart be fully contented."

This speech of Hepborne's very much moved
Assueton; he shifted his legs down from the
wall and up again at least a dozen times, and
his tattoo now became so rapid, that it would
have troubled the legions for whom the march
may have been originally composed, to have
kept their feet trotting in time to its measure.

" Nay, verily, Hepborne," said he seriously,
" thou dost thy sister but scrimp justice, methinks. The Lady Isabelle was anything but
tiresome to me; nay, if I may adventure to say
so much, she hath sense and judgment greatly
beyond what might be looked for from her age
and sex; there is something most truly pleasing
in her converse—something, I would say, much
superior to anything I have heretofore chanced
to encounter in woman. But, methinks, thou
art rather hasty in thy disposal of her. The
damosel is young enow, meseems, to be thrust

forth of her father's boure, perhaps to take upon her the weight of formal state that appertaineth to the Madame of some stiff and stern vavesoure. Perdie, I cannot think with patience of her being so bestowed already; 'twould be cruel, methinks—nay, 'twould, in good verity, be most unlike thee, Hepborne, to throw thy peerless sister away on some harsh lord, or silly gnoffe, merely to rid thy father's castle of her for thine own convenience. Fie on thee; I weened not thou could'st have even thought of anything so selfish."

"Nay, be not angry, Assueton," said Hepborne, "thou knowest that they have all a wish to wed them. But 'tis somewhat strange, methinks, to hear thee talk so; the poppet seems to have made more impression on thee than ever before was made by woman. What means this warmth? or why should'st thou step forth to be her knight?"

"'Tis the part of a good knight," replied Assueton, hastily, "to aid and succour all damosels in distress."

"Nay, but not against a distress of the knight's own fancying, yea, and contrary to the wishes of the damosel herself," replied Hepborne. "What! would'st thou throw down the gauntlet of defiance against thy friend, only for being willing to give to his sister the man of her own heart?"

" And hath she then such?" exclaimed Assueton, his face suddenly becoming the very emblem of woe-begone anxiety.

" Yea, in good truth hath she, Assueton," replied Sir Patrick. " I did but suspect the truth last night, but this day I have been confirmed in it."

" Then am I the most wretched of knights," cried Assueton, at once forgetting all his guards; and rising hastily from his seat, he struck his breast, and paced the room in a frenzy of despair.

Hepborne could carry on the farce no longer. He burst into a fit of laughter that seemed to threaten his immediate dissolution; then threw himself on the couch, that he might give full way to it without fear of falling on the floor, and there he tossed to and fro with the reiterated convulsions it occasioned him. Assueton stood in mute astonishment for some moments, but at last he began to perceive that his friend had discovered his weakness, and that he had been all this time playing on him. He resumed his seat and position at the hearth, and returned again to his tattoo.

" So," said Hepborne—" so!—ha, ha, ha!

—so!—ha, ha!—so!—Oh, I shall never find breath to speak—ha, ha, ha! So, Sir John'Assueton, the woman-hater, the Knight of Adamant, he who was wont to be known in France by the surnoms of the Knight sans Amour, and the Chevalier cœur caillou—who, rather than submit to talk to a woman, would hie him to the stable, to hold grave converse with his horse —who railed roundly at every unfortunate man that, following the ensample of his great ancestor Adam, did but submit himself to the yoke of love—who could not bear to hear the very name of love—who sickened when it was mentioned—who had an absolute antipathy to it,' as some, they know not why, have to cats or cheese—who, though he liked music to admiration, would avoid the place if love but chanced to be the minstrel's theme;—he, Sir John Assueton, is at last enslaved, has his wounds bound up by a woman, and wears her scarf—plays the lady's knight, and leads her palfrey rein—rownes soft things in her ear, hangs o'er her harp, and drinks in the sweet love-verses she sings to him!"

" Nay, nay, Hepborne, my dearest friend," said Assueton, starting up, and clasping his hands together in an imploring attitude, " I. confess, I confess; but sith I do confess, have mercy on me, I entreat thee; 'tis cruel to sport with my sufferings, since thou knowest, alas, too surely that I must love in vain."

" But, pr'ythee, ' why should'st thou afflict thyself, and peak and pine for a silly girl?' " said Hepborne ironically, bringing up against him some of the very expressions he had used to himself at Norham. " ' A knight of thy prowess in the field may have a thousand baubles as fair for the mere picking up; let it not erk thee that this trifle is beyond thy reach.' " And then rising, and striding gravely up to Assueton, and shaking his head solemnly—" ' Trust me, women are dangerous flowers to pluck, and have less of the rose about them than the thorn.' Ha, ha, ha! Oh, 'tis exquisite—by St Denis, 'tis the richest treat I ever enjoyed."

" Nay, but bethink thee, my dear friend," said Assueton, with an imploring look—" bethink thee, I beseech thee, what misery I am enduring, and reflect how much thou art augmenting it by thy raillery. Depardieu, I believe thou never didst suffer such pain from love as I do now."

" ' No, thank my good stars,' " said Hepborne, returning to the charge, and again assuming a burlesque solemnity of air and tone,

" ' and I hope, moreover, I never shall be so be-sotted; it makes a very fool of a man.' "

" Well, well," said Assueton, sighing deep-ly, " I see thou art determined to make my fa-tal disease thy sport; yet, by St Andrew, it is but cruel and ungenerous of thee."

" Gramercy, Assueton, I thought my inno-cent raillery could do thee no harm," said Hep-borne; " methought that ' thou might'st be said to have no ears for such matters.' But if thou, in good truth, hast really caught the fe-ver, verily I shall not desert thee, ' my friend-ship for thee shall make me listen to thy ra-vings;' yea, and ' compassion for thy disease shall make me watch the progress of its symp-toms. Never fear that I shall be so little of a Christian knight as to abandon thee when thy estate is so dangerous.' But what, I pr'ythee, my friend, hath induced this so dangerous ma-lady?"

" Hepborne," replied Sir John, " thy ange-lic sister's magnanimity, her matchless beauty, her enchanting converse, and her sweet syren voice."

" Ay, ay," said Hepborne, roguishly, " so 'twas her voice, her warbles, and her virelays, that gave thee the coup-de-grace? Nay, it must be soothly confessed, thou didst hang over her chair to-night in most proper love-like fashion, as she harped it; yet her verses ' were silly enough in conscience, methought'—and then, thou knowest, thou dost ' rarely listen to music when love or its follies are the theme.' "

" Hepborne," said Assueton gravely, and with an air of entreaty, " it was not after this fashion that I did use thee in thine affliction at Norham. Think, I beseech thee, that my case is not less hopeless than thine. But who, I entreat thee, is the happy knight who is blessed by the favouring smile of thy divine sister, of the Lady Isabelle Hepborne, whom I now no longer blush to declare to be the most peerless damosel presently in existence ?"

" He is a knight," replied Hepborne, "whose peer thou shalt as rarely meet with, I trow, as thou canst encounter the make of my sister, the Lady Isabelle. He is a proper, tall, athletic, handsome man, of dark hair and olive complexion, with trim moustaches and comely beard—nay, the very man, in short, to take a woman's eye. Though as yet but young in age, he is old in arms, and hath already done such doughty deeds as have made him renowned even in the very songs of the minstrels. Moreover, he is a beloved friend of mine, and one much approved of my father, and he shall gladly have our consent for the espousal of my sister."

. ˜" Nay, then," said Assueton, in the accents of utter hopelessness, " I am indeed but a lost knight, and must hie me to some barren wilderness, to sigh my soul away. But lest my disease should drive me to madness, tell me, I entreat thee, the name of this most fortunate of men, that I may keep me from his path, lest, in my blind fury, I might destroy him in some ill-starred contecke, and through him wrack the happiness of the Lady Isabelle, now dearer to me than life?"

" Thou knowest him as well as thou dost thyself, my dear Assueton," said Hepborne. " Trust me, he is one to whom thou dost wish much too well to do him harm; his name is— Sir John Assueton."

" Nay, mock me not, Hepborne, drive me not mad with false hopes," said Assueton; " certes, thy raillery doth now exceed the bounds that even friendship should permit."

" Gad-a-mercy," said Hepborne, " thou dost seem to me to be mad enough already. What! would'st thou quarrel with me for giving thee assurance of that thou hast most panted for? By the honour of a knight, I swear that Isabelle loves thee. 'Tis true, I heard it not from her lips; but I read it in her eyes, the which, let me tell thee, inexperienced in the science, and all unlearned in the leden of love as thou art, do ever furnish by far the best and soothest evidence on this point that the riddle woman can yield. Never doubt me but she loves thee, Assueton. She drank up the words thou did'st rowne in her ear, with a thirst that showed the growing fever of her soul. And now," continued he, as he observed the happy effects of his intelligence upon the countenance of his friend —" and now, Assueton, tell me, I pr'ythee, at what hour in the morning shall I order thine esquire and cortege to be ready for thy departure?"

" Hepborne," said Assueton, running to embrace him, " thou hast made me the happiest of mortals. Go! nay, perdie, I shall stay at Hailes till thou dost turn me out."

" But, my dearest Assueton," cried Hepborne, smiling, " consider thy mother, and the friends and the scenes of thy boyhood—consider what thou——"

" Pshaw, my dear Hepborne," cried Sir John, interrupting him, " no more on't, I entreat thee. Leave me, I beseech thee, to dreams of delight. Good night, and may the blessed Virgin and St Andrew be thy warison, for this ecstacy of jovinaunce thou hast poured into my soul."

"Good night," said Hepborne, with a more serious air—" good night, my dear and long-tried brother-in-arms; and good night, my yet dearer brother by alliance, as I hope soon to call thee."

The meeting of the lovers on the next day, was productive of more interesting conversation than any they had yet enjoyed; and although Assueton was, as his friend had said, a novice in the science and language of love, yet he caught up the knowledge of both with most marvellous expedition, and was listened to with blushing pleasure by the lovely Isabelle.

As the party was seated at breakfast, the sound of trumpets was heard, followed by that of the trampling of horses in the courtyard, and immediately afterwards a herald, proudly arrayed, and followed by his pursuivants, was ushered into the hall.

"Sir Patrick Hepborne," said he, "and you, Sirs Knights, I come to announce to you and to the world, that on the tenth day of the next month, the noble John Dunbar, Earl of Moray, will hold a splendid meeting of arms on the Mead of St John's; and all princes, lords, barons, knights, and esquires, who intend to tilt at the tournament, are hereby ordained to lodge themselves within his Castle of Tarnawa, or in pavilions on the field, four days before the said tournament, to make due display of their armouries, on pain of not being received at the said tournament. And their arms shall be thus disposed : The crest shall be placed on a plate of copper large enough to contain the whole summit of the helmet, and the said plate shall be covered with a mantle, whereon shall be blazoned the arms of him who bears it; and on the said mantle, at the top thereof, shall the crest be placed, and around it shall be a wreath of colours, whatsoever it shall please him. God save King Robert."

The herald having in this manner formally pronounced the proclamation intrusted to him, was kindly and honourably greeted by Sir Patrick Hepborne, and forthwith seated at the board, and hospitably entertained; after which he arose, and addressed the knight.

" Sir Patrick Hepborne," said he, " myself and my people being now refreshed, I may not waste my time here, having yet a large district to travel over. I drink this cup of wine to thee and to thy roof-tree, with a herald's thanks for thy noble treatment. Say, shall the Lord of Moray look for thy presence at the Tournay?

I know it would be his wish to do thee and thine particular honour."

" Of that I judge by his sending thee to Hailes," said Sir Patrick, courteously. " But in truth I cannot go. I must leave it to thee to tell the noble earl how sorely grieved I am to say so; but my heart has been ill at ease of late."

" Thine absence will sorely grieve the noble earl, Sir Knight," replied the herald; " but, nathless, I shall hope to see thy gallant son and the renowned Sir John Assueton, chiefest flowers in the gay garland of Scottish knights, who shall that day assemble at St John's. Till then adieu, Sirs Knights, and may God and St Andrew be with ye all."

The trumpets again sounded, and the herald, being waited on by the knights to the court-yard, mounted his richly-caparisoned steed, and rode forth from the Castle, again attended by all the pomp of heraldry.

" Assueton," said Hepborne, with a roguish air of seriousness, as they returned up stairs, " goest thou to this tournay ?"

" Nay, of a truth," replied Assueton, with his eyes on the ground, " I cannot just at present yede me so far. Besides, these wounds in

2

my bridle-arm do still pain me grievously, rendering me all unfit for jousting."

" Then, as I am resolved to go," said Hepborne, " I do beseech thee make Hailes Castle thy home till my return, and play the part of son to my dear father in mine absence."

CHAPTER XIII. .

As the way was long, and the day of the
tournament not very distant, Sir Patrick Hepborne the younger resolved to leave Hailes
Castle next morning for the North, that he
might save himself the necessity of forced marches. He accordingly made instant preparations
for his journey; his father gave immediate orders for securing him such a cortège as should
not disgrace the name he bore; and his horses,
arms, and appointments of every description,
were perfectly befitting his family and rank.
When the morning of his departure arrived, he
took an affectionate leave of his father and Assueton, who left the Castle with their attendants,
at an early hour, for the purpose of hunting together. The Lady Isabelle would gladly have
made one of the party with her father and her
lover, but, attached as she was to Sir John Assueton, her affection for her brother was too
strong to permit her to leave the Castle till he

should be gone. That he might enjoy her society in private till the last moment, Hepborne
dispatched his faithful esquire, Master Mortimer Sang, at the head of his people, to wait for
him at a particular spot, which he indicated, at
the distance of about a mile from the Castle ;
and he also sent forward the palfrey he meant
to ride, for his noble destrier Beaufront was to
be led by a groom during the whole march.

His fond sister Isabelle resolved to walk with
him to the place where he was to meet his attendants, and accordingly the brother and sister
set out together arm in arm.

Sir Patrick, resolving to probe his sister's
love, adroitly turned the conversation on his
friend Assueton, and, with extreme ingenuity,
touched on those agrémens and virtues which
his friend evidently possessed, as well as on a
number of weak and faulty points, both in person and manner, which he chose, for certain
purposes, to feign in him, or greatly to exagge-
rate. In praising the former, the Lady Isabelle
very much surpassed her brother ; for, however
highly he might laud his friend, she always
found something yet more powerful and eloquent to say in his favour ; but whenever Sir
Patrick ventured to hint at anything like a
fault or a blemish, the lady was instantly up

in arms, and made as brave a defence for him against her brother, as she had done for him some days before against the wolf. This light skirmishing went on between them until they reached a knoll covered with tall oaks, whence they beheld the party, about to take shelter in the appointed grove of trees, on the meadow by the river's side, at a considerable distance below them.

"Isabelle," said Hepborne, taking her hand tenderly, "thou hast walked far enough, my love; let us rest here for an instant, and then part. Our converse hath not been vain. My just praise of Assueton, as well as the faults I pretended to find in him, were neither of them without an object. I wished, ere I left thee, to satisfy myself of the true state of thy little heart; for I should have never forgiven myself had I discovered that I had been mistaken, and that I had told what was not true, when I assured Assueton, as I did last night, that thou lovest him."

"Told Sir John Assueton that I love him!" exclaimed the Lady Isabelle, blushing with mingled surprise and confusion; "how could'st thou tell him so? and what dost thou know of my sentiments regarding him?—Heavens! what will he think of me?"

" Why, well, passing well, my fair sister,"
said Hepborne; " make thyself easy on that
score. He loves thee, believe me, as much as
thou lovest him; so I leave thee to measure the
length, breadth, heighth, and depth, of his attachment by the dimensions of thine own. But
as to knowing the state of thy heart—tut! I
could make out much more difficult cases than
it presents; for well I wot its state is apparent
enough, even from the little talk I have had
with thee now, if I had never heard or seen
more. But, my dear Isabelle, after my father,
thou and be are the two beings on earth whom
I do most love. Ye are both perfect in mine
eyes. I could talk to thee of Assueton's qua-
lities and perfections for days together, and of
virtues, which as yet thou canst not have dreamt
of; but I must leave thee to the delightful task
of discovering them for thyself. All I can now
say is, may Heaven make ye both happy in each
other,—for I must be gone. And so, my love,
farewell, and may the blessed Virgin protect
thee."

He then threw his arms about his sister's
neck, pressed her to his bosom, and, having
kissed her repeatedly with the most tender affection, tore himself from her, ran down the
hill, and, as she cleared her eyes from the tear-

drops that swelled in them, she saw him disap-
pear in the shade of the clump of trees where
his party was stationed. A good deal of time
seemed to be lost ere the whole were mounted,
and in motion; but at last she saw them emer-
ging from the wood-shaw, and winding slowly,
in single files, up the river-side. She sat on the
bank, straining her eyes after them, until they
were lost in the distant intricacies of the surface, and then turned her steps slowly homewards, ruminating agreeably on her brother's
last words, as well as on the events of the preceding days, which had given her a new and
more powerful interest in life than she had ever
before experienced.

" Oh, my dear brother," said she to herself,
" thou didst indeed say truly that I do love him;
and if thou sayest as soothly that he doth love
me, then am I blessed indeed."

It was courtesy alone that induced Sir John
Assueton to agree to Sir Patrick Hepborne's
proposal of going that morning to the woodlands to hunt the deer. He went with no very
good will; nay, when his host talked of it, he
felt more than once inclined, as he had done
with his friend about the tournament, to plead
his wounded arm as an excuse for remaining at
home with the Lady Isabelle; and perhaps, if it

had not been for absolute shame, he might have
yielded to the temptation. Hence he had but
little pleasure in the sport that day, although it
was unusually fine; and he was by no means
gratified to find himself led on by the chase to a
very unusual distance. But to leave Sir Patrick
was impossible. He was therefore compelled,
very much against his inclination, to ride all
day like a lifeless trunk, whilst his spirit was
hovering over the far-off towers of Hailes Castle. The deer was killed so far from home, that
it was later than ordinary before the party returned.

" I am surprised Isabelle is not already here
to receive us," said Sir Patrick, as they entered
the banquet-hall; " I trowed she might have
been impatient for our return ere this.—Gabriel," said he to the old seneschal, " go, I
pr'ythee, to Mary Hay, and let her tell her
lady that we are come home, and that we have
brought good appetites with us."

Gabriel went, and soon returned with Mary
Hay herself, who appeared in great agitation.

" Where is thy lady?" demanded Sir Patrick,
with an expression of considerable anxiety.

" My lady! my good lord," said the terrified
girl; " holy St Baldrid, is she not with thee
then?"

" No," said Sir Patrick, with increasing amazement and alarm, " she went not with us. We left her here with my son, when we rode forth in the morning."

" Nay, I knew that," said the terrified Mary Hay, " but—good angels be about us—I weened that her pages and palfrey might have gone with thee, and that she might ha' been to join thee in the woods, after having given her brother the convoy."

" Merciful powers! did she leave the Castle with her brother?"—" Good Heavens! hath she never been seen since morning?" exclaimed Sir Patrick and Assueton, both in the same breath, and looking eagerly in the faces of the people around them for something satisfactory; but no one had seen her since morning. Some of the domestics ran out to question those who had kept guard; but though she had been seen as she went out with her brother, neither warder nor sentinel had observed her return. Meanwhile the whole Castle was searched over from garret to cellar by Assueton, Sir Patrick, and the servants, all without success.

The consternation and misery of the father and the lover were greater than language can describe. Broken sentences burst from them at short intervals, but altogether void of connexion. A thousand conjectures were hazarded, and again abandoned as impossible. Plans of search without number were proposed, and then given up as hopeless; while all they said, thought, or did, was without concert, and only calculated to show their utter distraction. But matters did not long continue thus.

" My horse, my horse !" cried the agonized and frenzied father; and "My horse, my horse !" responded Assueton, in a state no less wild and despairing.

Both rushed down to the stable, and the horses which yet remained saddled from the chase being hurriedly brought out, they struck the spurs into their sweltering sides, and, almost without exchanging a word, galloped furiously from the gateway, each, as if by a species of instinct, taking a different way, and each followed by a handful of his people, who mounted in reeking haste to attend his master. They scoured the woodlands, lawns, and alleys, from side to side, and all around; they beat through the shaws and copses, and hollowed and shouted to the very cracking of their voices. By and by, to those who listened from the walls, their circles appeared to become wider, and their shouts were no longer heard. Forth rushed, one by one, as they could horse them in haste, or gird themselves for running, grooms, lacqueys, spearmen, billmen, bowmen, and foresters, until none were left within the place but the men on guard, the old, the feeble, and some of the women. Even Mary Hay ran out into the woods, beating her breast, tearing her hair, screaming like a maniac, and rummaging the bushes, even less rationally than those who had gone before her.

Sir Patrick, as he rode, began, in the midst of his affliction, to collect his scattered ideas, and, calling to mind what they had told him of Lady Isabelle having gone to convoy her brother, he immediately halted from the unprofitable search he was pursuing, and turned his horse's head towards that direction which they must have necessarily taken. He rode on as far as the knoll where the brother and sister had bid adieu to each other, and there being a cluster of cottages at the bottom of the hill, he made towards one of them himself, and sent his attendants to all the others in search of information. From several of the churls, and from their wives, he learned that his son had been seen taking an affectionate leave of a lady, whom they now supposed to have been the Lady Isabelle, among the oaks on the knoll, and that he had afterwards joined his party, waiting for him under the trees by the river's side, whilst the

lady seemed to turn back, as if to take the way
to the Castle. With this new scent, Sir Patrick
made his panting horse breast the hill, and, assisted by his men, beat the ground in close tra-
verse, backwards and forwards, from one side
to another, with so great care and minuteness,
that the smallest object could not have escaped
their observation. They tried all the by-routes
that might have been taken, but all without success; though they spent so much time in the
search, that darkness had already begun to descend over the earth, ere they were compelled
to desist from it as hopeless.

They returned towards the Castle, still catching at the frail chance, as they hurried thither,
that though they had been unsuccessful, some
one else might have been more fortunate, and
that probably the Lady Isabelle had been already brought back in safety. But unhappily
the guards, who crowded round them at the
gate, and to whom both master and men all at
once opened in accents of loud inquiry, had no
such heart-healing tidings to give them. They
obtained such intelligence, however, as had awakened a spark of hope. Sir John Assueton
had returned a short time before Sir Patrick,
with the horse he had ridden so exhausted, that
the wretched animal had dropped to the ground,

and died instantly after his rider had quitted the saddle. He had called loudly for fresh horses and a party of spearmen, and had then rushed into the Castle to arm himself in haste; and a number of those who had gone to search independently, having fortunately by this time dropped in, some fifteen or twenty bowmen, spearmen, and billmen, had been hastily got together, and provided with brisk and yet un-breathed horses. Without taking time, how-ever, to give the particulars of what he had ga-thered, or to say whither he was bound, Sir John had merely called out to the guard, as he was mounting, to tell Sir Patrick, if he should re-turn before him, that he had heard some tidings of the Lady Isabelle, and that he would bring her safely back, or perish in the attempt; and after having said so, he had given the word to his men, and scoured off at the head of them in a southern direction.

The miserable father was more than ever perplexed by this information. From the pre-parations Sir John had so effectually though hastily made, it was evident that the scene of the enterprise he went on was distant; and that it was not without doubt or danger, appeared from the few words he had let fall. Could Sir Patrick have had any guess whither to go, he

would have instantly armed himself, and such
men as he could have got together, to follow
and aid Sir John Assueton; but such a chase
was evidently more wild and hopeless than the
fruitless search he had just returned from; and
the pitchy darkness which by this time prevailed, was in itself an insurmountable obstacle
to his discovering the route that Sir John had
taken. He was compelled, therefore, most un-
willingly and most sorrowfully, to give up all
idea of further exertion for the present; but he
resolved to start in the morning, long ere the
first lark had arisen from its nest, and if he
should hear nothing before then, to ride towards England. He accordingly gave orders
to his esquires to have a body of armed horsemen ready equipped to accompany him, an hour
before the first streak of red should tinge the
eastern welkin.

Old Gabriel Lindsay, his dim eyes filled with
tears, and altogether unable to take comfort to
himself, came to make the vain attempt to ad-
minister it to his master, and to try to persuade
him to take some rest. But all the efforts of
the venerable seneschal were ineffectual, and
the heart-broken father continued to pace the
hall with agitated steps among his people, dis-
patching them off by turns, and often running

down himself to the gate, or to the ramparts, whenever his ear caught, or fancied it caught, a sound that might have indicated Assueton's return.

CHAPTER XIV.

But it is now time to state the circumstances of Assueton's search, as well as the cause of his abrupt departure. If Sir Patrick, on first starting from the Castle, had been so little master of himself as to lose time by galloping over ground, where it was next to impossible his daughter could be found, it was not at all likely that Sir John and his people, strangers as they were to the neighbourhood, could make a better selection. But it not unfrequently happens that chance, or, which is a much better word for it, Providence, does more than human prudence in such cases. After making two or three wild and rapid circles through the woods in the immediate vicinity of the Castle, like a stone whirled round in a sling, he flew off at a tangent southwards, and accidentally hit upon a solitary cottage, about a couple or more miles from the Castle, where he learned that a small body of English spearmen had halted that morning, and that the leader had made a number of inquiries about the late and future motions of his friend, the younger Sir Patrick Hepborne, and himself. These were well enough known, for the arrival of their young lord had excited universal joy among the population of his father's estate; the coming of the herald, with Hepborne's departure, were also matters too interesting to escape circulation; and the churl of the cottage had told, without reservation, all the circumstances to the strangers. He also learned, that the party had gone on to reconnoitre the Castle; and that afterwards, as the rustic was making faggots at some distance from his dwelling, he had seen them sweeping by towards England. Assueton could not elicit from the peasant whether it had appeared to him that the Lady Isabelle was with them, because the man had had but an indistinct view of them as they rode through the woodlands; but he and his people were agreed that these must have been the perpetrators of the outrage. His judgment, now that it had a defined object, began to come into full play. He saw that his own horse and the horses of his attendants were too much spent to enable him to pursue on the spur of the moment, and, had it not been so, that it would be vain to go on such an expedition so slenderly accoutred and accompanied. He therefore galloped back to the Castle as hard as the exhausted animal could carry him, followed at a distance by his straggling men; and there he made those rapid preparations and that hasty outset which we have already noticed.

The night became extremely dark before Assueton had gone many miles; but luckily for him, Robert Lindsay, the head forester, happened to be one of his company, for without him, or some other guide equally well acquainted with the country he had to travel over, his expedition must have been rendered abortive. Even as it was, he found difficulty enough in threading the mazes of the Lammermoors; and although Lindsay knew every knoll, stone, bog, flow, and rivulet that diversified their surface, they made divers deviations from the proper line, and were much longer in crossing the ridge than they should have been if favoured by the light of the moon. Towards morning, they judged it prudent to halt on the brow of the hills, ere they began to descend into the lower and more level country, that they might make observations by the first light, and determine both as to where they were, and as to their future movements.

As objects below them began to grow somewhat distinct, they found that they had posted themselves immediately over the hollow mouth of a glen, opening on the flat country, where a rivulet wound through some green meadows; and they soon began to descry several tents, pitched together in a cluster, with a number of horses piquetted around them.

" By'r lady," said Assueton, "yonder lie the ravishers. Let's down upon them, my brave men, ere they have time to be alarmed and fly."

He gave his horse the spur, and galloped down the slope at a fearful pace, followed by his party, and having gained the level, they charged towards the little encampment with the swiftness of the wind. The morning's mist that hung on the side of the hill, and the imperfeet grey light, had prevented the sentinels who were on the watch from seeing the horsemen approaching, until they had descended; but they no sooner observed them coming on at the *pas de charge,* than the alarm was given, and a general commotion took place among them. Out they came pouring from the tents to the number of forty or fifty; and there was such a hasty putting on of morrions and skull-caps, and seizing of weapons, and loosing of halters, and mounting of the few that had time to get on horseback, and such a clamouring and shouting, and so much confusion, as assured Assueton an easy victory, though their numbers were so much greater than his. He came on them at the head of his small body like a whirlwind, and before half of them had time to turn out, he was already within a hundred yards of their position. A few of them, armed with spears, had formed in line before the tents, apparently with the resolution of standing his charge, and at the head of these was an old man, hastily armed in a cuirass. He stood boldly planted with a lance in his hand, though his head was bare, and his white hairs hung loosely about his determined countenance. Sir John Assueton was on the very eve of bearing him and his little phalanx down before the irresistible fury of his onset, when he suddenly pulled up his reins, and halted his men.

" Sir Walter de Selby !" exclaimed he, with astonishment, and raising his vizor, that he might the better behold him.

" Sir John Assueton !" cried Sir Walter, " I crave truce and parley."

" Thou hast it, Sir Walter," said Assueton " but only on one condition, that I see not any one attempt to escape hence, or stir from the position he is now in, until all matters be explained betwixt us. Pledge me thine honour that this shall be so, and I shall parley with thee in friendship, till I shall see just cause for other acting. But, by the Rood of St Andrew, if a single knave shall seek to steal him away, or to quit the spot of earth that now bears him, I will put every man to death, saving thee only, whose white hairs and recent hospitality are pledges for thy security. Advance, Sir Walter; I swear by my knighthood that thy person shall take no hurt from my hands, or from the hands of any of my people."

" Thou comest, doubtless," said Sir Walter, " to seek after the Lady Isabelle Hepborne, the fair sister of thy friend Sir Patrick Hepborne."

" I do," said Sir John Assueton, eagerly; " and by the blessed Virgin, an she be not immediately delivered up scatheless into my custody, I will put every man but thyself to instant death. Shame, foul shame on thee, Sir Walter, to be the leader in a foray so disgraceful as this. Is this thy requital to Sir Patrick Hepborne for——But hold—I will not in my friend's name cast in thy teeth what he himself would scorn to throw at thee."

" Nay, Sir John Assueton, judge not so hastily, I entreat thee. What didst thou see in my behaviour at Norham, that should lead thee to suspect me of the foul deed thou art now so ready to charge me withal? Were I capable of any such, perdie, thou might'st well pour out all thy wrath and wrekery on this old head of mine. Listen to me, I beseech thee, with temper, and thou shalt soon know that I have had no hand in this unknightly outrage, the which nobody can more deplore than I do. It was Sir Miers de Willoughby who carried off the lady,—God pity me for being related to one who could so disgrace me! But on him be the sin and the shame of the act."

"Nay, Sir Knight," cried Assueton, hastily, "seeing that he did it in thy company, thou canst not, methinks, shake thyself free of a share of both. But where is the recreant, that I may forthwith chastise him? And where is the lady? By all the saints in the kalendar, if she is not instantly produced, I will make every man in thy troop breakfast upon cold steel."

"As God is my judge, Sir Knight," said Sir Walter, "as God is my judge, mine own afflictions weigh not more heavily on my old heart at this moment, than does the thought that I have been in some sort, though innocently, the occasion of this outrage having been done against the sister of the very knight for whom, of all others, gratitude would make me think it matter of joy to sacrifice this hoary

head to do him service.   There are some honourable gentlemen here present, who can vouch
for me, that, forgetful of mine own bereavement,
and the direful consequences that may follow it,
I had resolved to abandon my own quest, and to
go forward this morning to Hailes Castle, to
inform Sir Patrick Hepborne in person of all I
know of this ill-starred and wicked transaction;
and if thou wilt but listen to me, I shall tell it
thee in as few words as may be."

" But the lady, Sir Knight, the lady," cried
Assueton, in a frenzy; " produce the lady instantly, else the parley holds not longer."

" By mine honour as a knight," cried the old
man, " she is not here."

" Not here!" exclaimed Sir John Assueton,
" not here! What, hast thou sent her forward
to Norham? By the blessed bones of my ancestors," said he, digging his spurs through mere
rage into his horse's sides, and checking him
again, till he sprang into the air with the pain,
" I shall not leave a stone of it together.   Its
blaze shall serve to light up the Border to-night,
in such fashion, that every crone on Tweedside
shall see to go to bed by it."

" She is not at Norham, Sir Knight," said
Sir Walter, calmly; " she is not in my keeping,
I most solemnly protest to thee."

" Where is she, then, in the name of St Giles ?" cried Assueton. " Tell me instantly, that I may fly to her rescue. Trifle no more with me, old man ; thou dost wear out the precious minutes. Depardieux, my patience is none of the strongest e'en now; it won't hold out much longer, I tell thee, for I am mad, stark mad ; so tell me at once where she is, or my rage may overpower my better feelings."

" Nay, Sir John Assueton," said Sir Walter de Selby, with a forbearance and temper that, old as he was, he could never have exercised, had it not been for the feeling of what he owed to Sir Patrick Hepborne, and the consciousness that present appearances warranted the suspicion of his having been accessory to the outrage committed against the Lady Isabelle, " I beseech thee, Sir John Assueton, command thyself so far as to listen to me for but a very few minutes; hadst thou done so earlier, thou hadst ere this known everything. Interrupt me not, then, I implore thee, and thou shalt be the sooner satisfied. This is now the third morning since, unfortunate father that I am, I discovered the sad malure which hath befallen me, and that I was bereft of my daughter, the Lady Eleanore, who had been mysteriously carried off during the night. Certain circumstances——"

" Nay, but, Sir Knight," said Assueton, interrupting him, " what is thy daughter to me?
What is she to the Lady Isabelle Hepborne?
Ay, indeed, wretch that I am, what is she in
any way to the point?"

Sir Walter de Selby went on without noticing
this fresh interruption.

" Certain circumstances led some of the
people about me to believe that thy friend, Sir
Patrick, had had some hand in the rapt, and
that he, or some of his people, had returned at
night, and, by some unexampled topinage, found
means unaccountably to withdraw my daughter from the Castle. In the frenzy I was
thrown into by mine affliction, I was easily induced to believe anything that was suggested
to me; and getting together my people in a
haste, I——"

" So," cried Assueton, " I see how it is; a
vile thirst of vengeance led thee to make cap-
tive of the Lady Isabelle. Oh, base and unworthy knight!"

" Nay, indeed, not so," said Sir Walter, eager
to exculpate himself; " I have already vowed
I had no hand in anything so base. 'Tis true,
I set out with the mad intent of besieging Hailes
Castle, and demanding the restoration of my
daughter. To this I was much encouraged by

Sir Miers de Willoughby, who happened to be at Norham at the time, and who offered to accompany me. I got no farther than this place that night; and having had time to reflect by the way, on the nature of the enterprise I was boune on, as well as on the great improbability of so foul suspicion being verified against a knight of thy friend Sir Patrick's breeding and courtesy, I resolved to proceed with the utmost caution, lest I should even give cause of offence where no offence had been rendered. As the most prudent measure I could adopt, and as that least likely to excite alarm, I resolved to pitch my little camp in this retired spot, and to send forward Sir Miers de Willoughby, who readily volunteered the duty, towards Hailes Castle, to make such inquiry of the peasants, as might satisfy me of the truth or falsehood of my suspicions; and this, thou must grant me, Sir John Assueton, was as much delicacy as could be observed by me, in the anguished and bleeding state of my heart for the loss of my only child, and the impatience which I did na--turally feel to gain tidings of her." Here the old man's voice was for some moments choked by his tears; and Sir John Assueton was so much moved by them that he spake not a word. Sir Walter proceeded—

" De Willoughby returned here last night about-sun-set. He came to my tent alone, and he did tell me, that from all he could learn, he believed that my daughter had not been carried thither, either by Sir Patrick or any other person. ' But,' added he, ' be Sir Patrick Hepborne guilty or innocent of this outrage against thee, I have made a capture that will be either paying off an old score, or scoring the first item of a new account against these Scots, for I have carried off the Lady Isabelle Hepborne.' Struck with horror, and burning with rage to hear him tell this, I insisted on her being instantly brought to my tent, that I might forthwith calm her mind, and take immediate steps to return her in safety with honourable escort to her father. ' Give thyself no trouble about her,' said the libertine, treating all I said with contempt, ' for ere this she bonnes her over the Border, on a palfrey led by my people.' I was thunderstruck," continued the old man; " and ere I had time to recover myself so far as to be able to speak or to act, De Willoughby sprang to the door of the tent, and I heard the clatter of his horse's heels as he galloped off. I was infuriated; I felt that he had basely made me the scape-goat to his own caitiff plans, which I now began to suspect were not of recent batching.

I dispatched parties in every direction after him, but all of them returned, one by one, without having gained even the least intelligence of him. And all this is true, on the word of an old knight. God wot how well I do know to feel for the father of the damosel, sith I do suffer the same affliction myself."

The old knight was overpowered by his feelings; and Assueton, who had been at length prevailed on to hear his tale to an end, gave way at the conclusion of it to a paroxysm of rage and grief, which might have well warranted the by-standers in believing he was really bereft of reason. He threw himself from his horse to the ground, in despair. Roger Riddel, his esquire, a quiet, temperate, and, generally, a very silent man, did all he could to soothe his master; and even old Sir Walter de Selby, sorrowful as he himself was, seemed to forget his wretchedness in endeavouring to assuage that which so unmanned the Scottish knight.

After giving way for some time to ineffectual ravings, the offspring of intense feeling, and having then vented his rage in threats against Sir Miers de Willoughby, Assueton began by degrees to become more calm, and seeing the necessity of exerting his cool judgment, that he might determine how to act, he was at length persuaded by Sir Walter de Selby to go into his tent for a short time, till the horses and men could be refreshed. Sir Walter had no disposition to screen his unworthy relative from the wrath with which Assueton threatened him; or if he had, he conceived himself bound to make it give way to a sense of justice. He therefore readily answered the Scottish Knight's hasty questions, and told him, that it was more than likely that the lady had been carried to a certain castle belonging to De Willoughby, situated among the Cheviot hills.

Assueton's impatience brooked no longer delay. Accordingly, with a soul agonized by the passions of love, grief, rage, and revenge, he summoned his party to horse, and set off at a furious pace on his anxious but uncertain search.

CHAPTER XV.

Sir Walter de Selby, who was enduring all the bitterness of grief that a father could suffer whose only child, a daughter too, on whose disposal hung a whole legion of superstitious hopes and fears, had been rent from him in a manner so mysterious, broke up his little camp with as much impatience as Assueton had exhibited. But age did not admit of his motions being so rapid as those of the younger knight. He moved, however, with all the celerity he could exert, for he remembered the warning flame which had appeared on the fatal shield; and the very thought of his daughter's disappearance, with the frightful consequences which might result from her being thus beyond his control, filled his heart with horror and dismay. He was also exceedingly perplexed how the wizard, Master Ancient Haggerstone Fenwick, could have so erred in his divination, as to occasion him the fruitless and mortifying expedition into

Scotland; for Sir Walter, in the first fever of distraction he was thrown into by the discovery of his daughter's disappearance, had immediately made his way to the aerial den of the Ancient. The cunning diviner instantly recollected that he had seen Sir Patrick Hepborne going towards the rampart, where, he had reason to know, the Lady Eleanore de Selby had been walking, from which he was led to suspect an appointment between them. He was too artful to make Sir Walter aware of this circumstance, but proceeding upon it, he enacted some hasty farce of conjuration, and then, with all due solemnity, boldly and confidently pronounced that Sir Patrick Hepborne had secretly returned, and obtaining possession of the person of the Lady Eleanore, had carried her over the Border.

Some time after Sir Walter de Selby had gone into Scotland, however, a discovery was accidentally made that seemed to throw light on the disappearance of his daughter. The mantle she usually wore, had been found by a patrole, at several miles distance to the south of Norham, lying by the way-side leading towards Alnwick—a circumstance which left no doubt remaining that she had been carried off in that direction. But ere this could be communicated to Sir Walter on his return, his impatience for an interview with his oracle was so great, that, putting aside all obstructions, he hastened to climb to the den of the monster on the top of the keep.

"What sayest thou, Master Ancient Fenwick?" said the old man as he entered the caphouse door, his breath gone with the steepness of the ascent and the anxiety of his mind; "for once thy skill seemeth to have failed thee."

The Ancient was seated in his usual corner, immersed in his favourite study; a large circle was delineated on the floor, and in the centre of it lay the Lady Eleanore's mantle.

"Blame, then, thine own impatience and haste," said the Ancient. "The signs were drawn awry, and no wonder that the calculations were erroneous; but thou wert not gone half a day until I discovered the error; and now thou shalt thyself behold it remedied. Dost see there thy daughter's mantle?"

The old man instantly recognized it; and looking at it in silence for some moments, the feelings of a sorrowing and bereft parent came upon him with all the strength of nature: his heart and his eyes filled, and he burst into a flood of tears. He stepped forward to lift it up, and imprint kisses upon it; but the stern and unfeeling Ancient called out, in a harsh voice,—

" Touch it not, on thy life, else all my mystic labours have been in vain. Stand aloof there, and, if thou wilt, be a witness of the power I possess in diving into secrets that are hid from other men."

Sir Walter obeyed. The Ancient arose and struck a light; and having darkened the loophole window, he lighted his lamp and put it into a corner. He then approached the circle, and squatting down, he with much labour and difficulty drew his unwieldy limbs within its compass, and, kneeling over the mantle, he proceeded to mutter to himself, from a book of necromancy which he held in his hand, turning the pages over with great rapidity, and making, from time to time, divers signs with his forefinger on his face and on the floor. After this he laid his head down on the pavement, covered it with the mantle, and continued to mutter uncouthly, and to writhe his body until he seemed to fall into a swoon. He lay motionless for a considerable time; but at length he appeared to recover gradually, the writhing and the muttering recommenced, and raising up his body with the mantle hanging over his head and shoulders, he exposed his horrid features to view. To the

inexpressible terror of Sir Walter, the forehead
blazed with the same appalling flame which he
had seen it bear on the night of his long interview with the wizard.

"Seek thy daughter in the South," said the
Ancient, in a hollow voice; "seek her from Sir
Rafe Piersie. Remember thy destinies. The
balance now wavers—now it turns against thee
and thy destinies. If but an atom of time be
lost, they are sealed, irrecoverably sealed."

Quick as the lightning of heaven did the
ideas shoot through the old man's mind, as the
Ancient was solemnly pronouncing this terrific
response. He remembered that Sir Rafe Piersie had left Norham, in a litter, the very day
preceding the night his daughter had disappeared; and it flashed upon him, that some of the
grooms had remained behind their master, under pretence of one of his favourite horses having been taken ill, and had afterwards followed him during the night. That they must have
found means to carry the Lady Eleanore off
with them, was, he thought, but too manifest.
The very name of Piersie, when uttered by the
Ancient, had made Sir Walter's blood run cold,
from his superstitious belief of the impending
fate that was connected with it; and the weight
of his feelings operating on a body oppressed

with fatigue and want of sleep, and on a mind worn out with the agitation and affliction it had undergone, became too much for nature to bear. He grew deadly pale. He made an effort to speak, but his tongue became dry, and cleaved to the roof of his mouth, and his lips refused their office; an indistinct, mumbling, moaning sound was all that they could utter—his cheeks became rapidly convulsed—one corner of his mouth was drawn up to his ear, and he fell backwards on the floor, in a state of perfect insensibility.

Fenwick became alarmed. He started up with the ghastly look of a newly-convicted felon, and the fear of being accused of the murder of Sir Walter came upon him. He went towards the knight, and, raising him up, made use of what means he could to endeavour to restore him to life; but all his efforts were unsuccessful. Trembling from the panic he was in, he then lifted the old knight in his arms, and with great difficulty conveyed him down the narrow stair to his own apartment. Horror was depicted in the faces of the domestics when they beheld the hated but dreaded monster bearing the bulky and apparently lifeless body of their beloved master. A wild cry of grief and apprehension burst from them. The Ancient laid Sir Walter on the bed, and, as the atten-

dants stood aloof and aghast, he took up a
small knife that lay near, and pierced the veins
of both temples with the point of it. The blood
spouted forth, and the knight began to show
faint symptoms of life. Never negligent of any
circumstance that might raise his reputation for
supernatural power, the Ancient now began to
employ a number of strange necromantic signs,
and to utter a jargon of unintelligible words in
a low muttering tone, laying his hand at one
time on the face, and at another on the breast,
of the semi-animate body, that he might impress
the by-standers with the idea of his magic having
restored Sir Walter to life; for, seeing the blood
flow so freely, he anticipated the immediate and
perfect recovery of the patient. But he was mistaken in the extent of his hopes. Sir Walter
opened his eyes, stared wildly about him, and
moved his lips as if endeavouring to speak;
but he continued to lie on his back, altogether
motionless, and quite incapable of uttering a
word.

The dismayed Ancient shuffled out of the
apartment, and hastily retired to his lofty cita-
del. A murmur of disapprobation broke out
among the domestics the moment he was supposed to be beyond hearing. They crowded
about their master's bed-side, every one eager

to do something.   All manner of restoratives
were tried with him, but in vain.   He seemed
to be perfectly unconscious of what they did,
and he lay sunk in a lethargy, from which nothing could rouse him.

Sir Walter was the idol of his people and
garrison.   By degrees the melancholy news
spread through the keep of the Castle, and
thence into its courts, barracks, stables, guard-
houses, and along its very ramparts, until every
soldier and sentinel in the place became aware
of the miserable condition of their beloved governor, as well as of the immediate share which
Master Ancient Haggerstone Fenwick, the sorcerer, had had in producing it.   General la-
mentations arose.

" Our good Governor is bewitched !"—" The
monster Ancient hath bewitched him !"—" The
villain Fenwick drew his very blood from him
to help his sorcery !"—" What can be done?"
—" What shall we do?"—" Let us send forthwith for some holy man."—" Let us send for
the pious clerk of Tilmouth Chapel, he hath
good lore in sike cases."

The suggestion was approved by all, and accordingly a horseman was instantly dispatched
to bring the clerk with all possible haste.   The
messenger speedily returned, unaccompanied,

however, by the pious priest of Tilmouth, who chanced to be sick in bed, but who had sent them a wayfaring Franciscan monk, of whose potent power against magic he had largely spoken. The holy man was immediately ushered into the Governor's apartment. Having previously taken care to inform himself of all the particulars of the case, from the horseman behind whom he had been brought, he approached the bed with a solemn air, and surveyed Sir Walter for some time, as if in deep consideration of his state and appearance, with intent to discover his malady. He looked into his eyes, felt him carefully all over, and moved his helpless legs and arms to and fro. Meanwhile the officers of the garrison, the attendants, and even some of the soldiers, were awaiting anxiously in the room, about the door, on the stairs, and on the bridge below, all eager to learn the issue of his examination.

" Sir Walter de Selby is bewitched," said the Franciscan at length, " and no human power can now restore him, so long as the wretch, whoever he may be, who hath done this foul work on him, shall be permitted to live. If he be known, therefore, let him be forthwith seized and dragged to the flames."

An indignant murmur of approbation followed this announcement, and soon spread to those on the stairs, and from them to the soldiers in the court-yard below. Fortified by the spiritual aid of a holy friar, the most superstitious of them lost half of their dread of the Ancient's supernatural powers.

" Burn the Ancient !" cried one.—" Burn Haggerstone Fenwick !" cried another.—" Burn the Wizard Fenwick !" cried a third.—" Faggots there—faggots in the court-yard !"—" Raise a pile as high as the keep !"—" Faggots !"— " Fire !"—" Burn the Ancient !"—" Burn the Wizard !" flew from mouth to mouth. All was instant ferment. Some ran this way, and others that, to bring billets of wood, and to prepare the pile of expiation; so that, in a short time, it was built up to a height sufficient to have burnt the Ancient, if his altitude had been double what it really was.

This being completed, the next cry was— " Seize the Ancient—seize him, and bring him down !" But this was altogether a different matter; for although every one most readily joined in the cry, no one seemed disposed to lead the way in carrying the general wish into effect. The friar assumed an air of command—

" Let no one move," said he, " until I shall have communed with the wretch. I shall my-

self ascend to his den, and endeavour to bend his
wicked heart to undo the evil he hath wrought
on the good Sir Walter.   But let some chosen
and determined men be within call, for should
I find him hardened and obdurate, he must
forthwith be led out to suffer for his foul sorcery.   Meanwhile let all be quiet, let no sound
be uttered, until I shall be heard to pronounce,
in a loud voice, this terrible malison, ' *Body
and soul, to the flames I doom thee !*' Then let
them up without delay on him, and he shall be
straightway overcome."

The Franciscan was listened to with the most
profound deference, his commands were im-
plicitly obeyed, and every sound, both within
and without the Castle, was from that moment
hushed.

CHAPTER XVI.

The Ancient Haggerstone Fenwick had been by no means comfortable in his thoughts after he had retreated to the solitude of his cap-house, and had in fact anticipated in some degree the effect which would result from the state of insensibility Sir Walter had been thrown into. He was aware that the very mummery he had enacted over him, when he expected his immediate resuscitation, instead of operating, as in that event it would have done, to raise his fame as a healing magician, would now be the means of fixing on him the supposed crime of having produced his malady, and strengthened it by wicked sorcery. But he by no means expected that the irritation against him would be so speedy or so violent in its operation as it really proved, and he perhaps trusted for his safety from any sudden attack to the dread with which be well knew his very name inspired every one in the garrison.

He had crept into the farther corner of his den, where, in the present distracted state of his mind, it did not even occur to him to extinguish the lamp he had left burning, or to let in the daylight he had excluded. There he sat, brooding over the unfortunate issue of his divination, in very uneasy contemplation of the danger that threatened him in consequence, distant though he then thought it. A coward in his heart, he began to curse himself for having tried schemes which now seemed likely to end so fatally for himself. He turned over a variety of plans for securing his safety, but, after all his cogitation, flight alone seemed to be the only one that was likely to be really available. But then Sir Walter might recover; in which case he might still obtain the credit of his recovery, and his ambitious schemes be yet crowned with success. Thus the devil again tempted him; and he finally resolved to wait patiently until night, which was by this time at hand, and then steal quietly down to ascertain Sir Walter's state, and act accordingly. Should he find him worse, or even no better than when he left him, he resolved to go secretly to the ramparts, there to undo some of the ropes of the warlike engines that defended the walls, and to let himself down by means of them at a part where he knew the height would be least formidable, and so to effect his escape.

Occupied as the Ancient was with these thoughts, although he had heard the clamours and shouts rising from below, yet, buried in the farthest corner of his den, they came to his ear like the murmurs of a far distant storm; and accustomed to the every-day noise of a crowded garrison, they did not even strike him as at all extraordinary.

To divert these apprehensions which he could by no means allay, he opened one of his favourite books, and endeavoured to occupy himself in his usual study; but his mind wandered in spite of all his exertions to keep it fixed, and he turned the leaves, and traced the lines with his eyes without being in the least conscious of the meaning they conveyed. He roused himself, and began reading aloud, as if he could have talked himself into quiet by the very sound of his own voice. He went on without at first perceiving the particular nature of the passage he had stumbled on; but his attention being now called to it, he was somewhat horrified to observe that it contained the form of exorcism employed for raising the devil in person. By some unaccountable fatality, he went on with it, wishing all the while that he had never begun it, but yet most strangely afraid to stop; until at length, approaching the conclusion, he ended with these terrible words,—" *Sathanas, Sathanas, Sathanas, Sathanas, Prince of Darkness, appear !*"

He stopped, and looked fearfully around him, as soon as they had passed his lips. The door of the place slowly opened, and the head of the very Franciscan monk who had formerly visited him, the face deeply shaded by the projecting cowl, was thrust within the doorway.

" I am here—what would'st thou with me?" said he, in a deep and hollow voice.

The Ancient threw himself upon his knees, and drew back his body into the corner. His teeth chattered in his head, and he was deprived of speech. He covered his eyes with his hands, as if afraid to look upon the object of his dread. He now verily believed that he had been formerly visited by the Devil, and that the Arch-Fiend had again returned to carry him away. The Franciscan crouched, and glided forward into the middle of the place.

" What becomes of him, lossel," said he, in a tremendous voice—" What becomes of him who takes the Devil's wages, and doeth not his work? What becomes of him who vainly tries to deceive the Devil his master? Fool! didst

thou not believe that I was the Prince of Darkness ?"

The terrified Ancient had now no doubt that
he was indeed the Devil; still he kept his hands
over his eyes, and drew himself yet more up,
in dread that every succeeding moment he
should feel himself clutched by his fiery fangs.

" Hast thou not tried to cheat me, wretch—
me, who cannot but know all things ?" conti-
tinned the Franciscan.

" Oh, spare me, spare me !—I confess, I
confess.—Avaunt thee, Sathanas !—Spare !—
Avaunt !—Spare me, Sathanas !" muttered the
miserable wretch, altogether unconscious of what
he uttered.

" Spare thee, thou vile slave !" cried the
Franciscan with bitterness, " I never spared
mortal that once roused my vengeance; and
thou hast roused mine to red-hot fury.   Answer me, and remember it is vain to attempt
concealment with me—Didst thou not fail of
thy promise to rouse Sir Walter de Selby to
my purpose, as it affected Sir Rafe Piersic ?"

" Oh, I did, I did—Oh, spare me, spare me,
Sathanas !" cried the Ancient.

" Didst thou not rather stir him up to reject and spurn the noble knight ?" demanded
the Franciscan.

".Oh, yes, I did—Oh, yes—Spare me, spare me!—Avaunt thee, Sathanas!—Spare me— Oh, spare me!"

" Spare thee!" cried the Franciscan, with a horrid laugh of contempt—" spare thee! What mercy canst thou hope from me? No, thou art given up to my power, not to be spared, but to be punished. Thine acts of sorcery, which have murdered Sir Walter de Selby, have put thee beyond the pale of mercy, nor canst thou now look elsewhere for aid.—Thou art fitting food for hell," continued he, with a fiendlike grin of satisfaction; and retreating slowly out of the doorway, and raising his voice into a shriek, that re-echoed from every projection and turret of the building, he pronounced the last fatal words, " *Body and soul, to the flames I doom thee!*"

An instantaneous shout arose from the court-yard below, and a clamour of many voices came rapidly up the stairs in the interior of the keep. It quickly swelled upon the ear, and the clattering noise of many feet was heard approaching. Out they came on the platform of the keep, one by one, as they could scramble forth and as the stoutest spirits naturally mounted first, the Franciscan was instantly surrounded by a body of the most determined hearts in the garrison.

"In on the servant of Sathanas," cried he; "in on the cruel sorcerer, who hath bewitched thine unhappy Governor, and who refuseth to save him again; in on the monster, tear him from his den, and drag him to the flames. Fear him not; his supernatural powers are quenched. Behold!" and pulling a wooden crosslet from his bosom, he held it up to their view—"In on him, I say, and seize him."

The door was instantly forced open, and one or two of the boldest entered first; then two or three more followed, to the number of half a dozen in all, for the place could hardly contain more. The Ancient had now become frantic from terror, and his reason so far forsook him, that he saw not or knew not the faces of those who came in on him to attack him, though many of them were familiar to him; he was fully possessed with the idea that a legion of devils were about to assail him, to drag him down to instant and eternal punishment. They sprang upon him at once by general concert. The Ancient was an arrant coward; but a coward so circumstanced will fight to the last, even against an infernal host; and so he did, with the desperation of a maniac. In the interior of the place, the scuffle was tremendous; the very walls and roof of it seemed to heave and labour with its tumultuous contents. The keep itself shook to its foundation, and the shrieks, groans, and curses that came from within appalled the by-standers.

" Pick-axes, crows, and hatchets !" cried the friar; and the implements were brought with the utmost expedition at his command.

" Unroof his den," cried he again; and two or three of the stoutest men mounted forthwith on the flags of the roof, and by means of the crows and pick-axes, began to tear them up with so much expedition, that they very soon laid the wood bare, and following up their work of devastation with the same energy, speedily and entirely demolished the roof, letting in the little light that yet remained of day upon the combatants.

The Ancient Fenwick was now discovered lying on his back, his jaws wide open, his huge tusks displayed, and his mouth covered with foam, while his opponents were clustered over him, like ants employed in overpowering a huge beetle. All their efforts to drag him out at the door had been quite unavailing. Though there were no weapons of edge or point among the combatants, many severe wounds and blows had been given and received, and blood flowed on the pavement in abundance. The Ancient's teeth seemed to have done him good service after his arms had been mastered and rendered ineffectual to him, for many of his assailants bore deep and lasting impressions of his jaws on their hands and faces.

" In on the savage wizard now, overwhelm and bind him," cried the Franciscan, with a devilish laugh of triumph.

At his word they scaled the roofless walls, and jumped down on the miserable wretch in such numbers, that the place was literally packed. But the more that came on him, the more furiously the Ancient defended himself, kicking, and heaving, and tossing some of them, till one of their number, laying his hand on a huge folio, made use of his code of necromancy against himself, and gave him a knock on the head that stunned him, and rendered him for some time insensible. Taking advantage of this circumstance, cords were hastily employed to bind his arms behind him; and a set of ropes being passed under him, he was with great difficulty hoisted from his den, and laid out at length upon the platform of the keep. There he lay, breathing to be sure, but in a temporary state of perfeet insensibility.

Availing themselves of the swoon into which he had fallen, the assailants began to hold council how they were to get his unwieldy and unmanageable carcase down to the courtyard. To have attempted to carry it by the stairs would have been hopeless; a week would have hardly sufficed to have manœuvred it through their narrow intricacies. The only possible mode, therefore, was to let him down by means of ropes, over the outside walls of the keep. Accordingly strong loops were passed around his legs, and under his arm-pits; and by the united exertions of some dozen of men, he was lifted up and projected over the battlements.

As they were lowering him down slowly and with great care, the wretched Ancient, recovering from his swoon, found himself dreadfully suspended between sky and earth; and looking upwards, and beholding the grim faces of the men who managed the ropes scowling over the battlements, strongly illuminated by the light of the torches they held, he was more than ever convinced that they were demons, nor did he doubt that he was in the very commencement of those torments of the nether world, which he had been condemned to undergo for his iniquity. He shrieked and kicked, and made such exertions, that the very ropes cracked, so that he ran imminent risk of breaking them, and of tumbling headlong to the bottom. Afraid of this, the people above began to lower him away more quickly, and the darkness below not permitting them to see the ground, so as to know when he had nearly reached it, his head came so rudely in contact with it, that he was again thrown into a state of insensibility.

The whole men of the garrison, both within and without the keep, having now assembled around him, a white sheet was brought out by order of the Franciscan, and he was clothed in it as with a loose robe. A black cross was then painted on the breast, and another on the back of it, from the charitable motive of saving his soul from the hands of the Devil, after it should be purified from its sins by the fire his body was destined to undergo. A parchment cap of considerable altitude, and also ornamented with crosses, was next tied upon his head; and two long flambeaux were bound firmly, one on each side, above his ears. He was then carried to the pile of wood, and extended at length upon the top of it. The torches attached to his head were lighted, and the Franciscan, approaching the pile with a variety of ceremonies, set fire to it with much solemnity; a grim smile of inward satisfaction lighting up his dark and stern features as he did so.

" Thus," said he, " let all wizards and sor-
cerers perish, and thus let their cruel enchant-
ments end with them."

The anticipation of the horrific scene which
was to ensue operated so powerfully on the vulgar crowd around, that a dead silence prevailed; and even those who, a few minutes before,
had shouted loudest, and fought most furiously
against the Ancient, now that they beheld the
wretched victim laid upon the pile, and the fire
slowly gaining strength, and rising more and
more towards him—already hearing in fancy
the piercing agony of his screams, and beholding in idea the horrible spectacle of his half-consumed limbs writhing with the torture of the
flames—stood aloof, and, folding their sinewy
arms and knitting their brows, half averted their
eyes from the painful spectacle.

Up rose the curling smoke, until the whole
summit of the broad and lofty keep was enveloped in its murky folds; while the flames,
shooting in all directions through the crackling
wood, began already to produce an intolerable heat under the wretched and devoted man,
though they had not yet mounted so high as to
catch the sheet he was wrapt in. Life began
again to return to him. He stretched himself,
and turned his head round first to the right,

and then to the left; and, beholding the dense group of soldiers on all sides of him, their eyes glaring red on him, from the reflection of the flame that was bursting from beneath him, and being now sensible of the intolerable heat, and half·suffocated with the gusts of smoke that blew about him, his belief that he was in the hands of demons, and that his eternal fiery punishment was commencing, was more than ever confirmed. He bellowed, writhed, and struggled; and his bodily strength, which was at all times enormous, being now increased tenfold by the horrors that beset him, he made one furious exertion, and, snapping the cords which bound his arms behind, and which, fortunately for him, had been weaker than they otherwise would have been, had those who tied them not believed that he was already nearly exanimate, he sprang to his feet, and rent open the front of the white robe they had put round him. Down came the immense and loosely-constructed pile of faggots, by the sheer force of his weight alone, and onward he rushed, with the force and fury of an enraged elephant, overturning all who ventured to oppose him, or who could not get out of his way, the flambeaux blazing at his head, and his long white robe streaming behind him, and exposing the close black frieze

dress he usually wore. The guards and sentinels at the first gate, aware of what was going
on, and conceiving it impossible for human
power to escape, after the precautions which
had been taken, when they saw the terrible figure advancing towards them, with what appeared to them to be a couple of fiery horns on
his head, abandoned their posts and fled in terror. Those at the outer gate were no less fright-
ened, and retreated with equal expedition. But
the drawbridge was up. Luckily for the Ancient, however, he, like many other fortunate
men, was on the right side for his own interest
on this occasion. Without hesitation he put the
enormous sole of one foot against it,—down it
rattled in an instant, chains and all, and he
thundered along it.

By this time the panic-stricken soldiers of
the garrison had recovered from their alarm,
and started with shouts after the fugitive, being
now again as eager to take him, and much more
ready to sacrifice him when taken, than they
had even been before. On they hurried after
him, yelling like a pack of hounds, and cheered
to the chase by the revengeful and bloodthirsty
Franciscan, their pursuit being directed by the
flaming torches at his head; and forward he
strode down the hollow way to the mead of

Norham, and, dreading capture worse than death itself, he darted across the flat ground, flaming like a meteor, and, dashing at once into the foaming stream of the Tweed, began wading across through a depth of water enough to have drowned any ordinary man; until at length, partly by swashing, and partly by swimming, during which last operation the lights he bore on his head were extinguished, he made his way fairly into Scotland.

His pursuers halted in amazement. The whole time occupied in his escape seemed to have been but as a few minutes. Fear once more fell upon them, and they talked to one another in broken sentences, and half-smothered voices.

" Surely," said one, " the Devil, whose servant he was, must have aided him."

" Ay, ay, that's clear enow," said another.

" He was stone-dead, and came miraculously alive again," said a third.

" Nay," said a fourth, " he came not alive again; 'twas but the Devil that took possession of his dead body."

" In good troth thou hast hit it, Gregory," said a fifth, with an expression of horror; " for no one but the Devil himself could have broken the cords that tied his hands, or kicked down the drawbridge after such a fashion."

" Didst see how he walked on the water ?"
cried a sixth.

" Ay," said a seventh, "and how he vanished
in the middle o' Tweed in a flash o' fire that
made the very water burn again ?"

Having thus wrought themselves into a belief that the spectre they had been following
was no other than the Devil flying off with the
already exanimate body of Ancient Fenwick,
they trembled at the very idea of having pursued him ; and they crept silently back to the
garrison, the blood in their veins freezing with
terror, and crossing themselves from time to
time as they went.

As for the Franciscan, he disappeared, no one
knew how.

CHAPTER XVII.

SIR JOHN ASSUETON'S fury and distraction
carried him on with great rapidity, until he
reached the banks of the Tweed, and his own
horse, as well as the horses of his small troop
of spearmen, were right glad to lave their smoking sides in its cool current, as he boldly swam
them to the English shore. He tarried but short
time by the way, to refresh either them or his
men; and towards nightfall, found himself winding into a green glen, thickly wooded in some
parts, opening in smooth pasture in others, and
watered by one of those brisk streams that descend into Northumberland from the Cheviot
hills.

The sight of those lofty elevations, now so
near him, brought the object of his hasty march
more freshly to his mind, too much agitated
hitherto by the violence of the various passions
that possessed it, to permit him to act or think
coolly. But he began now to reflect, that al-

though he had learned that the Castle of Burnstower, to which Sir Miers de Willoughby was
supposed to have carried off the Lady Isabelle,
lay somewhere among the intricacies of these
hills, his rage and impatience had never allowed
him to inquire further, or to advert to the very
obvious circumstance of the extent of the hilly
range, which was so great, that he might search
for many days before he could discover the spot
where it was situated. It was therefore absolutely necessary that he should avail himself of
the very first opportunity which occurred of
procuring information, both as to the Castle he
was in search of, and the owner of it, of whom
he had in reality as yet learned nothing. He
rode slowly up the glen, therefore, in expectation of seeing some cottage, where he might
halt for a short time to gain intelligence, or of
meeting some peasant, from whom he might
adroitly gather the information he wanted, without exciting suspicion as to the nature of his
errand.

Fortune seemed to be so far favourable to
him, that he had not ridden any great distance
ere he descried a forester, standing under a
wide-spreading oak, by the side of a little glade,
where the glen was narrowest. He had a cross-

bow in his hand, and appeared to be on the
watch for deer.

"Ho, forester," cried Assueton to him,
"methinks thou hast chosen a likely pass here
for the game; hast thou sped to-day?"

"Not so far amiss as to that," said the forester, carelessly leaving his stand, and loun-
ging towards the party, as if to reconnoitre
them.

"Dost thou hunt alone, my good fellow?"
said the knight.

"N-nay," said the forester, with hesitation;
"there be more of us in company a short way
off."

"Hast thou any cottage or place of shelter
hereabouts, where hungry travellers might have
a mouthful of food, with provender, and an hour's
rest for our weary beasts?" demanded Assueton. "Here's money for thee."

"As to a cottage like," replied the forester,
"I trow there be not many of them in these
wilds; but an thou wilt yede thee wi' me, thou
shalt share the supper my comrades must be
cooking ere this time; and as for thy beasts,
they canna be muckell to dole for, where the
grass grows aneath their feet. Thy money we
care not for."

"Thine offer is fair and kind, good forester,"

said Assueton; " we shall on with thee right
gladly, and give thee good thanks for thy syl-
van hospitality, such as it may be. Lead on
then."

The forester, without more words, walked
cleverly on before Sir John Assueton, who followed him at the head of his party. As they
advanced a little way, the wooding of the glen
became much more dense, and rocks projecting
themselves from the base of the hills on either
side, rendered the passage in the bottom between
them and the stream excessively narrow, so that
the men of the party could only move on singly,
and were more than once obliged to dismount
to lead their horses. The way seemed to be very
long, and night came on to increase its difficulties. Assueton's impatience more than once
tempted him to complain of it ; but he restrain-
ed himself, lest his eagerness might excite suspicion that he had some secret and important
hostile object in view, and that he might thus
lose all chance of gaining the information he so
much wanted. He kept as close as he possibly
could to his guide, however, for he began to
have strange doubts that he might be leading
him into some ambush ; and he had resolved
within his own mind to seize and sacrifice him,

the instant he had reason to be convinced he had betrayed them.

After forcing their way through a very wild pass, where the rocks on both sides towered up their bold and lofty fronts, the glen widened, and the party entered a little gently-sloping glade or holme, bounded by the high and thickly-wooded banks, which here retired from the side of the stream, and swept irregularly around it. A blazing fire appeared among the trees.

" Ay," said the forester, " these are my comrades : I reckon we come in good time, for yonder be the supper a-cooking."

The party now crossed through the luxuriant pasture, that, moistened with the evening dew, was giving out a thousand mingled perfumes from the wild flowers that grew in it, and speedily came within view of about a dozen men, clad in the same woodland garb worn by their guide. Some of them were sitting about the fire, engaged in roasting and broiling fragments of venison ; while others were loitering among the trees, or sitting under their shade. A number of cross-bows and long-bows hung from the branches, several spears rested against their stems ; and these, with swords, daggers, and anelaces, seemed to compose the arms of this party of hunters. They appeared to have had good sport, for six or eight fat bucks were hanging by the horns from the boughs overhead.

" Here is a gallant knight and his party," said their guide to a man who seemed to be a leader among them, " who would be glad of a share of our supper."

. The person he addressed, and who came forward to receive Assueton, was a tall and uncommonly handsome man; and although his dress differed in no respect from that of the others, except that he wore a more gaudy plume in his hat, and that his baldrick, the sword suspended from it, his belt and dagger, and the bugle that hung from his shoulder, were all of more costly materials and rarer workmanship. But there was something in his appearance and mien that might have graced knighthood itself. He bowed courteously to Assueton.

" Sir Knight," said he, " wilt thou deign to dismount from thy steed, and partake with us in our woodland cheer ? Here," said he, turning to the people around him, " let more carcases be cut up; there is no lack of provisions. Will it please thee to rest, Sir Knight?"

" I thank thee, good forester, for thy willing hospitality," said Assueton, alighting, and giving his horse to his squire; " I will rest me on that green bank under the holly busket there, and talk with thee to wile away time and beguile my hunger. This is a merry occupation of thine," added he, after they had sat down together.

" Ay," replied the forester, " right merry in good sooth, were we left at freedom to enjoy it. But, by the mass, that is not our case here, for there wons in this vicinage a certain discourteous knight, who letteth no one kill a deer on his ground that he may know of; so we be forced to steal hither, at times when we may ween that he is absent, or least on the watch. The red and roe-deer much abound in these glens; and, by the Rood, 'tis hard, methinks, that the four-footed game should be given by nature for man's food, and that he should be reft of his right to take it."

" And who may this discourteous knight be ?" said Assueton, wishing to feel his way with the stranger.

" His name," said the forester, " is Sir Miers de Willoughby, of a truth, a most cruel and lawless malfaitor, and as bold a Borderer as ever rode through a moss. He rules everything here, and gives honest folks the bit to champ, I promise thee. Would that some such gallant knight as your worship might meet with him and humble him, for verily he is a scourge to the country."

Sir John Assueton inwardly congratulated himself upon his good luck in having thus so fortunately stumbled on a man, who, having himself suffered from De Willoughby's oppression, was manifestly so inimical to him: he felt much inclined to speak out at once, but he checked himself, and thought it wiser to proceed with caution.

" Is he so very wicked, then, this Sir Miers de Willoughby of whom thou speakest?" said he to the forester.

" By the mass is he, Sir Knight," replied the forester. " He will soar ye from his border, keep like a falcon, and pounce on any prey that may come within his ken; and als he be so stark as to others using his lands for their honest and harmless occupation of hunting, by'r lady, he minds not on what earth he stoops, if so be that there be anything to clutch from off its surface. 'Twas but some three days ago that he yode hence on some wicked emprise, for 'twas his absence that led us hither; and this morning, as we lay concealed in these woodshaws, we saw him and his men ride by this very spot, bearing home with him some worthy man's gentle cosset he had stowne away."

Assueton perfectly understood the forester to have used the word cosset, a pet lamb, in a metaphorical sense; but, to draw him on, he pretended to have taken him up literally.

" A cosset !" cried he, with feigned surprise. " A poor pet lamb was but a wretched prey indeed for so rapacious a lorrel as thou would'st make this same Sir Miers to be, good forester."

" Nay, nay, Sir Knight," replied the forester, " I meant not in very simplicity a pet lamb, but a fair damosel, who looked, meseemed, as if she had been the gentle cosset of some fond father. 'Twas a damosel, Sir Knight, a right fair and beauteous damosel; and she shrieked from time to time in such piteous fashion, that, by the Rood, it was clear she went not with him willingly."

Assueton's blood boiled, so that it was with difficulty he could longer restrain his fury. He, however, kept it within such bounds as it might well enough pass for the indignation natural to a virtuous knight upon hearing of such foul outrage done to any damsel.

" Unworthy limb of knighthood," said he, " thus to play the caitiff part of a vile lossel ! Show me the way to his boure, and by the blessed bones of the holy St Cuthbert, he shall dearly rue his traiterie."

" Marry, 'tis no wonder to see a virtuous knight so enchafed at such actings," said the forester; " yet can the damosel be little to thee; and 'twere scarce, methinks, worth thy while to step so far from thy path. Had she been thine own lady, indeed——"

" Nay," said Assueton, hastily, but endeavouring to conceal his emotion, " thou knowest, good forester, that 'tis but my duty as a true knight, to redress this foul wrong; and whosoever the lady may be, and wheresoever I may be bound, I must not scruple to step a little out of my way to punish so wicked a coulpe."

" Right glad am I, Sir Knight," said the forester, " to see thee so ready to do battle against this caitiff, Sir Miers, and full willing should I be to conduct thee to the sacking of his tower; but in good verity, 'twere vain to go so accoutred and attended as thou art. He keeps special good watch and ward, I promise thee, and he is too much wont to have his quarters beat up, not to be for ever on the alert. He hath scouts stationed all around him, in such a manner that no one may approach his stronghold of Burnstower by day or by night withouten ken, and he is straightway put on the alert long ere he can be reached. If those who come against him be strong and well armed, more than his force can overcome, then he hies him away to the fastnesses of his mosses and hills, where no one but the eagle may follow him, and leaves only his barren walls to the fury of the besiegers. But if the party be small, and such as his wiles may master, he is sure to lead them into some ambush, and to put every man of them to the sword. Trust me, wert thou to go clad in steel, and with such a party of spearmen at thy back, he would take the alarm, and thou would'st either have thy journey and thy trouble for thy guerdon, or thou and thy people might fall by cruel traiterie."

"Then what, after all, may be the best means of coming at him?" said Assueton; "for thou hast but the more inflamed my desire to essay the adventure."

The forester seemed to consider for a time— "In truth," said he at length, "I see no other way than one the which thou would'st spurn, Sir Knight."

"Name it," said Assueton; "depend on't, I shall not be over nice in this affair."

"Wert thou," said the forester, "and, it might be, no more than two of thy people, to venture thither in disguise, with one or two of us to guide thee, thou mightest peradventure pass hither without begetting alarm, and be re-

ceived into the Castle as lated and miswent travellers, lacking covert for the night. But then
all that would be but of small avail, for what
could'st thou do with thy single arm, and so
small a force to aid it?"

"Nay, good forester," said Assueton, "be
it mine to see to that, and be it thine to bring
me thither. Knights are but born to conquer
difficulties, and, perdie, I have never yet seen
that which did not, with me, give greater zest
to the adventure I went upon. By the blessed
Rood, I shall with thee. Let us forthwith have
our disguises, then, and these two men of my
company," pointing to Riddel and Lindsay,
"shall share the glory of mine emprise. So
let us, I pr'ythee, snatch a hasty meal, and set
forward without delay."

"By the mass, but thou art a brave knight,"
said the forester; "yet doth it grieve me to see
thee go on so hopeless an errand. Nathless, I
shall not baulk thee, nor back of my word;
verily I shall wend with thee, to show thee the
way thither. But I would fain persuade thee
even yet to leave this undertaking untried."

"Nay," said Assueton, "I have said it, and
by God's aid I will do it, let the peril be what
it may; so let us use dispatch, if it so please
thee."

Seeing that the bold and dauntless knight was resolved, the forester ordered some of the venison that was by this time cooked to be set before Assueton, and some also to be served to those who were to accompany him; and after all had satisfied their hunger, Assueton doffed his armour, clad himself in a suit of plain Lincoln green, such as the foresters wore, and unperceived by any one slipped his dagger into his bosom. He then openly girt his trusty sword by his side, and leaving orders with his party to remain with the friendly foresters until they should see him, or hear from him, he and his two people, who were also disguised, mounted their horses, and set off under the guidance of the leader of the hunting party and two of his men, whom he took with him, as he said, to bear him company on his return.

CHAPTER XVIII.

THEIR route lay up the glen, and the darkness of the night, with the roughness of the way, very much impeded their progress. At one time they were led along the very margin of the stream, and at another climbed diagonally up the steep sides of the hills that bounded it, and wound over far above, to avoid some impediment which blocked all passage below. Now they penetrated extensive thickets of brushwood, and again wound among the tall stems of luxuriant oaks, or passed, with greater ease to themselves and their weary horses, over small open glades among the woods. At length they began to rise over the sides of the hills, to a height so much beyond any that they had hitherto mounted, that Assueton thought the deviation strange and unaccountable, and was tempted to put some questions to his guide.

" Whither dost thou lead us now, good fo-

rester?" said he; " thou seemest to have aban-
douced the glen altogether, and methinks thou
art now resolved to soar to the very·clouds.   I
much question whether garron of mosstrooper
ever climbed such a house-wall as this."

" Sir Knight," replied the forester, " I but
intend to lead thee over the ridge of a hill here
by a curter cast.   The glen maketh a wicked
wide courbe below, and goeth miles about. This
gate will save us leagues twayne, at the very
shortest reckoning. Trust me, I am well up to
all the hills and glens of these parts, by night
as well as by day."

" Nay, good forester," said Assueton, " I
doubt thee not; but, by our Lady, this seemeth
to me to be a marvellous uncouth path."

" T'other, indeed, is better, Sir Knight," said
the forester; " but bad as this may be, 'twill
haine us a good hour's time of travel."

Assueton was satisfied with this explanation,
and the ground getting more level as they advanced, he soon discovered that they were crossing a wild ridge of moorland, and hoped that
the impediments to a speedier progress would
be fewer.   But the way seemed, if possible,
to be even more puzzling and difficult than
ever. They wound round in one direction, and
then went zigzag to the opposite point of the

compass; then they wormed their way through bogs and mosses—then stretched away Heaven knows where, and then making a little detour, they (as it seemed to Assueton) returned again in a line nearly parallel to that which they had just pursued. Hours appeared to glide away in this wearisome and endless maze, and Assueton's impatience became excessive.

" Good forester," said he, " methinks we are never to get out of this enchanted labyrinth."

" Nay, Sir Knight," said the forester, " 'tis an enchanted labyrinth in good soberness; for, verily, full many a good steed hath been ygraven in the flows that surround us. There be quaking bogs here that would swallow a good-sized tower. Nay, halt thee, Sir Knight, thou must of needscost turn thee this gate again."

" By St Cuthbert," said Assueton, " meseems it a miracle that thou should'st have memory to help thee to thread the intricacies of so puzzling a path, maugre the darkness that yet prevails."

" 'Tis indeed mirk as a coal mine," said the forester, " but I look for the moon anon."

After better than half an hour more of such travelling as we have described, they at length wound down a very precipitous hill, where their necks were in considerable peril, and found

themselves again in the glen, and by the side
of its stream. As well as Assueton could guess,
they had now travelled fully three or four hours,
the greater part of which time they had spent
on the high ground. The state of their horses,
too, bore out his calculation, for they showed
symptoms of great exhaustion, from this so large
addition to the previous severe journey. They
pushed them on, however, as fast as the nature
of the ground would admit, the glen presenting
the same variety of woods, glades, and thickets,
it had formerly done.

At length they came to a place where the
hills approached on each side, and the glen nar-
rowed to a wild gorge, where all passage was
denied below, except for the stream, and they
were consequently again compelled to ascend
the abrupt banks by a diagonal path. But
they had no sooner gained the summit, than
the moon arose, and threw its silver light full
over the scene into which they were about to
advance. Above the gorge, the valley was split
into two distinct glens, or rather deep ravines,
that each poured out its stream, and these, uniting together, formed that which they had so
long traced upwards. Above the point of their
union arose a green-headed eminence, swelling
from among the rich woods that everywhere

clothed it, and all the other lower parts of the space within their view. The round top of the eminence was crowned with a rude Border Tower; and the whole was backed, a good way behind, by a semicircular range of hilly ridges. The moonlight shone powerfully on the building, the keep of which seemed to be of no great size, but very strong in itself; and the outworks, consisting of massive walls defended here and there by round towers, showed that it was a stronghold where determined men might make a powerful resistance.

" Yonder is the peel of Burnstower," said the forester, pointing to it; " thou must ford the stream there below, under the hill whereon it stands, and so make thy way up through the woods by a narrow path, that will lead thee to the yate. I shall yet go with thee as far as the ford, to show thee the right gate through the water; but I must then bid thee farewell, nor canst thou lack mine aid any longer."

" Good forester," said Assueton, " certes thou hast merited the guerdon of my best thanks for thine obliging and toilsome convoy. When I join thee again, trust me they shall be cheerfully paid thee, together with what more solid warison thou mayest see fit to accept, in token of my gratitude.   Meanwhile, I beseech thee take good charge of my brave men."

"Nay, fear me not in that, Sir Knight," said the forester; "they shall be well looked after, I promise thee. My men have doubtless already taken good care of them and of their steeds too."

Having descended the hill, they pushed their way through the opposing brushwood, and reached the bank of one of the streams, immediately above the spot where it united itself to the other. The forester indicated the ford to Assueton, and then took an abrupt leave, diving into the thicket with his two followers.

Assueton stood for a moment on the brink of the stream before he entered, and took that opportunity of telling his two attendants to be particularly on their guard, to watch his eye, attend to his signals, and be ready to act as these might appear to suggest to them. They were also to bear in mind, that for the present they were to pass as equals. He then cautiously entered the ford, and, followed by Riddel and Lindsay, soon reached the farther bank.

They now found themselves on a low grassy tongue of land, which shot out between the two streams from the woods at the base of the eminence the Castle stood on, and which, though

of considerable length, was nowhere more than
a few yards wide. Along this they pushed
their horses, as fast as the weary animals could
advance. A few trees straggled down over it
at the farther extremity, where it united itself
to the base of the hill; and just as they had
entered among these, all their horses were at
one and the same moment tumbled headlong
on the ground. An instant shout arose from
the thickets on either side, and about a dozen
men sprang from them on the prostrate riders;
and, after a short and ineffectual struggle on
their part, Assueton and his two attendants
were bound hand and foot, and blindfolded.
All this time not a word was spoken; and excepting the shouts that were the signal of the
onset, not a sound was heard. But the prey
was no sooner fairly mastered, than a loud bu-
gle-blast was blown, and immediately answered by another, that rung from the woods at
some distance. The horses were then extri-
cated from the toils of ropes which had been
so treacherously though ingeniously employed
to ensure their prostration, and on regaining
their legs, their late riders were lifted up, and
laid across them like sacks, and they were led
by the villains who had captured them up the
steep and devious ascent, through the thick

wood, to the Castle. The party then entered
the gateway, as Assueton judged from the noise
made in raising the portcullis, and the prisoners
being lifted from their horses, were carried each
by two men into the main tower.

Whither they took his two attendants, Assueton had no means of guessing; but he was borne
up a long and winding stair, as he supposed to
the top of the building, and then through several
passages. There he heard the withdrawing of
rusty bolts, and the heavy creaking of hinges;
and being set down on the floor of his prison,
his arms and legs were unbound, his eyes uncovered, and he was left in utter darkness and
amazement.

After sitting for some moments to recover
from the surprise occasioned by this sudden and
unlooked-for annihilation of all his plans, and of
all the hopes he had cherished from them, he
arose, and, before yielding to despair, groped
his way to the walls, and felt them anxiously
all round. Not a crevice or aperture could he
discover but the doorway, and that was blocked
by an impregnable door, crossed and recrossed
by powerful bars of iron, so that he saw no
hope of its being moved by any strength of human arm, unassisted by levers or other such
instruments. The walls and floor were of the

most solid masonry in every part; yet he felt the balmy air of a soft night blow upon his face, and, on looking upwards, he could just descry a faint glimmer of light, that broke with difficulty through the enormous thickness of the building, by a narrow window immediately over where he then stood. This opening, however, was quite beyond his reach, being at least a dozen feet above him.

As he moved backwards to get from under the wall where the window was, that he might obtain a better view of it, his head came in contact with something hanging behind him. He turned round, but his eyes were not yet sufficiently accustomed to the obscurity, to enable him to discover anything more than that there was some dark object suspended from above. He put up his hands to ascertain what it was, and, to his inexpressible horror, felt the stiffened legs of a corpse, which swung backwards and forwards at his touch. Bold and firm as he was, Assueton started involuntarily back, and his heart revolted at the thought that he was to be so mated for the night. He retired to a corner, where he had discovered a heap of straw, with a coarse blanket, and he sat him down on it; but it immediately occurred to him that this had probably been the bed of the unfortunate man who

now dangled lifeless from the centre of the
vault, and he could sit on it no longer.   That
the poor wretch had been put to death in the
very chamber which had been his prison, seemed
to argue a degree of hardened cruelty and sum-
mary vengeance in those in whose power he
had now himself the misfortune to be, that left
him little room to hope for much mercy at their
hands.

Having moved to an opposite corner, nearly
under the little window, he seated himself on
the floor, and gave up his mind to the full bitterness of its thoughts.   The first recollection
that presented itself was that of the Lady Isabelle, torn from her home, her father, and himself, by an unprincipled and abandoned villain.
His reflections on this painful theme banished
every thought of his own captivity, as well as
every speculation as to what its result might
be, excepting, indeed, in so far as it might affect
the fate of her who was now the idol of his
heart.   He ran over his past conduct, and seeing that he could now have no hope of being the
instrument of her rescue, he blamed himself in
a thousand ways.   He accused himself bitterly
for not having sent back a messenger from the
place where he had met Sir Walter de Selby,
to inform Sir Patrick Hepborne the elder of the

intelligence he had obtained from the Captain
of Norham; then unavailing regrets and self-
accusations arose within him for having negleeted to obtain more full information from
Sir Walter, when he had it in his power to do
so; but, above all, he cursed his folly for having abandoned his stout-hearted spearmen,
who would have backed him against any foes
to the last drop of their blood. He turned over
the circumstances of his rencontre with the
foresters, and, recalling the whole conduct of
their leader, he now began to be more than
half suspicious that they had played him false.
This last reflection made him tremble for the
fate of his people whom he had left with them;
and remembering his guide's parting assurance,
" that they should be well looked after," he felt
disposed to interpret it in a very opposite sense
to that he had put upon it at the moment it
was uttered. He had no doubt, that, if the
foresters really were villains, as he had now so
much reason to believe, they would easily fall
on means to deceive his innocent men, nay,
perhaps to murder them in cold blood.

He then again recurred to the Lady Isabelle.
Why had he gone a-hunting on the day she was
carried off, when he had been repeatedly warn-
ed, by something within his own breast, that

he ought to stay at home with her? Alas!
where was she now? The question was agony
to him.   Could she be within these walls? To
know that she, indeed, really was so, would
have been cheering to him even in his present
state of desponding uncertainty, as it might
have given him some frail hope of yet being
of use to her.   He listened for distant sounds.
Faint female shrieks came from some part of the
building far below.   Again he heard them yet
more distinctly; and full of the maddening idea
that they came from the Lady Isabelle, he started up, unconscious of what he was doing, flew
like a madman to the door, and began beating
at it with his fists, screaming out, " Villains!
murderers!" But his voice, and the noise of
his furious knocking, returned on his ear with
a deadened sound, and speedily convinced him
that nothing could be heard from the lofty, solitary, and massive walled prison in which he
was immured.

With a heart torn and distracted, and almost
bereft of reason, he paced the floor violently
backwards and forwards.   His ear then caught,
from time to time, the distant and subdued
shouts of merriment and laughter.   These again
stung him to fury.

" What!" cried he aloud, " do they make

sport of her purity and her misery? Villains!
demons! hellhounds!" And he again raved
about his prison with yet greater fury than before, a thousand horrible ideas arising to his
heated and prolific imagination.

At length he flung himself on the floor, utter-
ly exhausted both in body and mind by the intensity of his sufferings, and lay for some moments in a state of quiet, from absolute inability
to give further way to the extravagance of ac-
-tion excited by his feelings. He had not been
long in this state, however, when the distant
and faint chanting of a female voice fell upon
his ear. He started, and raising himself upon
his elbow, listened anxiously, that he might
drink in the minutest portion of the sound which
reached him. Though evidently coming from
some far-off chamber below, he distinctly caught
the notes, which he recognized to be those of a
hymn to the Virgin, from the vesper service.
The melody was sweet and soothing to his lace-
rated soul. Again it stole on him.

"The voice," said he to himself, "that can
so employ itself, must come from one who may
be unhappy, but who cannot suppose herself to
be in any very immediate peril; nor, if her
mind had been so lately suffering urgent alarm,
could she have by this time composed it so far,

as to be able to lift it to Heaven in strains so gentle and placid."

Though immediately afterwards convinced of the folly of such an idea, he, for a moment, almost persuaded himself that he recognized the voice of the Lady Isabelle Hepborne in that of the pious chantress. He threw himself upon his knees, and offered up his fervent orisons for help in his affliction. The voice came again upon him—and again he fancied he knew it to be that of her he loved; but although he found himself, in sound reason, obliged to discard all idea of the possibility of such a recognition, yet it clung to his broken spirit, and was as a healing balm to it, in despite of reason.

It produced one happy effect, however, by causing his agonizing thoughts to give way, at last, to the immense bodily and mental fatigue he had undergone. He dropped asleep on the bare pavement, notwithstanding the horrors that hung over him, the uncertain fate that awaited him, and the complication of misery by which he was oppressed.

CHAPTER XIX.

SIR JOHN ASSUETON'S sleep was deep and uninterrupted until the first dawn of morning, when he awoke, and rubbed his eye-lids, having, for a moment, forgotten where he was, and all that had befallen him. The first object that presented itself when he looked upwards, was the figure and countenance of the dead man, hanging almost immediately over the spot where he lay. The features were horribly distorted and discoloured, by the last agonies of the violent death he had died; the tongue was thrust out, and the projected eye-balls were staring fearfully from their sockets. The sight was appalling and heart-sickening.

He could now observe, that the dress of the unfortunate man was that of a forester. The arms were rudely tied behind the back, and the body was suspended from a huge iron ring, that hung loose in an enormous bolt of the same metal, strongly built in vertically between the key-

stones of the vault, the height of which was very
considerable. It seemed as if the wretched man
had been dragged from his couch of straw to
instant punishment, or rather perhaps murder;
for portions of the straw yet littered the floor,
as if dragged along with him in his ineffectual
struggles, and some fragments of it still adhered
between his ankles, to the rough woollen hose
he wore, as if retained there by the last dying
convulsion that had pressed and twisted the
limbs unnaturally together. Then the fatal
rope was not like one intended for such a use.
It was thicker than seemed necessary, and looked as if it had been hastily taken, as the readiest instrument for the murderous deed. After
passing through the ring, where it was fastened
by two or three turns, it stretched down diagonally to one corner of the place, where it lost
itself in an immense coil. It had manifestly
been hastily brought there, to effect the destruction of the unfortunate wretch, and afterwards
left on the floor uncut, that it might not be rendered unfit for the purpose to which it had been
originally dedicated.

It may seem strange, that Assueton should
have derived anything like pleasure from a spectacle so truly appalling; but it is nevertheless
true, that a faint gleam of hope broke upon the

miserable despair that had possessed him. He saw that the coil of rope was of sufficient extent, to give him good reason to believe that, when untwisted, it might reach to the base of the tower, at the top of which he was now confined, if he could only detach it from what went upwards, and conceal it till night. But how was he to sever it? He remembered that he had concealed his dagger in his bosom at the time he put on his disguise. Those who seized and bound him had immediately deprived him of his sword, but they had not suspected his being possessed of any other weapon, and his dagger, therefore, had escaped their notice. He drew it joyfully forth; but just as he was about to divide the rope, he paused, and observing that there were at least fourteen or sixteen feet stretching diagonally between the coil and the ring, he hesitated to cut it. To throw away so considerable a portion of it, when perhaps that very piece might be essential to the preservation of his life, would have been the height of absurdity; yet to get at that portion there was but one way, and this was so disgusting, and so repugnant to his feelings, that the very idea of it made him shudder.

- But liberty, and perhaps life, depended on it; and what will not the desire of liberty and life compel human nature to attempt? To him both were now more precious than ever, since they might yet be the means of saving her, without whom he could value neither. He hesitated not a moment longer, but screwing up his resolution to the revolting alternative, laid hold of the legs of the dead man, swung himself up from the ground, and catching at his clothes, at last got the rope within his gripe, and thus continued to climb, hand over hand, until he reached the fatal ring. Holding by one sinewy arm, he drew forth his dagger, and was again on the eve of cutting the rope close to the ring, when prudence once more stopped him. He had been from the first aware, that it was absolutely necessary to leave the dead body hanging, lest, when his jailors should visit him, they might have their suspicion awakened by its removal. What made him hesitate, then, whilst hanging by one arm to the ring and bolt in the arch of the vault, was the idea that, by loosening the turns that were made in it, he might be enabled to hoist up the body a few feet higher, then to fasten the turns of the rope again, and thus gain so many more feet of hope. All this, with immense fatigue of arm, he effected, and then dividing the rope with his dagger, and descending to the floor, he lifted up the large coil, and removing the straw of the bed, he hid it underneath, covering it up with the greatest care. He was fully aware of the possibility of its being missed from its place, sought for, and removed from the concealment he had put it into; but it was also possible, that the wretches who had done the deed might not be among those who should come to visit him, in which case its absence could never attract their observation.

He now sat down to consider and arrange his plans. He at once saw, that it would be useless to attempt his descent while day-light remained, or, indeed, while the people in the Castle might be supposed to be still stirring, as, if he did try it then, he must do so with hardly a chance of escaping detection. To lessen the risk of being observed and seized, therefore, it was absolutely essential that he should postpone his enterprise until night. But then the risk of his rope being discovered before night crossed his mind: his judgment wavered, and he was filled with the most cruel and perplexing doubts. He remembered that the state of the moon, which left the earlier part of the night excessively dark, made that by far the most favourable time to risk his fate; and he at length determined, that, a descent in day-light being perfectly hopeless, he must be content to take his chance of the other alternative. But what was he to do if the rope should be missed, sought for, and detected? After some consideration, he resolved, that in that event he would draw his dagger, spring unawares on those who might visit him, and so make a desperate endeavour to effect his escape, by striking down all that might oppose him.

But another and a different thought now occurred to him. What if the very first visit that might be paid him should be for the purpose of taking down the murdered body from the ring, only to hang him up in its place? Brave as he was, he shuddered at the contemplation of such a fate. He had already often faced death in bloody field, led on by glory and the laudable thirst of fame; but to be hung up like a dog by the hands of murderous ruffians, in this lone chamber, far from every human ear or eye but those of his clownish and unfeeling executioners, who would take small account of him after witnessing his passing agonies, or perhaps leave him, as they had done the wretch who had gone before him, till his place was wanted for a successor, and then throw his half-consumed body into some unholy spot, over which his perturbed ghost might hover, seeking in vain for repose,—this was to strip death of the fascinating drapery which men have contrived to throw over him, and to unveil all his terrors. But he steeled himself for the worst, and, resolving to wait firmly, and to act as circumstances might suggest, he determined that, happen what might, he would sell his life dearly, should he be reduced to the unhappy alternative of doing so.

With his mind thus wound up, he sat him down on the couch of straw, that he might appear unconcerned to any one who might enter; and there he remained, waiting patiently for the issue. He had been seated in this way about a couple of hours, when he heard the heavy tread of feet approaching along the passages. The key was inserted in the lock of the door, and considerable force exerted before it could be turned.

" Be quick with you, old churl," cried an impatient voice; " thou wilt be all day working at it."

The door half opened, and two or three heads were thrust in at once. Seeing their prisoner calmly seated on the straw at the farther wall, four men entered. One of these, a thick,-squat, large-headed old man, with a rough, cloddish, unfeeling countenance, and long, thick, grizzled hair hanging about it, was clad in a close wool-

len jerkin and hauselines, and appeared ·to be
the jailor, for several enormous keys hung from
divers straps attached to his leathern belt.· He
stationed himself with his back at the door. The
other three men were younger, but the expression of their features betrayed such depraved
and lawless spirits, as might make them ready
instruments to perpetrate any cruelty or crime
at the mere nod of a master. Their dress was
similar to that in which the murdered body was
clothed. Two of them, armed with short swords
in their hands, placed themselves at the door, in
front of the old jailor, while the third, with a
pewter-covered dish under his left arm, an earth-
en jug of ale in his left hand, and his naked
sword in his right, advanced a little way, and
deposited the provisions on the pavement. Turning his eyes round, he beheld the dead body
hanging.

" Heyday, Daniel Throckle," said he, with à
careless laugh to the jailor, " how camest thou
to leave our comrade Tim Ord here, to keep
watch over this young man all night? By the
mass, methinks he was but a triste companion
for him."

" 'Twas none o' my doing, Master Ralpho
Proudfoot; 'twas Wat Withe that did the deed
himsell. He got the key from me, and thou

knowest he doth not ever care overmuch, so he gets his job done, whether the work-shop be cleaned out or no. He thinks that be none o' his business."

"Nay, but, fine fellow as he thinks himself, he may come and take down his own rubbish for me," said Ralpho Proudfoot; "I clean out after no sike cattle, I promise thee. An thou likest to do his dirty work thou mayest, seeing thou art custodier of the place." Then turning to Assueton, who had sat quite still all this time, "Here, sir," said he, "is thy morning's meal —better eat it whiles it be hot—thou mayest not have a many deal of sike like;" and as he said so, he threw his eye sideways up towards the dead man. "Thou seest we be sometimes rather more curt than courteous ;—thou canst not tell when it may be thy turn."

"Young man," said Assueton, composedly, and still without rising from his sitting posture, "canst thou tell me why I have been so traitorously seized and conveyed hither, and why I am thus immured, and treated as a foul felon?"

"Nay, as to being treated like a felon, *young man*," replied Ralpho Proudfoot, evading his question, and laying particular emphasis on the words in italics, "meseems 'tis but ungrateful of thee to say so, seeing I have brought thee a

dish of hot steaks, cut from the rump of a good
Scottish ront; and then for ale, never was better brewed about the roots of the Cheviots, as
well thou knowest, honest Daniel Throckle."

The jailor replied by a significant chuckle,
indicating his perfect acknowledgment of Proudfoot's assertion.

"Well," continued Proudfoot, "we may e'en
leave thee, *young man*, to the full enjoyment of
this pleasing sunshiny day, such as thou may'st
have on't through yonder window on high, for
thou may'st see even less on't to-morrow." And,
wheeling round, he was on the eve of departure,
when he suddenly stopped—"But hold," said
he, "had we not better ripe him, to see that he
hath nothing of weapon sort about him? Come
forward, *young man*; and do thou, old Daniel,
approach, and feel his hide all over, as thou
wouldst do a fat sheep fed for the slaughter.
And who knows how soon it may be his lot?
Approach, I say: we shall stand by here, and
see that he doeth thee no harm."

Assueton perceived that resistance would be
vain, and he also knew that it was unnecessary.
Before they entered, he had taken the precaution to remove his dagger from his bosom, and
conceal it among the straw near where he sat,
yet in such a manner as he could have easily

seized it had he seen any necessity for using
it. He arose indignantly, and then, with assumed carelessness, submitted to be searched; not,
however, without considerable inward alarm,
that they might not be contented with the mere
examination of his person, but proceed to rummage the straw also. Should they do so, all his
hopes were gone; but his heart kept firm, and
he stood with so easy and indifferent an air, that
the villains were soon satisfied.

" No, no," cried Proudfoot, " I see all is
sicker. So a jolly morning to thee, *young man.*
Come, lads, let us be trooping. We have work
before us, as ye well know."

" Had I not better shake up his straw for
him?" said one of the others; " he may not be
used to make his own bed."

" Nay, nay," said Proudfoot, " he may learn
to make it then; he can never learn younger,
I ween. Besides, hath he not Tim Ord there to
help him?—ha! ha! ha! By St Roque, but
they will have pleasant chat together."

" Nay, Daniel Throckle," said the other man,
" but thee shouldest come back ere long, and
remove this grim mate from his dortoure."

" Umph," said Throckle, as if in doubt; " it's
a plaguy long stair to climb, and I may not get

hands to help me. But, nathless, I'll see what
may be done. Wat Withe may peraunter——"

"Come, come," cried Proudfoot, impatiently,
"we are wanted ere this. Off, I say—off;" and
with these words they all four left the prison;
the door was bolted and barred with the utmost
precaution, and their heavy lumbering steps
were heard retreating along the passages.

It was strange, perhaps, but it was most true,
that the shutting of the rusty bolts sounded almost as sweetly in Assueton's ear, as if they
had been opened to give him liberty. The relief he felt at the retreat of the four men was
so great, that, like a pious knight, he knelt
down and offered up his heartfelt gratitude,
in fervent thanksgivings to Heaven, that his
plans were as yet unfrustrated. He took up
the food that had been left with him, and made
a hearty and cheerful meal. He then began
turning in his mind the circumstances that
were likely to occur to him before night, and
again some cruel anticipations obtruded themselves. Were Throckle to return to remove the
body, perhaps it might be of little consequence;
but if, as he seemed to hint at when he was interrupted—if he should call in the aid of Wat
Withe, as they had nicknamed the executioner,
then all his schemes for escape must be ruined.

Nay, what if the coil of rope, the villain had so hastily taken, should happen to be wanted before night for the purpose it had been originally intended for? The thought was most alarming. Assueton immediately removed the straw from it, that he might examine it narrowly, and his mind was very much relieved when he discovered that it was everywhere quite rough and new, as if it had never been used. But still nothing presented itself to him, to rid him of the apprehension of the return of Watt Withe, who could not fail to remark the disappearance of the coil. A thousand times during the day he fancied he heard steps approaching, and more than once he grasped his dagger to prepare for bloody work. But it was all fancy. The only sound he heard was that of the trampling of horses, the jingling of bridles, and the clattering of weapons, mingled with the voices of men, as if some party was riding forth.

CHAPTER XX.

THE time passed slowly and heavily until within about an hour of nightfall, when steps were again distinctly heard approaching Assueton's prison. Much to his relief, however, they seemed to be those of a single person; something was put down on the pavement on the outside; the bolts were tardily withdrawn, and the great head of Daniel Throckle alone appeared through the partially opened door, as if to ascertain in what part of the chamber his prisoner was, ere he should venture farther. Seeing Assueton seated as formerly, on the straw, he hastily pushed within the door-way vessels containing food and drink, as before, and instantly retreating, turned the bolts behind him, and departed without uttering a word.

Now Assueton's hopes beat high, and again on his knees he returned his fervent thanks to Heaven. He then determined to avail himself

6

of the small portion of day-light which yet remained, to make everything ready for his escape.

Disgusting and revolting as it had been to
him, on the first discovery of the murdered
body, that it should have been left as his night-
ly and daily companion, he had now good reason to be glad that it had been so; for even if
its removal had not occasioned the discovery of
his appropriation of the coil of rope, without it
he could have had no means of reaching the
ring in the centre of the vault, the only thing
within it to which he could have attached the
end of his rope, and it would have been there
only to have mocked his hopes.

After he had succeeded in making it fast, he
had still an appalling difficulty before him; for
the window was so high above the floor of the
vault that it was quite beyond all reach. There
was, to be sure, a small fragment of rusty iron,
that projected an inch or two from the centre of
the sole of it, like the decayed remains of a
stanchion, that had once divided the space vertically within; but it was little better than a
knob. It yet remained to be proved, therefore,
whether he should succeed in throwing a part
of his rope over this frail pin of iron, so as to
furnish him with the means of pulling himself up
to the window; and he lost no time in making

the experiment. But this, so absolutely essential part of his operations, he found most difficult to effect. He threw, cast, and jerked the
rope, trying every possible way he could think
of; but the piece of iron was so short, that although he often succeeded in throwing the rope
over it, he could never manage to make it hold.
The day-light ebbed away fast, and still he la-
boured, but without success. At length he
grew desperate, and threw the rope up time
after time with mad and senseless rapidity. It
became darker and darker till pitchy night closed in, yet still he persevered in throwing furiously and at random; bnt it was the perseve-
rance of despair, all attempt at skill being utter-
ly abandoned. At length, when he had almost
become frantic, it caught as he pulled back after
an accidental throw; he felt it hold against him,
and keeping it down to the floor tight with one
foot, to prevent it from slipping, he laid the
whole weight of the coil upon it, and then dropping on his knees, returned thanks to Heaven
for his success. It was but a small matter throwing a coil of rope over a projecting fragment of
iron; yet on that trifle depended all his hopes,
for by means of that small piece of iron alone
could he escape.

He now sat him down on the coil to wait pa-

tiently for the hour when he might think it safe
to make his bold attempt.

Judging at length that the night was sufficiently far advanced for his purpose, he offered
up a prayer for divine aid and protection, and
tying the blanket of the bed around him in
case of need, laid hold of the rope and hoisted
himself up by his arms, until he had reached
the window. Having lodged himself fairly in
its aperture, he discovered that the wall was at
least six or eight feet thick. He now laid himself on his side, with his feet hanging inwards,
and by slow degrees pulled up the rope, until
he got the whole coil deposited safely within
the small area of the window. The space was
barely sufficient to admit of his creeping easily
through. Altering his position, therefore, and
advancing his feet, he wormed himself forward, when, just as he expected to thrust them
into the open air, he felt them suddenly arrested by a vertical bar of iron. His heart was
chilled by its touch. He tried the width of the
vacancies on either side of it, but neither afforded space enough to admit of the passage of
his body.

Much disheartened by this unexpected obstruction, he withdrew himself, and with great
difficulty again changed his position, and ad-

vanced head foremost, until he brought his hands
near enough to the bar to feel it all over. It
was much decayed by rust, but yet by far too
strong to be broken by the mere force of his
arm. After a little consideration, he drew his
dagger, and making use of its point, worked
away the lead and the stone where the lower
end of the stanchion was inserted; and after
labouring. unceasingly for a considerable time,
he found he had weakened the stone and removed the lead so much, that he had some
hopes of assailing it successfully with his feet.
He was now, therefore, obliged to retreat again
and change his position, so that he again projected his feet till they came in contact with the
bar. Having fixed himself firmly in the place
by means of his arms, that he might bring all his
-orce to bear against it, he was about to strike violently at it with the soles of his feet, when he remembered that the sound might be heard below.
His situation made him fertile in expedients.
He slipped forward a part of the blanket, and
adjusting two or three folds of it over the bar,
he began to drive his feet furiously against it.
It gradually gave way before them, and then it
suddenly yielded entirely. He ceased working for an instant, and, to his no small alarm,
heard a piece of the stone he had driven off fall

in the court-yard below. He listened anxiously
for a time, but no alarm seemed to have been
excited. He again felt at the bar with his feet,
and recommencing his attack upon it, after a
succession of hard blows, bent it so far outwards as to leave no doubt that he could pass
himself through the aperture.

Commending himself to God, then, he slipped himself forward, and, committing his weight
gently to the rope, began descending by shifting his hands alternately and slowly one below
the other, always pulling out more and more of
the coil of rope as he wanted it, until the end
of it being unwound, it fell perpendicularly below him. Still he went on descending till, to
his no small dismay, he found that he had reached the last foot of its length. For an instant he
hung in awful doubt. He cast his eyes below,
but the night was so dark, that the ground beneath was invisible, and he could not possibly
calculate the height that yet remained. He
thought for a few moments; and finally, resign-
ing himself to the care of Providence, loosen-
ed his grasp of the rope and fell. His fall was
dreadful, and his death must have been certain,
had not his descent been interrupted by a fortunate circumstance. The blanket he had wrapped round him caught in the branches of a yew

tree growing close to the wall, and although it did not keep its hold, yet the force of the fall was so much broken that he escaped comparatively uninjured.

He lay stunned for some moments under the tree; and then, recovering himself, he was about to rise, when reflecting that he must proceed with caution, he crept silently forth from his covert, and listened to hear if there was any one stirring. All was quiet. He then moved forward, and, dark as the night was, he could yet perceive the outer walls and towers of the building rising against the pale glimmer of the sky. His first step was to steal around the base of the keep, that he might reconnoitre it in all directions; and, as he did so, he passed by its entrance, which he found open. Wishing to examine farther, he went on listening, but all was silent around. At length, as he moved onwards to another side of the building, he descried a light breaking from a loop-hole window near the foundation of the keep, and heard the sound of human voices, with now and then a peal of boisterous laughter. He approached with extreme caution and silence, until he was near enough to see and hear all that passed within.

The place he looked down into appeared to be a sort of cellar, being surrounded with huge

barrels placed against the walls, near one of
which, on an inverted tub, sat the old jailor,
Daniel Throckle, with a great wooden stoup of
ale on his knee, and with no small quantity of
the fumes of the same fluid in his brain, as was
evident from the manner in which his eyes ogled
in his head. Almost close by him stood a good-
looking wench in conversation with him; and
the group was lighted by a clumsy iron-lamp
placed on the top of one of the largest of the
tuns.

" Coum, coum, Daeniel Throckle," said the
girl, " thee hast had enow o' that strong stuff;
that stoup but accloyeth thee. Blessed Mary!
but thine eyes do look most fearsome askaunce
already."

" Nay, nay, my bellebone," replied Throckle,
" I mun ha' a wee drop more yet. Coum, now,
do sit thee down, and be buxom a bit,—a—a—
Thee knawest—a—that I loves thee dearly—he!
he! he! Sit thee down, now, I say,—a—a; sit
thee down, my soft, my soote virginal!—By St
Cuthbert, there be not a he that yalt the gate
through sun and weet—a—a—that—a—a—he!
he! he!—that loveth thee more than I do.—
Sit thee down, I say—a—a—and troll a roundel
with me. Hear ye, now, do but—a—a—do but
join thy sweet voice with mine.—Nay, then, an

thou wont, I mun e'en—a—a—sing by mysell
—a—a—

> Oh I am the man,
> That can empty a can,
> And fill it again and again, ah!
> A—a—And empty and fill,
> And the barley-juice swill,
> Till a tun of the liquor I dram, ah!
>
> A—a—Then it lightens mine eye,
> And my liard jokes fly,
> And it warms my old blood into pleasure.
> A—a—a—Then out comes my song,
> Trolling glibly a—a—along,
> And merrily clinks in the measure.
>
> Oh—a—a—a—And then should I see
> A sweet pusell like thee,
> She catches mine eye, as I cock it;
> And then at her, gadzooks!
> I throw such winning looks,
> As soon turn both of hers in the socket.
>
> So then—a—a———

A murrain on't! how should I forget the rest
on't ?—

> So then I—a—a—then—a———

The red fiend catch it, for I can't!—So my
bonny mistress, Betty Burrel, do thee—a—do
thee sit thee down here, whiles I but drink this
single can—a—a—of double ale; and, sin' we
canna sing the rest o' the stave,—a—a—sit thee
down, and let me kiss thee."

" Na, na, Daeniel Throckle," said the girl ;
" thee knawest thou'rt ower auld for me—
thou'rt ower auld to be make o' mine."

" Ower auld!—a—a—thou scoffing—thou
scoffing giglet, thou!" cried Throckle. "Thou'lt
find me—a—kinder—a—thou'lt find me kinder
at least than that cross-grained, haughty knave.
Ralpho Proudfoot. A pestilent rascal!—Thou
knawest—a—a—a—thou knawest, I say, how
ill he used thee—a—but last night, no farther
gone. Did he not beat thee—a—yestreen—a—
till he made thee rout out like any Laverdale
cow, when—a—she hath been driven—a—
across the Border—a—and hath left her calf
behind her ?"

" In troth, Daeniel Throckle," said the wench,
" he did use me hard enow, that's certain, now
when a's done. But rise thee up, Daeniel. Bethink thee, thou'rt a' that be left to guard the
Castle, an it be na mysell, and auld Harry
Haddon standing sentry at the yett. Ise warrant he's asleep or this time :—And what 'ud
coum o' us an the prisoners were to break
out ?"

" Phoo !" said Daniel, sticking one arm akim-
bo, and assuming the most ridiculous air of importance—" Phoo ! I would not care that—a —
a—snap of my finger, look you now, for—a—a
N 2

—for the whole bunch of 'em. A stout, able-bodied—a—courageous—a—warlikesome—a—Southron like me—well fortified and charged with potent double ale—against three lousy Scottish louns! Phoo! I'd put 'em all down with my thumb. But—a—a—but, look ye here, my bonny Betty Burrel; here they are—a—a—all safe at my girdle. This mockell knave here," continued he, laying hold of the keys that hung from his belt, " this mockell knave—a—I call Goliah; he—a—a—he locks me up and maketh me sicker—a—the tall dark wight—a—that hath been put in durance in the hanging vault at the top o' the keep: he's—a—he's fast enow, I warrant thee, and, ha! ha! ha! hath got jolly company wi' him, I wot. Poor Tim Ord, thou knawest—a—was strung up for traiterie; and, ha! ha! ha!—sure I canna help loffen to but think on't; ha! ha! ha! ha! he hangs yonder aside the poor Scottish knight they took yestreen—a bonny jolly comrade for him to spend the night wi', I trow."

" Poor Tim Ord!" said the girl, " thou gar'st mine heart creep to think on hoo hasty they war wi' 'im."

" Hasty," cried Throckle, " ay, I trow, he lay not among his straw an hour—a—till Wat Withe and some others broke his dreams, to

send him to a sounder sleep, ha ! ha ! ha ! But
—a—a—'tis the gate, wench—a—'tis the gate
that a' sike traitrous faitours should yede them."

" But what key is that other wi' the queer
courbed handle?" inquired the curious Betty
Burrel.

" Wilt thou—a—a—wilt thou gie me a buss,
then, and I'll tell thee?" said Throckle.

Betty Burrel advanced her head within his
reach. Old Throckle kissed her, and endeavoured to detain her, but, after some little romp-
ing, she escaped.

" Tell me now," said she, " sin' I gied thee
the kiss."

" That courbe-hafted key," said Throckle,
lifting it up; "that—a—a—I call—a—a—a—
I call Crooked-hold-him-fast : he locks the donjon vault at the end of the passage—a—the passage aneath the stair. There—a—there lie the
twy rogues wha were cotched i' the same trap
wi' the wight in the hanging vault. This third
key—a—this here is called Nicholas-nimble-
touch : he—a—he openeth the range of vaults
on the north side. They are tenantless; but
an the Knight and his bandon have good luck,
they may be filled ere the morn's night. This—
a—this other key—a—I call Will-whirl-i'-the-

wards—a: he opens—a—opens the dark vault
i' the middle, in which—a—in which is the
mouth o' the donjon pit.

"An' what be that sma' tiny key?" said
Betty Burrel.

"That," said Throckle, "that—a—a—that is
merry Mrs Margery-of-the-mousetrap, though—
a—a—that is but an ill-bestowed name, seeing
that—a—a—it be's more of a bird-cage, I wis.
But—a—a—Mrs Margery keeps—she—a—she
keeps the door—a—the door of the ladies' room
—the ladies' room off the passage—a—the passage leading to the hall, thou knawest—a—thou
knawest there be's a linnet bird there encaged.
The Knight—a—the Knight can't at no rate
make her warble—a—warble as he would ha'
her. But she's but new caught—a—and she
may sing another measure—a—ay, ay, and
dance too, when he comes back again. Nay,
but now I ha' told thee all—a—sweet Mistress
Betty Burrel—a—sweet Betty, sit thee down—
a—a—a—and sing—a—a—sing one roundel.
Coum! here's to thy health, my—a—a—my
bonny blossom."

He put the wooden stóup to his head, and
drained it to the bottom.

"A—a—" said he then, attempting to rise

and lay hold of Betty; "a—a—coum—a—a—
sit thee—a—a—a—sit thee down—sit thee
down—a—one roundel—one kiss—a—a—."

" Nay, nay," cried Betty Burrel, moving
off, " I maun to my bed i' the kitchen, Master
Throckle ; I be wearisome tired and sleepy."

" Now, see," cried Throckle, standing up,
" now see—a—see what it is—a—see what it is
to be between liquor and love—a. Wise as thou
art, Master Daniel Throckle, thou be'st but as
the ass i' the fable between the tway hay-cocks
—a—Shalt thou after—a—shalt thou after the
Rownsyvall jade now?—or shalt thou—a—shalt
thou have one stoup more—ay—one stoup more?
—Daniel, one stoup more will make thee a—
will make thee—a—one stoup the stouter.—
Coum, then—a."

He opened the spigot, and, holding the stoup
with both hands, tried to catch the ale as it spouted forth, gallons of it spilling on the floor for
the drops that entered the mouth of the vessel.

" A murrain—a—a—a murrain on it, I say—
a—May I die—a—die of thirst—a—if the barrel be not dronkelew—a—It canna—a—a—it
canna stand fast—a—a—stand fast only till I—
a—a—till I fill mine stoup—a—a—But hold !
—a—a—hold, I say—it runs over now—a—a
—over now like a fountain.—Oh ! I am the man

a—a—to empty a can—a—a—and fill it—a—
a.—Hiccup—fill it again and again—ah !—a—
a—so here goes."

And, leaving the spigot to run as it might,
he put the stoup to his head, and, drinking it
out, staggered forward a step or two towards
the door, and, losing his feet and his balance at
the same moment, fell backwards with a tremendous crash on the pavement, where he lay
senseless in a sea of ale that deluged the floor.

CHAPTER XXI.

ASSUETON had no sooner witnessed the prostration of Master Daniel Throckle, than he
hastened round to the door of the keep; and,
having noted the part of the building where the
cellar lay, he slipped down a stair, and, groping
along a passage, was soon led to it by the light
of the lamp. He entered hastily, and, unbind-
ing the belt from the drunken beast's body,
made himself master of the keys. He then seized
the lamp, stole silently out by the door, and,
taking the directions Throckle had so gratui-
tously given him, explored a passage, at the
end of which he found a stair leading upwards.
Beneath it was the strongly-barred door of a
vault. Having singled out the key called Crooked-hold-him-fast, he applied it to the door, and
found it answer perfectly to the lock. He turned the bolt, and, to his no small delight, his
lamp showed him his esquire Roger Riddel, and
Robert Lindsay, both sound asleep on separate

heaps of straw. He gently waked first one, and then the other; and, laying his finger on his lips, he cautioned them to be perfectly silent. The poor fellows were so confounded by their unexpected deliverance, that they rubbed their eyes, and could hardly believe that they were really awake.

" Bestir thee, but not a word," said the knight to them; " the Castle is all our own. There are but two men within the walls. One I have left in a cellar, senseless as a hog, rucking and wallowing in his ale : from him we have nothing to fear, but the other yet standeth sentinel at the outward gate. So we must approach him cautiously; and when I whistle, pounce on him like falcons. But there is yet a woman in the place, whom we must first secure, to prevent all chance of alarm."

" Yea," said Roger Riddel, gravely, " woman's tongue be's a wicked weapon."

The knight and his followers hastened to find out the kitchen; and, having peeped in, they descried Betty Burrel, either asleep, or pretending to be so ; and, remarking that the windows were strongly barred, so that she could not escape that way, they gently shut the door, and turned the key in the lock.

They now ascended the stair, and, having

set down the lamp, Assueton, to guard against
all possibility of accident, took the large key
from the door of the keep, as they passed out.
They then stole towards the gateway, where,
after prying about for some time, they discovered the watchful warder of the garrison, lying
within a door-way, sound asleep, on the steps
of the stair leading up to a barbican that over-
looked the gate. Assueton immediately sprang
on him, and threw the blanket over his head;
and, having taken the keys of the gate from
him, they muffled him so completely up as to
stop his utterance, and, crossing his arms behind his back, bound all tightly together with
Master Throckle's leathern belt. They then
hoisted the knave on the broad back of Roger
Riddel, who marched merrily away with his
burden, and deposited him in the vault, on the
very straw from which he had himself so lately
risen. Proceeding next to the cellar, they lifted
up the drunken jailor, who, being perfectly senseless, had run no small risk of being drowned
externally, as well as internally, by a flood of
ale; and having carried him also to the vault,
and put him among the straw that had been
Robert Lindsay's bed, they turned Crooked-
hold-him-fast upon both of them.

Lighting another lamp, which they had found extinguished, 'the two squires then went to the stables to look for horses. Meanwhile Assueton ascended the stairs alone, to discover the ladies' chamber of which Throckle had spoken, and, by attending to the description the jailor had given, soon discovered it. He tapped gently at the door;—a deep sigh came from within;—he tapped again.

"Who knocks there at this hour?" said a female voice.

The voice made Assueton's heart bound with joy, for it was the voice of the Lady Isabelle Hepborne.

"Who knocks there?—who comes thus to break the hour of rest, the only one I have been blessed with since I entered these wicked and impure walls. If it be thou, false and traitorous knight, know thou may'st kill, but thou canst never subdue me."

"Lady Isabelle," cried Assueton, in transport, "it is no traitor; it is I, who will dare to call myself thy true and humble slave—thine own faithful knight, who, by God's blessing, has come to undo the bars of thy prison, and to set thee free."

"Sir John Assueton," cried the fair Isabelle, overpowered by amazement and joy—"Sir John

Assueton !—Blessed Virgin !—and how camest
thou here ?—But thou art in dreadful danger.
For mercy's sake—for my sake—I entreat thee
not to speak so loud," continued she, tripping
lightly towards the door, and whispering softly
through the key-hole ; "speak not so loud, lest
thou should'st be overheard and surprised by
some of the caitiff knight's cruel followers. I
will brave all danger to fly with thee."

" Nay, fairest lady," said Assueton, " thou
hast now but little cause of dread. The Castle,
and everything in it, is in my power; but I am
rather meagrely attended, and 'twere better we
should lose as little time as may be. I shall
unlock thy door, and keep watch for thee in the
hall hard by, until thou art ready to wend with
me."

The knight accordingly passed into the hall,
where he found a long board, covered with the
wrecks of feast and wassail, everything in the
apartment betokening the riotous and reckless
life that was led by the libertine owner of the
place. The walls were hung round with arms
of various kinds, and, to his great surprise, he
perceived the very armour he had worn, and
which he had left with his people when he
changed his dress, together with his shield,
lance, and trusty sword, all forming a grand

trophy, at one end. He soon removed them from
their place, and speedily equipped himself like
a knight as he was; and he had hardly done so,
when his eye caught the very baldrick and bugle worn by thé leader of the foresters who had
acted as his guide. He took them also down, and
hung them from his own neck, in memorial of
the treachery he had suffered. He then stood
anxiously listening, nor did he wait long until he heard the light step of the Lady Isabelle,
dancing merrily along the passage. He flew to
meet her, and the joy of both was too great to
be controlled. Yet they trifled not long to give
way to their feelings. Assueton gave his arm to
the fair prisoner, and they descended the stair
together. On reaching the court-yard, he found
Riddel and Lindsay busy in the stable. His
squire was employed in putting the furniture
and harness on the very steed the knight had
ridden from Hailes; but what gave rise to most
unpleasant speculation in the mind of Assueton,
was the discovery that the horses and equip-
ments of his whole party were there. As he
looked at the steeds and trappings of his brave
spearmen, his heart sank within him at the
thought of the cruel death that treachery had
probably wrought on the gallant fellows who
had used them. A palfrey was soon selected and

prepared for the Lady Isabelle; and the other three horses being ready, Assueton ordered them to be led out. Before they mounted, however, Roger Riddel, who never gave himself the trouble of speaking except when he had something of importance that compelled him to use his tongue, addressed his master.

" Methinks, your worship," said he, " we should be the better of a lantern to light us on our way till the moon rises."

" Go seek one, then," said Assueton; " but do not lose time, for it is but a chance thou shalt find one."

"Fasten the horses to that hook, then, Rob," said Riddel to Lindsay; " I shall want thee to help me to light it."

The two men went into the keep-tower together, where they remained some time, and at length they came out, each bearing a burden on his back.

" What, in the name of St Andrew, bearest thou there ?" demanded Assueton.

" 'Tis but the dronkelew jailor and the watchful warden," said Riddel; " methinks they will lie better in the stable."

" Tut !" said Assueton peevishly, " why waste our time with them ?"

But Roger and his comrade deposited their

burdens quietly in the stable, and then returned
again into the keep-tower, where they remained
so very long that Assueton lost all patience. By
and by female shrieks were heard from within.
They became louder, and seemed to approach
the door of the keep, when out stalked Roger
Riddel with much composure, carrying Betty
Burrel like any infant in his arms. The damsel, who was in her night attire, was wrapped
in a blanket, and was screaming, kicking, and
tearing the squire's face with her nails, like any
wild-cat. But the sedate Roger minded her
not, nor did her scratching in the least derange
the gravity of his walk.

"This is too much, Riddel," said Assueton,
loosing temper: "What absurd whim is this?
Is the Lady Isabelle Hepborne to be kept standing here all night, till thou shalt find a new bed
for Betty Burrel?"

Roger turned gravely about, with the kicking and scratching Betty Burrel still in his
arms—

"Surely," said he, "Sir Knight, thou hast
too much Christian charity in thee to see the
poor pusell burnt alive?"

"Burnt!" cried Assueton with astonishment;
"what mean ye?"

But now came the explanation of all Roger

had said and done; for volumes of smoke began to burst from the different open loop-holes of the keep, and to roll out at the door, sufficiently explaining what Roger Riddel had meant by a lantern. The squire hastily deposited the kicking and screaming Betty Burrel in the stable, to which there was no risk of the fire communicating, and locking the door, put the key quietly into his pocket. The Lady Isabelle and Assueton mounted, while the squire and Lindsay went before them, to raise the portcullis and open the gates; and the whole party sallied forth from the walls, right glad to bid adieu to Burnstower. Their two attendants went before them, leading their own horses down the hill, and along the narrow tongue of land, towards the ford, lest there might have been any such trap in their way as they formerly fell into. But all was clear, and they got through the ford with perfect safety.

From the summit of the rising ground above the ford, that is, from the same spot where the moon had given Assueton the first and only view of Burnstower, on the night of his approach, they now looked back, and beheld the keep involved in flames, that broke forth from every opening in its sides, and forced their way through various parts of its roof. The reader is already aware of the grandeur of the surrounding scene, closely shut in all around by high backing hills, and the two deep glens, with their streams uniting under the green-headed eminence, that arose from the luxuriant forest, which everywhere covered the lower grounds : let him conceive all this, then, lighted up as it was by Roger Riddel's glorious lantern, which, as they continued to look, began to shoot up jets of flame from its summit, so high into the air that it seemed as if the welkin itself was in some danger from its contact, and he will have in his imagination one of the most sublime spectacles that human eye could well behold.

The party, however, stopped not long to look at it, but urged onwards through the thickets and sideling paths of the glen, now losing all sight of the burning tower, and now recovering a view of it, as they occasionally climbed upwards to avoid some impassable obstruction below. At length a turn of the glen shut it altogether from their sight, and the place where it lay was only indicated by the fiery-red field of sky immediately over it.

Assueton resolved to follow the course of the glen, and in doing so he found that the forester had completely deceived him in regard to the path, that below having occupied about one-tenth part of the time which was consumed the former night in unravelling the mazes of the hill-road. The moon now arose to light them cheerily on their way; objects became more distinct; and, as they were crossing a little glade, they observed a man running, as if to take shelter under the trees.

" After him, Riddel," cried Assueton; " we must know who and what he is."

The squire and Lindsay charged furiously after the fugitive, and ere he could gain the thicket, one rode up on each side of him, and caught him. The Knight and Lady Isabelle immediately came up, when, to their no small delight, they discovered that it was a trooper of Assueton's party, and, on interrogating him, they learnt that all the others were lodged safely among the brushwood, at no great distance. The man was instantly dispatched for them, and when they appeared, the whole villainy of the pretended foresters was explained. The knight and his two attendants had no sooner left them, than they were largely feasted with broiled venison, after which liberal libations of potent ale had been administered to them; and they now firmly believed that the liquor had been drugged with an opiate; for though the excessive fatigue they had undergone might have accounted for their being immediately overcome with drowsiness, yet it could have furnished no adequate explanation of their sleeping for the greater part of next day, as they had all done to a man, without once awakening. When at length they did arise from their mossy pillows, their horses and accoutrements, as well as the knight's armour, had vanished with the foresters, and nothing remained but part of the carcase of a deer, left, as it appeared, to prevent them from starving. In this helpless state the men were quite at a loss what to do. To advance with the hope of meeting their leader, even if he were not already the victim of a worse treachery than they had experienced, would have been vain; yet, unarmed as they were, the brave fellows could not entirely abandon him; and after much hesitation they had at last resolved, towards evening, to wander up the glen, to see what discoveries they could make. They had got thus far, when the darkness of the night compelled them to halt until the moon rose; and the man whom Assueton first descried, had been sent out by the rest as a scout, to ascertain whether they were yet safe in proceeding.

Assueton's mind being now relieved as to the safety of the party, he resolved to send back Lindsay to guide the spearmen to Burnstower, that they might horse and arm themselves in the stables. Meanwhile he proposed, that he, the Lady Isabelle, and the squire, should halt in the thickets, near the spot where they then were, and wait patiently for their return.

"Stay," said Roger Riddel to one of the men, as soon as he had heard his master's arrangement, "stay, here is the key, and be sure thou shuttest the stable-door after thee. Thou can'st not mistake the way, even had'st thou no guide, for there is a lantern burning in the castle of Burnstower that enlighteneth the whole valley."

CHAPTER XXII.

THE party led by Robert Lindsay marched off, and Roger Riddel proceeded to seek out a retired spot, where the Lady Isabelle might enjoy a little rest. A mossy bank within the shelter of the wood was soon discovered, and there the knight and his fair companion seated themselves, whilst the squire secured their horses at no great distance. Assueton was extremely desirous to learn the history of the lady's capture, and she proceeded to satisfy him.

As she was passing through the woodlands, on her return towards Hailes Castle, after parting from her brother, she was suddenly surrounded by Sir Miers de Willoughby's party, seized, put on horseback, and carried rapidly off. She was compelled to travel all that day and all next night, halting only once or twice for a very short time, to obtain necessary refreshment for the horses and people; and early next morning they arrived with her at the Castle of Burnstower, where, although every comfort was provided for her, she was subjected to confinement as a prisoner. Sir Miers de Willoughby had taken every opportunity that so rapid a journey afforded, to tease her with offers of love and adoration; and after they reached Burnstower, he had spent several hours in making his offensive addresses to her. The lady had repulsed him with a spirit and dignity worthy the daughter of Sir Patrick Hepborne, called upon him boldly to release her at his peril, and made a solemn appeal to Heaven against his treachery and baseness. At length she was relieved from his presence, by his being called on some expedition, from which, fortunately, for her peace, he did not return till a very late hour, and she saw no more of him that night. But next morning, he came again to her apartment, where he compelled her to listen for some hours to addresses which she treated with scorn and indignation. He became enraged, and, in his fury, talked of humbling her pride by other means than fair speeches, if he did not find her more compliant on his return from an expedition he was about to proceed upon. She trembled to hear him; but fortunately his immediate absence saved her from farther vexation, until she was finally rescued from the villain's power by Sir John Assueton.

Having completed her narrative, the Lady Isabelle anxiously demanded a similar satisfaction from Assueton, who gave her all the particulars of his adventures, the recital being characterized by the modesty which was natural to him. The lady shuddered and trembled alternately at the perils to which he had been exposed on her account, and her eyes gave forth a plenteous shower of gladness and of gratitude when he had finished. He seized the happy moment for making a full declaration of his passion, and he was repaid for all his miseries, fatigues, dangers, and anxieties, by the soft confession he received from her.

After their mutual transports had in some degree subsided, Assueton called Roger Riddel from the spot where, with proper attention to decorum, he had seated himself beyond earshot of their conversation, and interrogated him as to what had occurred to him and Lindsay. Their story was short, and Roger, who was always chary of his words, did not add to its length by circumlocution.

" Why, Sir Knight," said he, " they carried us like bundles of straw to the drearisome vault, and locked us up in the dark. Next day came one Ralpho Proudfoot, with divers rogues—Caitiff lossel had some old pique at good Rob Lindsay—swore he would now be ywreken on him—threatened him with hanging—and would háve done it with his own hands then, but they would not let him till he got his master's warrant—swore that he would get the warrant and do execution on Rob to-morrow. So we got beef and ale to breakfast and supper, and slept, till your honour waked us to wend with thee."

Sir John now prevailed on the Lady Isabelle to take a short repose, whilst he and Riddel, watched over her safety. In a little time afterwards, Robert Lindsay returned at the head of his remounted cavalry. Assueton was now himself again, and, with spirits light as air, he and the lady got into their saddles, and proceeded slowly down the glen. To prevent all chance of surprise, Robert Lindsay preceded them with half the party as an advanced guard, whilst Roger Riddel brought up the rear with the remainder.

The night was so far spent, that day dawned ere they had threaded the pass that formed the entrance into the territory of Sir Miers de Willoughby. The sun rose in all his glory, and threw a flood of golden light over the romantic scenery they were passing through.

All nature rejoiced under the benignant influence. of his cheering rays; a thousand birds raised their happy wings and melodious voices to heaven; nay, all vegetable as well as animal life seemed to unite in one general choir to pour out their grateful orisons. Nor did the souls of the lovers refuse to join in the universal feeling. They each experienced inwardly a joy and a gratitude that surpassed all the power of expression, but which was perhaps best uttered in that silent, but not less fervent language, used by the devout spirit, when, impressed with a deep sense of the blessings it has received, it rises in secret thanksgivings to its Creator. Each being thus separately occupied in thought, they rode gently on until they had cleared the defiles, and were entering the wider pastures, where the space in the bottom was more extended, and the trees that clothed the sides of the hills, or dropped down occasionally on the more level ground, grew thinner and more scattered.

As they were entering one of those little plains, through which the stream they had followed meandered, they were surprised by the appearance of a party of armed horsemen, approaching from the other extremity of it. Assueton immediately called forward his esquire.

- " Riddel," said he, " we know not as yet whether those who come towards us may prove friends or foes; but be they whom they list, to thy faithful charge do I consign the care and protection of the Lady Isabelle; leave not her bridle-rein, whatever may betide. Take three of the spearmen, and let her be always kept in the midst. Should that bandon yonder, that cometh so fast, prove to be hostile, remember thou art in no wise to act offensively unless the lady be attacked; but be it thy duty, and that of those I leave with thee, to think only of defending her to the last extremity. I shall myself ride forward with the rest, to see who these may be."

The Lady Isabelle grew pale with alarm, partly because her lover was probably about to incur danger, but even yet more, if possible, because, in the knight who was approaching at the head of the troop, she already recognized the figure and the arms of him from whose power she had so lately escaped.

" Blessed Virgin protect us," cried she, " 'tis the caitiff knight De Willoughby who advanceth!"

" Is it so?" cried Assueton, his blood boiling at the intelligence; " then, by the Rood of St Andrew, he shall not hence until I shall have questioned him for his villainy."

He staid not to say more, but galloping forward, he reined up his steed in the middle of the way, and instantly addressed the opposite leader.

"Halt!" cried he, in a voice of thunder; "halt, Sir Knight, if yet thou mayest deserve a title so honourable; for, of a truth, thou dost not, if thou art he whom I take thee to be. Say, art thou, or art thou not, that malfaitour Sir Miers de Willoughby?"

"Though I see no cause why I should respond to a rude question rudely put, yet will I never deny my name," replied the other. "I am so hight; and now what hast thou to say to Sir Miers de Willoughby?"

"That he no longer deserves to be called a knight, but rather a caitiff robber," replied Assueton.

"Robber!" retorted the other; "dost thou call me robber, that dost wear my baldrick and bugle hanging from thy shoulder?"

"Thine!" replied Assueton; "if they be thine, 'tis well thou hast noted them so; I wear them as the gage of my revenge; and I have sworn to wear them till thou payest dearly for the wrong thou hast done to the virtuous Lady Isabelle Hepborne, for I speak not of the base treachery thou didst use towards myself."

" Nay, then," replied De Willoughby, " it
seems thou art determined that we shall do instant battle.   Come on, then."

And so saying, he put his lance in the rest,
and ran his course at Assueton.   The Scottish
knight couched his, and exclaiming aloud, "May
God and St Andrew defend the right," he put
spurs to his horse, and rushed at his opponent.
They met nearly mid-way.   Sir Miers de Willoughby's lance glanced aside from Assueton's
cuirass, without doing the firmly-seated knight
the smallest injury; but Assueton's point entering on one side, between the joinings of Sir
Miers's helmet and neck-piece, bore him headlong from his saddle, and stretched him, grievously wounded, on the plain.   Meanwhile, before Assueton had time to recollect himself, on
came the party of De Willoughby, and with the
natural impression that he would dismount to
put their leader to death, charged him *en masse.*
His own spearmen rushed to his rescue, but
before they came, he had so well bestirred himself that he had prostrated three or four of the
enemy.   The battle now became general; but
though the numbers were on the other side, yet
the victory was very soon achieved by the prowess of Assueton and his people, who left not a
man before them, all, save one only, being either

thrown to the ground, or forced to seek safety in flight.

That one, however, was Ralpho Proudfoot, who at the first onset had singled out Robert Lindsay, with a bloody thirst of long-cherished hatred. Their spears having been splintered in the shock, he had grappled Lindsay by the neck, and the latter seizing his antagonist in his turn, they were both at once dragged from their horses. Rising eagerly at the same moment, however, they drew their swords and attacked each other. Some of Lindsay's comrades having now no antagonist of their own to oppose, were about to assist him.

· " Keep off," cried he immediately, " keep off, my friends, if ye love me; one man is enow in all conscience, upon one man : so let him kill me if he can, but interfere not between us."

They rained down their blows on each other with tremendous force, and the combat hung doubtful for a considerable time. Proudfoot's expression of countenance was savage and devilish. He tried various manœuvres to break through Lindsay's cool determined guards, but without effect; and being more desirous of wounding his adversary than of saving himself, he received some severe thrusts. At length, as he attempted to throw his point in on Lindsay's

body, he received a cut from him that laid his
arm open from the shoulder to the wrist, and
at once rendered it useless. The sword dropped
from his hand, and fainting from the loss of
blood that poured from his other wounds, he
staggered back a few paces, and fell senseless
on the ground. The generous Lindsay, forgetting the brutal threats Proudfoot had uttered
against him, ran up to his assistance.

" He was my companion when we were
boys," cried he; " oh, let me save him if I
can."

And so saying, he ran to the stream, filled his
morrion with water, and poured it on Proudfoot's face. He then bathed his wounds, and
bound up his arm, and tried to stanch the
bleeding from the thrusts he had given him.
Nor were his pious and merciful exertions un-
attended with success. Proudfoot opened his
eyes, and, his senses returning to him, gazed
with silent wonder in the face of the man, who
had a moment before fought so manfully against
him, and who was now so humanely employed
in endeavouring to save his life, and assuage the
acuteness of his pains. His own villainous and
cruel determinations against Lindsay, which he
had been contemplating having it in his power
to carry into execution that very night, now

rushed upon his mind. His conscience, long hardened by guilt and atrocity, was at once melted by that single, but bright ray of goodness, which darted on it from the anxious eye of Lindsay; and days long since past recurring to his memory, he remembered what he had been, and burst into an agony of tears.

Assueton had no sooner rid himself of his enemies, than he went to assist the wounded and discomfited Sir Miers de Willoughby; and on unlacing his helmet, discovered, to his no small surprise, the features of the very forester who had guided him to Burnstower.

The evidence of Sir Miers de Willoughby's villainy was now complete; yet was not the gallant Assueton's compassion for his hapless state one atom diminished by the discovery. The wound in his neck, though not mortal, bled most profusely, and he lay in a swoon from the quantity of blood he had already lost. The Lady Isabelle and the esquire now coming up, every means were used to stop the effusion, and, happily, with success, but he still remained insensible. Assueton, therefore, ordered his people to catch some of the horses of those who had fallen; and having placed De Willoughby, Proudfoot, and one or two others of whose recovery there seemed to be good hope, across their saddles, they proceeded cheerily onwards, and after some hours slow travel, brought them safely to Carham, and lodged them under the care of the Black Canons of its Abbey.

Having rested and refreshed themselves and their horses there, they crossed the Tweed, and being impatient to return to Hailes, that they might relieve the anxious mind of the elder Sir Patrick Hepborne, they arrived there by forced marches.

The joy of Sir Patrick at the unexpected return of his daughter may be conceived. He had, as he resolved, gone in pursuit of Assueton, and had used every means in his power to discover the direction in which the Lady Isabelle had been carried; but all his efforts had been fruitless—and they found him in the deepest despair. It is easy to guess what happiness smiled upon that night's banquet.

CHAPTER XXIII.

OUR history now returns to the younger Sir Patrick Hepborne, whom we left about to commence his journey towards the North. He had no sooner parted from his sister the Lady Isabelle, and joined his esquire and cortège, under the trees by the side of the Tyne, than he espied a handsome youth, clad in the attire of a page, who came riding through the grove towards a ford of the river. He was mounted on a sorry hackney, carrying his valise behind him, and guided by a clown, who walked by his bridle. The boy showed symptoms of much amazement and dismay on finding himself thus so unexpectedly surrounded by a body of armed men; and he would have dropped from his horse, from sheer apprehension, had not Sir Patrick's kind and courteous salutation gradually banished his alarm.

" Who art thou, and whither goest thou,

young man ?" demanded the knight, in a gentle
tone and manner.

" I am a truant boy, Sir Knight," replied
the youth, in a trembling voice; " I have fled
from home, that I might see somewhat of the
world."

" And where may be thy home ?" demanded
Sir Patrick.

" On the English bank of the Tweed," replied the boy.

" Ha !" exclaimed Sir Patrick, " and why
hast thou chosen to travel into Scotland, rather
than to explore the southern parts of thine own
country ?"

" Verily, because I judged that there was
less chance of my being looked for on this side
the Border," replied the boy. " Moreover, the
peace that now prevails hath made either side
safe enow, I hope, for travel."

" Nay, that as it may happen," said the
Knight. " But why didst thou run away from
thy friends, young man ? Was it that thou
wert evil-entreated ?"

" Nay, rather, Sir Knight, that I was over
charily cockered and cared for," replied the
boy; " more especially by my mother, at home,
who, for dread of hurt befalling me, would give
me no license to disport myself at liberty with

other youths. I was, as it were, but a page of
dames. But, sooth to say, I have been long
tired of dames and damosels, and knitting, and
broidery, and all the little silly services of wo-.
men."

" Nay, in truth, thou art of an age for something more stirring," replied Sir Patrick; " a
youth of thine years should have to do with
gay steeds, and armour, and 'tendance upon
knights."

" Such are, indeed, the toys that my heart
doth most pant for," replied the boy; " and.
such is mine excuse for quitting home. I sigh.
for the gay sight of glittering tourneys, and
pageants of arms, and would fain learn the noble trade of chivalry."

" If thou hast no scruple to serve a Scottish
knight," replied Sir Patrick, " that is, so long
as until the outbreak of war may call on thee
to appear beneath the standard of thy native
England, I shall willingly give thee a place
among my followers; and, by St Genevieve,
thou dost come to me in a good time, too, as
to feats of arms, being that I am now on my
way to the grand tournament to be held on the
Mead of St John's. So, wilt thou yede with
me thither, my young Courfine?" The boy
made no reply, but hung his head, and looked.

abashed for some moments. "Ha! what sayest thou?" continued the knight; "wilt thou
wend with me, or no? Thine answer speedily,
yea or nay, young man, for I must be gone."

"Yea, most joyfully will I be of thy company, Sir Knight," replied the boy, his eyes glistening with delight; "and while peace may
endure between our countries, I will be thy
true and faithful page, were it unto the death."

"'Tis well, young man," replied Sir Patrick;
"but thou hast, as yet, forgotten to possess me
of thy name and parentage."

"My name, Sir Knight," replied the boy, with
some confusion and hesitation—"my name is
Maurice de Grey—my father, Sir Hargrave de
Grey, is Captain of the Border castle of Werk
—and the gallant old Sir Walter de Selby, captain of the other Border strength of Norham, is
mine uncle."

"Ha! is it so?" exclaimed Hepborne, with
great surprise and considerable agitation—
"Then thou art cousin to the La——? then
thou art nevoy to Sir Walter de Selby, art
thou? Nay, now I do look at thee again, thou
hast, methinks, a certain cast of the features of
his family. Perdie, he is a most honourable sib
to thee. Of a truth thou art come of a good
kindred, and if thou wilt be advised by me,

sweet youth, thou wilt straightway hie thee back again to thine afflicted mother, doubtless ere this grievously bywoxan with sorrow for loss of thee."

"Nay, good Sir Knight, I dare not now adventure to return," replied the boy; "and sith thou hast told me of that tourney, verily thou hast so much enhanced my desire to go with thee, that nothing but thy refusal of what thou hast vouchsafed to promise me shall now hinder me."

"Had I earlier known of whom thou art come, young man," replied Sir Patrick gravely, "I had been less rash in persuading thee with me, or in 'gaging my promise to take thee; but sith that my word hath already passed, it shall assuredly be kept; nor shall thy father or mother have cause to regret that thou hast thus chanced to fall into my hands. Come, then, let us have no more words, but do thou dismiss thy rustic guide, and follow me without more ado."

The youth bowed obedience, and taking the peasant aside, gave him the reward which his services had merited, and, after talking with him for some little time, sent him away, and prepared to follow his new master. Meanwhile

Sir Patrick called Mortimer Sang, and gave him strict charges to care for the boy.

" Be it thy duty," said he to him, " to see that the young falcon be well bestowed ·by the way. Meseems him but a tender brauncher as yet; he must not be killed in the reclaiming. Let him be gently entreated, and kindly dealt with, until he do come readily to the hand."

All being now in readiness, the troop moved forward; and Sir Patrick Hepborne, who wished to know something more of his newly acquired page, made the boy ride beside him, that they might talk together by the way. Maurice displayed all the bashfulness of a stripling when he first mixes among men. He hung his head much ; and although the knight's eye could often detect his in the act of gazing at him, when he thought he was himself unobserved, yet he could never stand his master's look in return, but dropped his head on his bosom. The knight, however, found him a lad of intelligence and good sense much beyond his years, and ere they had reached Edinburgh,, the boy had. perfectly succeeded in winning Sir Patrick's good affections towards him.

On their arrival in the capital, Sir Patrick bestowed on the page a beautiful milk-white palfrey, of the most, perfect symmetry of form

and docility of temper, and added rich furniture
of velvet and gold to complete the gift. He accoutred him also with a baldrick, and sword and
dagger, of rare and curious workmanship—presents which seemed to have the usual effect of
such warlike toys on young minds, when the
boy is naturally proud of assuming the symbols
of virility. He fervently kissed the generous
hand that gave them, and blushed as he did so;
then mounting his palfrey, rode with the knight
up the High Mercat Street, to the admiration
of all those who beheld him. The very popu-
lace cheered them as they passed along, and all
agreed, that a handsomer knight or a more beautiful page had never graced the crown of their
causeway.

Yet though the boy seemed to yield to the joy
inspired by the possession of these new and precious treasures, his general aspect was rather
melancholy than otherwise, and Hepborne that
very evening caught him in tears. He dried
his eyes in haste, however, as soon as he saw
that he was observed, and lifting his long dark
eye-lashes, beamed a smile of sunshine into the
anxiously inquiring face of his master.

" What ails thee, Maurice?" said Hepborne,
kindly taking his hand—" what ails thee, my
boy? Thy hand trembles, and thy cheeks flush

—nay, the very alabaster of thine unsullied forehead partakes of the crimson that overrunneth thy countenance. 'Tis the fever of home-leaving that hath seized thee, and thou weepest for thy mother, whom thou hast left behind thee; silly youth," said he, chucking him gently under the chin, " 'tis the penalty thou must pay for thy naughtiness in leaving them. Doubtless thou hast made them weep too. But say if thou would'st yet return? for if thou dost, one of mine attendants shall wend with thee, and see thee safe to Werk; and——"

" Nay, good Sir Knight," cried the boy, interrupting him, " though I weep for them, yet would I not return to Werk, but forward fare with thee."

"Nay," said Hepborne, " unless thou should'st repent thee of thy folly, young man, I shall leave thy disease to run its own course, and to find its own cure. And of a truth, I must confess, I should part with thee with sorrow."

" Then am I happy," cried the boy, with a sudden expression of delight: " Would that we might never part!"

" We shall never part whilst thou mayest fancy my company," said Hepborne, kissing his cheek kindly, and infinitely pleased with the unfeigned attachment the boy already showed him. " But youth is fickle, and I should not .choose to bind thy volatile heart longer than it may be willing; for it may change anon." '

The boy looked suddenly to heaven, crossed his hands over his breast, and said earnestly, " I am not one given to change, Sir Knight; thou shalt find me ever faithful and true to thee."

After leaving Edinburgh, Hepborne travelled by St Johnstoun, and presented himself before King Robert the Second at Scone, where he then happened to be holding his court. The venerable monarch received him in the most gracious and flattering manner.

" Thy renommie hath outrun thy tardy homeward step, Sir Knight," said his Majesty, " for we have already heard of thy gallant deeds abroad. Perdie, we did much envy our faithful ally and brother of France, and did grudge him the possession of one of the most precious jewels of our court, and one of the stoutest defences of our throne. We rejoice, therefore, to have recovered what of so good right belongeth to us, and we hope thou wilt readily yield to our command, that thou should'st remain about our royal person. Since old age hath come heavily upon us, marry, we the more lack such stanch and trusty props."

" My most gracious Liege," said Hepborne,
" I shall not be wanting in my duty of obedience
to your royal and gratifying mandate. At present I go to attend this tourney of my Lord of
Moray's, and I go the more gladly, that I may
have an opportunity of meeting with my peers of
the baronage, of Scottish chivauncie, whom my
absence in France hath hitherto prevented my
knowing. Having your royal leave to follow
out mine intent, I shall straightway render myself in your grace's presence, to bow to your
royal pleasure."

" By doing so, Sir Patrick," said the King,
" thou wilt much affect us to thee. We have of
late had less of thy worthy father's attendance on
our person than we could have wished. Man-
sucte as he is in manners, sage in council, and
lion-hearted in the field, we should wish to see
him always in our train. But we grieve for the
sad cause of his retirement. Thy virtuous mother's sudden death weighed heavily on him,
yet must he forget his grief. Let a trentall of
masses be said for her soul;—he must bestir
himself anon, and restore to us and to his country the use of those talents, of that virtue and
bravery with which he hath been so eminently blessed, and which were given him for our
glory and Scotland's defence. If thou goest by

the most curt and direct way into Moray-land, thou wilt pass by our son Alexander Earl of Buchan's Castle of Lochyndorbe. Him must thou visit, and tell him that we ourselves did urge thee to claim his hospitality."

Hepborne readily promised that he would obey his Majesty's injunctions in that respect, and took his leave, being charged with a letter for the earl, from the King, under his own private signet.

His route lay northwards, through the centre of Scotland. As he journeyed onwards, through deep valleys and endless forests, and over high, wide, and barren wastes, he compared in his own mind the face of the country with the fertile regions of France, which he had so lately left. But still, these were the mountains of his father-land that rose before his eye, and that name allied them to his heart by ties infinitely stronger than the tame surface of cultivation could have imposed. His soul soared aloft to the summits of the snow-topt Grampians, and the hardy and untameable spirit of Scotland seemed to sit enthroned among their mists, and to bid him welcome as a son.

He made each day's journey so easy, on account of the tender page, that a week had nearly elapsed ere he found himself in the upper part

of the valley of the Dee.   It was about sunset
when he reached a miserable-looking house,
which had been described to him as one accustomed to give entertainment to travellers.   It
was situated under some lofty pines on the edge
of the forest.   The owner of this mansion was
a Celt; a tall, stout, athletic man of middle age,
clad in the garb of the mountaineers.   Having
served in the wars against the English, he had
acquired enough of the Southron tongue to enable Hepborne to hold converse with him.   The
knight, and the page, whom, notwithstanding
his injunction to Mortimer Sang, he had yet
kept always within his own eye, were ushered
together into a large sod-built apartment, where
a cheerful fire of wood burned in the middle of
the floor.   The squire and the rest of the party
were bestowed in a long narrow building of the
same materials, attached to one end of it.   The
night had been chilly on the high grounds they
had crossed, and the fire was agreeable.   They
sat them down therefore on wooden settles close
to it, and the rude servants of their host hastened to put green boughs across the fire, and
to lay down steaks of the flesh of the red-deer
to be cooked on them.

Meanwhile the host entered with a wooden
stoup in his hand, and poured out for them to

drink, into a small two-eared vessel of the same material. The liquor was a sort of spirit, made partly from certain roots, and partly from grain; and was harsh and potent, but rather invigorating. Hepborne partook of it, but the page would on no account taste it.

" Fu !" said Duncan MacErchar, for that was their host's name, " fu ! fat for will she no drink ?"

" He is right," said Hepborne; " at his age, water should be his only beverage."

The host then went with his stoup to offer some of its contents to the knight's followers, most of whom he found less scrupulous than the page. During his conversation with the men, he soon learned who was their master; but he had no sooner heard the name of Hepborne, than he became half frantic with joy, and hastily returned into the place where Sir Patrick was sitting.

" Master Duncan MacErchar," said Hepborne to him as he entered, " thou must e'en procure me some mountaineer who may guide me into Moray-land. I be but a stranger in these northern regions, and verily our way among the mountains hath been longer than it ought, for we have been often miswent. Moreover, I am altogether ignorant of thy Celtic

leden, so that when we have had the good fortune to meet with people by the way, we have
not been able to profit by the information they
could give us."

"Ugh!" cried MacErchar, with a strong
expression of joy, and rubbing his hands as he
spoke; " but she'll go with her hersell, an nae-
body else can be gotten to attend her. Ugh ay,
surely she'll do that and twenty times more for
ony Hepborne, and most of all for the son of
the noble, and brave, and worthy Sir Patrick,
and weel her part. Och ay, surely!"

" And how comest thou to be so very friendly
to the Hepbornes, and, above all, to our family?" demanded Sir Patrick.

" Blessings be upon her!" said MacErchar,
" she did serve mony a day with her father, the
good and the brave Sir Patrick against the English, and mony was the time she did fight at her
ain back. She would die hersell for Sir Patrick,
or for ony flesh o' his."

Hepborne's heart immediately warmed to the
honest Celt; he shook him cordially by the
hand, and MacErchar's eyes glistened with pleasure.

" Depend on it, Master MacErchar," said
he, " my father shall know thine attachment to
him."

" Ou fye," said MacErchar, " it would be an honour and a pleasure for her to see Sir Patrick again, to be sure!—ugh ay !" And he stopped, because he seemed to lack language to express all he felt.

" Thou livest in a wild spot here," said Hepborne ; " but thou art a soldier, and hast travelled."

" Ou ay, troth she hath done that," said Duncan, with a look of conscious pride ; " troth hath she travelled mony a bonny mile in England, not to talk o' Ireland, where she did help to take Carlinyford. Troth she hath seen Newcastle, and all thereabouts, for she was with the brave Archembald Douglas, the Grim Lord of Galloway. Och! oich! it was fine sport!— She lived on the fat o' the land yon time; and, u-hugh! what spulzie!—ay, ay, he! he! he !"

" Thou didst march into England, then, with the French auxiliaries who came over to St Johnstoun under Jean de Vian, Conte de Valentinois ?" demanded Sir Patrick.

" Ou ay, troth she was with the Frenchmens a long time," said MacErchar.—" *Peut parley Frenchy*, hoot ay can she. Fair befall them, they helped her to beleaguer and to sack two or three bonny castles. U-hugh! what bonny spuilzie !—sure, sure !"

He laid his finger with great significancy against his nose, and, having first shut the door, he lifted a brand from the fire, and went to one end of the apartment. There he removed a parcel of faggots, that lay carelessly heaped up against the wall, and, lifting a rude frame of wattle that was beneath them, uncovered an excavation in the earthen floor, from which he brought out a massive silver flagon, one or two small silver mazers, and several other pieces of valuable spoil; and besides these, he produced a plain black bugle-horn, and two or three coarse swords and daggers.

"Troth she would not show them to everybody," said he; "but she be's an honourable knight, and Sir Patrick's son;—she hath no fears to show the bonny things to her. But she has not had them out for mony a day syne."

Hepborne bestowed due admiration on those well-earned fruits of Master Duncan MacErchar's military hardships and dangers. Though of less actual value to the owner than the wooden vessel from which he had so liberally dealt out his hospitable cup at meeting, yet there was something noble in the pride he took in showing them. It was evident that the glory of the manner of their acquisition gave them their chief value in his eyes; for it was not those of most intrinsic worth that were estimated the highest by him.

"See this," said he, lifting the plain black bugle-horn; "this be the best prize of them all. She took this hersell off a loon that fought and tuilzied with her hand to hand: but troth she tumbled him at the hinder-end of the bicker. Fye, fye, but he was a sorrowful mockel stout loon.—This swords, and this daggers, were all ta'en off the loons she killed with her nane hand.—But uve, uve! she maunna be tellin' on her, though troth she needna fear Sir Patrick Hepborne's son. But if some of the folks in these parts heard of this things, uve, uve! they wouldna be long here."

Saying this, he hastily restored the several articles of spoil to the grave that had held them, and putting down the wattle over them, he threw back the billets into a careless heap against the wall.

"Thy treasure is so great, Master MacErchar," said Hepborne, "that thou art doubtless satisfied, and wilt never again tempt thy fate in the field?"

"Hoot, toot!" cried MacErchar, "troth, she'll be there again or lang; she maun see more o' the Southrons yet or she dies. But uve, uve ! what for is there nothing yet for her to eat ?"

He then burst out in a torrent of eloquence in his own language, which soon brought his ragged attendants about him, and the best that he could afford was put on a table before Sir Patrick and the page. Cakes made of rough ground oatmeal, milk, cheese, butter, steaks of deer's flesh, with various other viands, and abundance of ale, appeared in rapid succession, and both knight and page feasted admirably after their day's exercise. Hepborne insisted on their host sitting down and partaking with them, which he did immediately, with a degree of independent dignity that impressed Sir Patrick yet more strongly in his favour.

CHAPTER XXIV.

As they sat socially at their meal, they were suddenly interrupted by the door being burst open, when two gigantic and very savage-looking men entered, in most uncouth and wild drapery. They were clothed in woollen plaids of various colours and of enormous amplitude, and these were wrapt round their bodies, and kept tight by a belt of raw leather, with the hair on it, leaving the skirts to hang half-way down their naked thighs, while the upper part above the belt was thrown loosely over the shoulder, so as to give to their muscular arms and hairy knees the full freedom of nakedness. Their heads also were bare, except that they had the copious covering which nature had provided for them, the one having strong curly black hair, and the other red of similar roughness, hanging in matted locks over their features and about their ears. The forests which nature had planted on their faces, chins, and necks too, had been allowed to grow, untamed by shears; their legs were covered half way to the knee by strips of raw skin twisted round them, and their feet were defended by a kind of shoes made of untanned hides. Each had a dirk in his girdle, and a pouch of skin suspended before, while across their backs were slung bows and bunches of arrows. In their hands they brandished long lances, and several recently taken wolves' skins were thrown over their shoulders, but rather for carriage than covering. Five or six large wiry-haired wolf-dogs entered along with them.

MacErchar instantly started up when they appeared, and began speaking loudly and hastily to them in their own tongue, waving them from time to time to retire, and at length opened the door, and showed them the way to the other apartment.

" Who may be these two savage-looking men?" demanded Hepborne of his host as he entered.

" Troth, she no kens them, Sir Patrick," replied MacErchar, " she never saw them afore; but they tells her that they be's hunters from the north side of this mountains here."

" Live they in the way that I must needs

wend to-morrow towards Morayland?" asked Hepborne.

"Uch, ay," replied MacErchar; "but mind not that, Sir Patrick, for hersell will go wi' thee the morn."

"Nay," said Hepborne, "that may not be; that is, if these men are to return whence they came, and that their road and mine run nearly in the same direction. Perdie, I cannot in that case suffer thee to yede so far with me unnecessarily, when their guidance may suffice. Thou shalt give them knowledge of the point I wish to reach, together with all necessary directions touching the places where we may best halt, and spend the night; and they shall receive a handsome guerdon from me when they shall have brought me and mine in safety to the Castle of Lochyndorbe, whither I am first bound."

"Uu-huch! of a truth she would like to go with her," said MacErchar; "but troth, after all, she must confess that she kens but little o' the way beyond her ain hills there. Weel would it be her pairt to wend wi' her; but if yon loons ken the gate into Morayland, (as doubtless they have been there mony a time, an she does not mistake them,) they will be better guides, after

all. But what an she should ask some questions at them?"

" Thou hadst better do so," said Hepborne;
" best ask them whence they come, and what
parts of the country they know, before thou
dost teach them the object of thy questions."

`" Troth, and she's right there," said Duncan
MacErchar; " this salvage loons are not just to
lippen till; weel does she ken them; and uve,
uve! she maun take special care to look sharp
after them gin she should yede wi' them; they
are but little chancy in troth. But she'll call
them in now, and see what the loons will say."

The two uncouth-looking men were accordingly brought in. They made no obeisance,
but stood like a couple of huge rocks, immo-
vable, with all their thickets and woods upon
them. They even beetled over the tall and
sturdy form of Duncan MacErchar, who, though
above the middle size, might have passed as a
little man when placed beside those gigantic
figures. Duncan put several questions to them
in their own language, which they answered,
but always before doing so they seemed to consult each other's countenances, and then both
answered in the same breath. They eyed the
knight and his page from time to time, as the
inhabitants of all secluded and wild regions are

naturally apt to stare at strangers. After a good deal of colloquy had passed, MacErchar turned to Hepborne,—

" Sir Patrick," said he, " these men ken every inch of the country from here to the Frith of Moray. Shall she now ask them if they be willing to guide her honour to Lochyndorbe ?"

"Do so, I beseech thee," said Hepborne, "and tell them I will give them gold when they bring me thither."

MacErchar again addressed them in their own language. The men seemed to nod assent to the proposals he made them ; and after a few more words had passed between them,—

" Uch, Sir Patrick," said he, " they be very willing for the job. They'll bring her there in two days. They say that she must be off by sunrise in the morning."

This Sir Patrick readily undertook ; and Duncan MacErchar having wet the treaty with a draught of the spirits from his stoup, of which he poured out liberally to each, the men retired. Sir Patrick Hepborne then signified a wish to go to his repose. Two heather-beds of inviting firmness and elasticity were already prepared at the two extremities of the chamber where they were ; and the knight having occupied the one,

and the page the other, both were very soon
sound asleep.

About the middle of the night, Sir Patrick
was awakened by a noise. He raised himself
suddenly, and looking towards the door, whence
it seemed to have proceeded, he saw that it was
open. One or two of the great rough wolf-dogs
came slowly in, looking over their shoulders, as
if expecting some one to follow them—and making a turn or two round the expiring fire, and
smelling about them for a little while, walked
out again. Hepborne arose and shut the door,
and then threw himself again within his blan-
kets. He lay for some time awake, to see whether the wolf-dogs would repeat their unpleasant intrusion; and finding that there was no
appearance of their doing so, he again resigned
himself to the sweets of oblivion.

He had lain some time in this state, when he
was a second time awakened, he knew not how,
but he heard as if there were footsteps in the
place. The fire had now fallen so low, that he
could see nothing by its light, but by a glimmering moon-beam that made its way in, he saw
that the door was again open. As he looked towards it, he thought he perceived something like
a dog glide outwards. He started up, as he had
done before, and going to the door, he again shut

it; and that the wolf-dogs might no more torment him, he piled up the rustic table he had
supped on, and some of the stools and settles
against it. The precautions he thus took were
effectual, for the dogs were no more troublesome
to him all night; and the first interruption his
slumbers experienced, was from the overthrow
of the whole materials of his barricado, and the
exclamation of " Uve! uve!" that burst from
Duncan MacErchar, who came for the purpose
of rousing him to prosecute his journey. Hepborne explained the cause of his having so fortified the door.

" Uch ay," said MacErchar, "they be's powersome brutes—powersome brutes, in troth, and
plaguy cunning. I'se warrant they smelt the
smell of the rosten deer's flesh, and that brought
them in. But they got little for their pains, the
ragged rascals—not but they are bonny tykes,
poor beasts! and troth, 'tis better to have ane
o' them in the house than the wolves themselves,
that we're sometimes plagued with."

The host approached the side of Hepborne's
couch, with his everlasting stoup in his right
hand, and the wooden cup in his left, and poured him out of the spirits it contained. The
Knight sipped a little, and then MacErchar retired to see that his morning's meal was pro-

perly provided. It was no less copiously and comfortably supplied, according to his means, than the supper of the previous evening had been.

At length Mortimer Sang came to receive his master's orders; and when Hepborne asked him how he and his people had fared, he learned that they had been treated with everything the good host could procure for them. Oats were not to be had for the horses; but, in addition to the grass that was cut for them, Master Mac-Erchar had himself carried a large sack of meal to the stables and out-houses of turf, where the animals had with some difficulty been forced in, and he had most liberally supplied them with his own hands. He went round all the men of Hepborne's party, and gave each his morning's cup of spirits. In short, he seemed to think that it was impossible he could do enough from his small means, for the knight and every person and animal belonging to him.

When the horses were brought out, Hepborne called MacErchar to him, and offered him, from his purse, ten times as much money as the value of his night's entertainment and lodging would have cost.

" Uve! uve!" said Duncan, sore hurt, and half offended; " uve! uve! Sir Patrick! Hoot,

no. What! take money from the son of Sir Patrick Hepborne, the son o' the noble brave knight
that she has followed mony a days!—take money from his son for a bit paltry piece and a
drink!—Na! na!—Uve! uve!—Ou fye! ou
fye!—na, na!—Troth, she's no just so poor or
so pitiful as that comes to yet. Uve! uve!
Surely!"

Hepborne at once saw the mischief he had
done. He would have rather put his hand in
the fire than have hurt feelings that were so honourable to Duncan MacErchar; and he almost
began to wish that his purse had been there, ere
it had been the means of giving pain to so noble
a heart. He did all he could, therefore, to remedy the evil; for, putting his purse sheepishly
in his pocket, he called for the stoup of spirits,
and, filling the cup up to the brim, drank it off,
to the health, happiness, and prosperity of Master Duncan MacErchar; then shaking the mountaineer heartily by the hand—

"May we meet again, my worthy friend,"
said he; "and wherever it be, let me not pass
thee by unnoticed. Meanwhile, farewell, and
may the blessing of St Andrew be about thee!"

This courteous and kind behaviour completely salved the wound Hepborne had so unwittingly inflicted. Duncan was overjoyed with

it, and gratified beyond measure. He tried to express his joy.

" Och, oich! God's blessing, and the Virgin's blessing be about her. Och, och! Sir Patrick! uu-uch! God's blessing, and the Virgin's blessing—and uch-uch!—and, Sir Patrick—Sure, sure! ou ay—uu—u!"

His English failed him entirely, and he resorted to that language in which he was most fluent. Hepborne mounted his horse, and waving him another farewell, rode on to overtake his guides, who were standing on a distant eminence waiting for him; and as he receded from the humble mansion of Master Duncan MacErchar, he for several minutes distinguished his voice vociferating in pleased but unintelligible accents.

CHAPTER XXV.

Sir Patrick Hepborne and the Page, followed by Mortimer Sang and the rest of the
party, rode slowly on after their savage guides,
along sidelong paths worn in the steep acclivi-
ties of the mountains, by the deer, wild bisons,
and other animals then abounding in the wil-
dernesses of Scotland. The fir forests appeared
endless ; the trees were of the most gigantic sta-
ture, and might have been of an age coeval with
that second creation that sprung up over the
surface of the renovated and newly fructified
earth, after the subsiding waters had left their
fertilizing mud behind them. Long hairy moss
hung streaming from their lateral branches,
which, dried by the lack of air and moisture
occasioned by the increasing growth of the
shade above, had died from the very vigour of
the plant they were attached to. As Hepborne
beheld the two mountaineers striding before
him in their rough attire, winding among their

enormous scaly trunks, or standing on some
rocky point above, leaning against one of them,
to wait for the slow ascent of himself and his
party, he could not help comparing them with
those vegetable giants, and indulging his fancy
in the whimsical notion, that they were as two
of them, animated and endowed with the powers
of locomotion. The ground they travelled over
was infinitely varied in surface, hills and hol-
lows, knolls, gullies, rivers, and lakes; but all
was forest, never-ending forest. Sometimes,
indeed, they crossed large tracts of ground,
where, to open a space for pasture, or to banish
the wolves, or to admit a more extended view
around for purposes of hunting, or perhaps by
some accidental fire, the forest had been burnt.
There the huge trunks of the trees, charred black
by the flames, and standing deprived of everything but a few of their larger limbs, added to
the savage scenery around.

Before entering one of these wastes, in a little plain lying in the bottom of a valley, where
the devastation had been arrested in its progress
by some cause, before it had been carried to any
great extent, their guides descried a herd of
the wild bisons, which were natives of Scotland
for ages after the period we are now speaking
of. The animals were feeding at no very great

distance, and the mountaineers were instantly all eagerness to get at them. Pointing them
out to Hepborne, they made signs that he and
his party should halt. He complied with their
wishes; and they immediately secured their
dogs to the trees, to prevent the risk of their
giving any premature alarm, and, setting off
with inconceivable speed through the skirting
wood that grew on the side of the mountain,
were soon lost to view. Hepborne kept his eye
on the herd. They were of a pure milk-white
hue, and, as the sun was reflected from their
glossy sides, they appeared still more brilliant,
from contrast with the blackened ruins of the
burnt pines among which they were pasturing.
At their head was a noble bull with a magnificent mane.

As Hepborne and the page were admiring
the beauty and symmetry of this leader of the
herd, noting the immense strength indicated
by the thickness and depth of his chest, with
the lightness and sprightliness of his head, and
his upright and spreading horns, of a white ri-
valling that of ivory in lustre, and tipt with
points of jet black, they observed a fat cow
near to him suddenly fall to the ground, by an
arrow from the covert of the trees, while another having been lodged in his flank at the

same moment, he started aside, and bounded
off in a wide circuit with great swiftness, and
the whole herd being alarmed, darted after him.
Out rushed the mountaineers from their concealment, and making for the wounded cow,
soon dispatched her with their spears.

They then attempted to creep nearer to the
herd, and even succeeded in lodging more than
one arrow in the bull; but as none of them
took effect in a vital part, they only served to
madden the animal. He turned, and, ere they
wist, charged them with a fury and speed that
left them hardly time to make their escape.
They ran towards the place where Hepborne
and his party were concealed; and just as the
knight moved forward into the open ground,
they succeeded in getting up into trees. Sir
Patrick's manœuvre had the desired effect in
checking the attack of the bisons, for they stopped short in the middle of their career, gazed
at the party, and then, led by the bull at their
head, again galloped off in a wide circle, sweeping round a second time towards the knight,
and coming to a sudden stand beyond bow-shot.
After remaining at rest for some minutes, with
their heads all turned towards the party, the
bull began pawing the ground, and bellowing

aloud, after which he charged forward half the distance, and then halted.

. Hepborne, seeing him thus detached from his followers, put his lance in the rest, and was preparing to attack him; but just as he was rising in his stirrups, and was about to give his horse the spur, the page, with a countenance' pale as death, and a hand trembling with apprehension, seized his bridle-rein, and looking anxiously in his face—

" Do not peril thy life, Sir Knight," said he —" do not, I beseech thee, peril thy life against a vulgar beast, where thou canst gain no honour; do not, for the sake of the blessed Virgin—do not essay so dangerous and unprofitable an adventure."

. " Pshaw," said Hepborne, vexed with the notion that the boy was betraying pusillanimity; " is that the face, are those the looks, and is that the pallid hue of fear, thou dost mean to put on, as the proofs of thy fitness for deeds of manhood and warlike encounter ?"

The page dropped his head, ashamed and hurt by his master's chiding; but still he did not let go the rein—

" Nay, Sir Knight," said he calmly, " I did but argue that thy prowess, shown upon a vile brute, were but lost. Rather let me attempt to

3

attack yonder salvage : he better befits mine
unpractised arm than thine honoured lance,
which hath overthrown puissant knights."

" Tush, boy," said Sir Patrick, somewhat
better pleased to see the spirit that lurked in
the youth, " thou art much too young, and
thine arm is as yet too feeble to fit thee for
encounter with yonder huge mass of thewes
and muscles. Stand by, my dear boy, and let
me pass."

He gave his palfrey the spur, and sprang forward against the bull. The page couched his
slender lance, to which a pennon was attached,
and bravely followed the knight in the charge,
as fast as his palfrey could gallop. The bull
seeing Hepborne coming on him, bellowed aloud,
and, putting down his nose to the ground, he
shut his eyes, and darted forward against his
assailant. Hepborne wheeled his horse suddenly
out of his way, and, with great adroitness, ran
his lance through him as he passed him. But
his manœuvre, though manifesting excellent
judgment, and admirable skill and horseman-
ship, had nearly proved fatal to the page, whose
palfrey, coming up in a straight line behind that
of the knight, and seeing the bull coming directly upon him, sprang to the side, and by that
means unhorsing the boy, left him lying on the

ground, in the very path of the infuriated beast. In agony from his wound, the creature immediately proceeded to attack the youth with his horns. But the page having kept hold of his spear, with great presence of mind ran its point, with the flapping pennon attached to it, right into the animal's eyes. The creature instantly retreated a few steps, and before he could renew his attack, he was overpowered by the knight and his party, who immediately surrounded him, and was killed by at least a dozen spear-thrusts at once. A general charge was now made against the rest, that still stood at a distance, crowded together in a knot; when the whole of them, wheeling suddenly round, galloped off with the utmost swiftness, and were lost in the depths of the forest.

Hepborne leaped from his horse, and ran anxiously to assist Maurice de Grey, who still lay on the ground, apparently faint from the fall he had had, and perhaps, too, partly from the alarm he had been in. He raised him up, upon which the boy burst into tears.

"Art thou hurt, Maurice?" demanded Hepborne, with alarm.

"Nay," said the boy, "I am not hurt."

"Fye on thee, then," said Hepborne; "let not tears sully the glory thou hast but now

earned by thy manly attempt in so boldly riding
to my rescue. Verily thou wilt be a brave lad
anon. Be assured, my beloved boy," continued
he, as he warmly embraced him, " I feel as
grateful for thine affectionate exertions in my
behalf as if I now owed my life to them. But
dry up thy tears, and let them not henceforth
well out so frequently, lest thy manhood and
courage may be questioned."

" Nay, Sir Knight," said the boy, " these are
not the tears of cowardice; they are the tears
of gratitude to Heaven for thy safety; and methinks they are less dishonourable to me," continued he, with an arch smile of satisfaction,
" since I see that thine own manly cheek is
somewhat moistened."

Hepborne said no more, but turned away hastily, for he felt that what the boy said was true.
He had experienced very great alarm for Maurice's life, and the relief he received by seeing
him in safety, operating in conjunction with the
thought that the danger the page had thrown
himself into had been occasioned by a mistaken
zeal to defend him from the bull, grappled his
generous heart, and filled his eyes with a moisture he could not restrain.

The two mountaineers proceeded to skin the
animals, a work which they performed with

great expertness; then cutting off the finer parts of the flesh, and carefully extracting the tallow, they rolled them up in the hides; and each lifting one of them on his brawny shoulders, proceeded on their journey, after allowing their hungry dogs to gorge themselves on the remainder.

The knight and his party were now led up some of those wild glens which bring down tributary streams to the river Dee, and they gradually began to climb the southern side of that lofty range of mountains, separating its valley from that of the Spey. They soon rose above the region of forest, and continued to ascend by zigzag paths, where the horses found a difficult and precarious footing, and where the riders were often compelled to dismount. The fatigue to both men and animals was so great, that some of the latter frequently slipped down, and were with great labour recovered from the hazard they were thrown into. At length, after unremitting and toilsome exertions, they found themselves on the very ridge of the mountain group, from which they enjoyed a view backwards over many leagues of the wild but romantic country they had travelled through during the previous days.

They now crossed an extensive plain; the

greatest part of which was covered with a hardened glacier, while two high tops reared themselves on either side, covered with glazed snow,
that. reflected the sun-beams with dazzling
brightness. The passage across this stretch of
table-land was difficult, the horses frequently
slipping, and often falling, till, at length, they
came suddenly to the edge of a precipice, whence
they looked down into one of the most sublime
scenes that nature can well present.

The long and narrow trough of a glen, bounded on both sides by tremendously precipitous
rocks, rising from a depth that made the head
giddy to overlook it, stretched from under them
in nearly a straight line for perhaps six or seven
miles, being cooped in between the two highest
points of the Grampians. The bottom of the
nearer and more savage part of this singular
hollow among the mountains, was so completely
filled with the waters of the wild Loch Aven,
as to leave but little shore on either side, and
that little was in most places inclined in a steep
slope, and covered with mountainous fragments,
that had fallen during a succession of ages from
the overhanging cliffs. A detachment of pines,
from the lower forests, came straggling up the
more distant part of the glen, and some of them
had even established themselves here and there

in scattered groups, and uncouthly-shaped single trees, along the sides of the lake, or among
the rocks arising from it. The long sheet of water lay unruffled amidst the uninterrupted quiet
that prevailed, and, receiving no other image
than that of the sky above, assumed a tinge
of the deepest and darkest blue. The glacier
they stood on, and which hung over the brow
of the cliff, gave rise to two very considerable
streams, which threw themselves roaring over
the rocks, dashing and breaking into an infinite
variety of forms, and shooting headlong into the
lake below.

The sun was now sinking rapidly in the west,
and night was fast approaching. The great elevation they had gained, and the solitary wilderness of alpine country that surrounded them,
almost excluded the possibility of any human
habitation being within their reach. Hepborne
became anxiously solicitous for the page Maurice de Grey, who had for a considerable time
been manifesting excessive fatigue. Their dumb
guides seemed to stand as if uncertain how to
proceed, and Hepborne's anxiety increased. He
endeavoured to question them by signs, as to
where they intended the party to halt for the
night. With some difficulty he succeeded in
making them understand him, and they then

pointed out a piece of green ground, looped in
by á sweep of the river, that escaped from the
farther end of the lake. The spot seemed to be
sheltered by surrounding pine-trees, and wore
in every respect a most inviting aspect. But if
they had been endowed with wings, and could
have taken the flight of eagles from the region
of the clouds where they then were, the distance
must have been five or six miles. Taking into
calculation, therefore, the immense circuit they
must make with the horses in order to gain the
bottom of the glen beyond the lake, which must
necessarily quadruple the direct distance, together with the toilsome nature of the way, Sir
Patrick saw that Maurice de Grey must sink
under the pressure of fatigue before one-twen-
tieth part of it could be performed. He was
therefore thrown into a state of the utmost per-
plexity, for the cold was so great where they
then were, that it was absolutely impossible
they could remain there during the night, without the risk of being frozen to death.

One of the guides, observing Hepborne's un-
easiness and doubt, approached him, and pointed
almost perpendicularly downwards to a place
near the upper end of the lake, where the masses of rock lay thickest and hugest. The knight
could not comprehend him at first, but the man,

taking up two or three rough angular stones, placed them on the ground, close to each other, in the form of an irregular circle, everywhere entire, except in one point, where the space of about the width of one of them was left vacant; and then, lifting up a stone of a cubical shape, and of much greater size, placed the flat base of it on the top of the others, so as entirely to cover them and the little area they enclosed. Having made Hepborne observe that he could thrust his hand in at the point where the circle had been left incomplete, and that he could move it in the cavity under the flat base of the stone, he again pointed downwards to the same spot he had indicated near the upper end of the lake, and at last succeeded in calling Hepborne's attention to one of the fallen crags, much larger than the rest, but which, from the immensity of the height they were above it, looked like a mere handful. The guide no sooner saw that the knight's eye had distinguished the object he wished them to notice, than he turned and pointed to the mimic erection he had formed on the ground, and at length made him comprehend, that the fallen crag below was similarly poised, and afforded a like cavernous shelter beneath it. At the same time he indicated a zigzag path, that led precipitously down the cliffs, like a stair among the rocks, between the two foaming cataracts. This was altogether impracticable for the horses, it is true, but it was sufficiently feasible, though hazardous enough, for active pedestrians. The guide separated Hepborne and Maurice de Grey from the rest of the party, and then pointing to the men and horses, swept his extended finger round from them to the distant green spot beyond the end of the lake; and this he did in such a manner as to make the knight at once understand, that he meant to propose that the party should proceed thither by a circuitous route, under the guidance of his companion, whilst he should himself conduct Hepborne, and his already over-fatigued page, directly down to the sheltering stone below, where they might have comfortable lodging for the night. He further signified to Hepborne, that the horses might be brought for a considerable way up the lake, to meet him in the morning.

CHAPTER XXIV.

So much time had been lost in this mute kind of conversation, that the night was fast approaching, and Sir Patrick saw that he must now come to a speedy decision. The plan suggested by the guide seemed to be the best that could be followed, under all the circumstances, and he at once determined to adopt it. At the same time, he by no means relished this division of forces, and, remembering the caution he had received from Duncan MacErchar, he called Mortimer Sang aside, and gave him very particular injunctions to be on the alert, and to take care that his people kept a sharp watch over the mountaineer who was to guide them, and to be sure to environ him in such a manner as to make it impossible for him to dart off on a sudden, and leave them in the dark, in the midst of these unknown deserts. Had they once safely arrived at the green spot, where there was a temporary though uninhabited hunting-hut, and

plenty of grass for the horses, he had no fear of
his being able to join them with the page next
morning; for the trough of the glen was so direct between the two points, where they were
separately to spend the night, that it was impossible to mistake the way from the one to the
other. Mortimer Sang engaged to prevent all
chance of the savage mountaineer escaping. He
produced from one of the baggage-horses a large
wallet, containing provisions enough for the
whole party, which the good and mindful Master Duncan MacErchar had provided for them,
altogether unknown to Hepborne. From it he
took some cakes, cheese, butter, and other eat-
ables, with a small flask filled from the host's
stoup of spirits; these were added to their
guide's burden of the flesh of the wild bisons
they had slain; and, bidding one another God
speed, the party, under Sang, with one of the
Celts, and all the dogs, departed to pursue their
long and weary way.

Maurice de Grey had sat all this while on the
ground, very much exhausted; and when he
arose to proceed, he had become so stiff, that
Hepborne began to be alarmed for him. The
poor boy, however, no sooner remarked the unhappy countenance of his master than he made
an attempt to rouse himself to exertion, and ap-

proaching the edge of the precipice, he commenced his descent after the guide, with tottering and timid steps, dropping from one pointed
rock to another, and steadying himself from time
to time, as well as he could, by means of his
lance, as he quivered on the precarious footing
the rough sides of the cliffs afforded. The height
was sufficiently terrific when contemplated from
above; but as they descended, the depth beneath
them seemed to be increased, rather than diminished, by the very progress they had made. It
grew upon them, and became more and more awful at every step. The crags, too, hung over their
heads, as if threatening to part from their native
mountains, as myriads had done before, and to
crush the exhausted travellers into nothing beneath their ruins. They went down and down,
but the lake and the bottom of the valley appeared still to recede from them. The way became
more hazardous. To have looked up or down,
would have required the eye and the head of a
chamois. A projecting ledge increased the peril
of the path, and the page, tired to death, and
giddy from the terrific situation he saw himself
fixed in, clung to a point of the rock, and looked
in Hepborne's face, perfectly unable to proceed
or to utter a word. There he remained, panting
as if he would have expired. The Knight was

filled with apprehension lest the boy should faint, and fall headlong down, and the guide was so much in advance, that he alone could give aid to the page. Yet how was he to pass the boy, so as to put himself into a position where he could assist him? He saw the path re-appearing from under the projecting ledge, a little to one side of the place where the page hung in awful suspense, and taking one instantaneous glance at it, he leaped boldly downwards. He vibrated for a moment on the brink; and his feet having dislodged a great loose fragment of the rock, it went thundering downwards, awakening all the dormant echoes of the glen. He caught at a bunch of heath with both his hands; and he had hardly recovered his equilibrium, when Maurice de Grey, believing, in his trepidation, that the noise he had heard announced the fall and destruction of his master, uttered a faint scream, and dropped senseless from the point of rock he had held by. Hepborne sprang forward, and caught him in his arms. Afraid lest the boy might die before he could reach the Sheltering-Stone, he shouted to the guide, and waving him back, took from him the bottle, and put it to the page's lips. The spirits revived him, and he opened his eyes in terror, but immediately smiled when he saw that Hepborne was safe.

Sir Patrick now put his left arm around the page's body, and swinging him upwards, seated him on his left shoulder, keeping him firmly there, whilst, with his right hand, he employed his lance to support and steady his ticklish steps. The timorous page clasped the neck of his master with all his energy, and in this way the knight descended with his burden. Many were the difficulties he had to encounter. In one place, he was compelled to leap desperately over one of the cataracts, where the smallest slip, or miscalculation of distance, must have proved the destruction of both. At length he reached the bottom in safety, and there the page, having recovered from his terror, found breath to pour forth his gratitude to his master. He now regained his spirit and strength so much, that he declared himself perfectly able to proceed over the rough ground that lay between them and the Sheltering-Stone; but Hepborne bore him onwards, until he had deposited him on the spot where they were destined to halt for the night. The grateful Maurice threw himself on his knees before the knight, as he was wiping his manly brow, and embraced his athletic limbs from a feeling of fervent gratitude for his safety.

Sir Patrick now proceeded to examine the
curious natural habitation they were to be hou-
sed in. The fallen crag, which had appeared
so trifling from the lofty elevation whence they
had first viewed it, now rose before them in
magnitude so enormous as almost to appear
capable of bearing a castle upon its shoulders.
The mimic copy of it constructed by the guide,
furnished an accurate representation of the mode
in which it was poised on the lesser blocks it
had fallen upon. These served as walls to support it, as well as to close in the chamber beneath; and they were surrounded so thickly with
smaller fragments of debris, that no air or light
could penetrate between them, except in one or
two places. On one side there was a narrow
passage, of two or three yards in length, leading
inwards between the stones and other rubbish,
and of height sufficient to permit a man to enter
without stooping very much. The space within, dry and warm, was capable of containing a
dozen or twenty people with great ease. It was
partially lighted by one or two small apertures
between the stones, and the roof, formed of the
under surface of the great mass of rock, was
perfectly even and horizontal. It presented a
most inviting place of shelter, and it seemed to
have been not unfrequently used as such, for in

one corner there was a heap of dried bog-fir, and in another the remains of a heather-bed.

The mountaineer carefully deposited his burdens within the entrance, and then set about collecting dry heather, and portions of drift-wood, which he found about the edges of the lake; and he soon brought together as much fuel as might have kept up a good fire for two or three days. Having piled up some of it in a heap, he interspersed it with pieces of the dry bog-fir, and then groping in his pouch, produced a flint and steel, with which he struck a light, and soon kindled up a cheerful blaze. He then began to cut steaks of the flesh of the wild bison, and when the wood had been sufficiently reduced to the state of live charcoal, he proceeded to broil them over the embers, on pieces of green heather plucked and prepared for the purpose. Meanwhile the knight and the page seated themselves near the fire.

"How fares it with thee now, Maurice?" demanded Sir Patrick kindly, as he watched the cloud that was stealing over the boy's fair brow, and the moisture that was gathering under his long eye-lashes, as he sat with his eyes fixed in a fit of absence upon the ground— "What ails thee, my boy? Say, dost thou repent thee of thy rashness in having exchanged

the softer duties and lighter labours of a page
of dames, for the toils, dangers, and hardships
befalling him who followeth the noble profession of arms? Trust me, thy path hath been
flowery as yet, compared to what thou must
expect to meet with. Methinks thou lookest as
if thy spirit had flown homewards, and that it
were hovering over the gay apartment where
thy mother and her maidens may be employed
in plying the nimble needle, charged with au-
reate thread, or sewing pales upon their gor-
geous. paraments."

" Nay, Sir Knight," said Maurice de Grey,
" my thoughts were but partly of those at home.
Doubtless they have ere this ceased to think of
their truant boy!" He sighed heavily, and the
tears rolled down his cheeks.

" But why dost thou sigh so?" demanded
Sir Patrick, " and what maketh thy brow to
wear clouds upon it, like yonder high and snow-
white summit? and why weepest thou like
yonder mountain side, that poureth down its
double stream into the glen? Perdie! surely
thou canst not be in love at so unripe an age?
Yet, of a truth, those mysterious symptoms of
abstraction and sorrow thou dost so often display, when thou art left alone to thine own
thoughts, would all persuade me that thou art."

The page held down his head, blushed, and sighed deeply, but said nothing.

"Is silence, then, confession with thee, Maurice?" demanded Hepborne.

The page wiped his streaming eyes, and raised them with a soft and melancholy smile, till they met those of his master, when he again sighed, and dropping them with renewed blushes to the ground, "I am indeed in love," said the boy, "most unhappily in love, since I burn with unrequited passion. I did indeed believe, vainly believe, that I was beloved; but, alas! how cruelly was I deceived! I found that what I had mistaken for the pure flame was but the wanton flashing of a light and careless heart, that made no account of the pangs it inflicted on mine that was sincere."

The page's eyes filled again, and he sighed as if his heart would have burst. Sir Patrick Hepborne sighed too; for Maurice, whilst telling of his unhappy love, had touched his own case most nearly.

"Poor boy," said he kindly, and full of sympathy for the youth; "poor boy, I pity thee. I do indeed most sincerely feel for thee, that thou should'st have already begun, at so early an age, to rue the smart of unrequited or unhappy love. Trust me," continued the knight, sighing deeply, " trust me, I know its bitterness too well not to feel for thee." And again he sighed heavily.

" Then thou too hast loved unhappily, Sir Knight ?" inquired the page earnestly.

" Ay, boy," said Hepborne sadly, " loved ! —nay, what do I say—loved !—I still love— love without hope. 'Tis a cruel destiny."

" And hast thou never prospered in love ?" asked Maurice; " hast thou never fancied that thou hadst awakened the warm flame of love, and that thou wert thyself an object adored ?"

" Nay, boy," said Hepborne, " thou inquirest too curiously. Yet will I confess that I have had vanity enough to believe that I had excited love, or something wearing its semblance; but then she that did show it was altogether heartless, and I valued the cold and deceitful beam but as the glimmering marsh-fire."

Maurice de Grey made no reply, but hung down his head in silence upon his breast, and again relapsed into the dream he had been indulging when Hepborne first roused him. The knight, too, ceased to have any desire to prolong the conversation. His mind had laid hold of the end of a chain of association, that gradually unfolded itself in a succession of tender remembrances. He indulged himself by giving

way to them, and consequently he also dropped
into a musing fit.   Both were disturbed by their
savage guide, who, having finished his unso-
phisticated cookery, now made signs to them to
approach and eat.

Love, however fervent, cannot starve, but
must give way to the vulgar but irresistible
claims of hunger.   The day's fatigue had been
long, they were faint for want, and the odour
of the smoking hot steaks was most inviting.
They speedily obeyed the summons, therefore,
and made a very satisfactory meal.   Maurice
de Grey had no sooner satisfied the cravings of
nature, than, worn out by his exertions, and
overpowered by sleep, he wrapped himself up
in his mantle, and throwing himself on the
heather, under the projecting side of the huge
rock, his senses were instantly steeped in sweet
oblivion.

Sir Patrick Hepborne regarded the youth
with envy.   His own thoughts did not as yet
admit of his yielding to the gentle influence of
sleep.   He tried to divert them by watching
the decline of the day, and following the slow
ascent of the shadows as they crept up the rug-
ged faces of the eastern precipices, eating away
the light before them.   A bright rose-coloured
glow rested for a time on the summits, tinging

even their glazed snows with its warm tint; but in a few minutes it also departed, like the animating soul from the fair face of dying beauty, leaving everything cold, and pale, and cheerless; and darkness came thickly down upon the deep and gloomy glen. In the meantime, the mountaineer had been busying himself in gathering dry heath, and in carrying it in under the Shelter-Stone, for the purpose of making beds for the knight and the page.

While the guide was thus employed, Hepborne sat musing at the fire, listlessly and almost unconsciously supplying it with fuel from time to time, and gazing at the fragments of wood as they were gradually consumed. His back was towards the entrance-passage of the place where the mountaineer was occupied, and the page lay to his right hand, under the shadow of the rock.

As Sir Patrick sat thus absorbed in thought, he suddenly received a tremendous blow on his head, that partly stunned him, and almost knocked him forwards into the flames. The weight and force of it was such, that, had he not had his steel cap on, his brains must have been knocked out. Before he could rise to defend himself, the blow was repeated with dreadful clang upon the metal, and he was brought down upon his knees; but ere it fell a third time on him, a piercing shriek arose, and a struggle ensued behind him. Having by this time gathered his strength and senses sufficiently to turn round, he beheld the horrible countenance of their savage guide glaring over him, his eye-balls red from the reflection of the fire, his lips expanded, his teeth set together, and a ponderous stone lifted in both hands, with which he was essaying to fell him to the earth by a third blow. But his arms were pinioned behind, and it was the feeble page who held them. Hepborne scrambled to get to his feet, but weakened by the blows he had already received, his efforts to rise were vain. The murderous ruffian, furious with disappointment, struggled hard, and at length, seeing that he could not rid himself of the faithful Maurice whilst he continued to hold the stone, he quickly dropped it, and, turning fiercely round on the boy, groped for his dirk. Already was it half unsheathed, when the gleam of a bright spear-head came flashing forth from the obscurity on one side, and with the quickness of thought it drank the life's blood from the savage heart of the assassin. Down rolled the monster upon the ground, his ferocious countenance illumined by the light from the blazing wood. In the agony of death his teeth ground against each other; his right hand, that still clenched the handle of the dirk, drew it forth with convulsive grasp, and raising it, as if for a last effort of destruction, brought it down with a force that buried the whole length of its blade in the harmless earth. Hepborne looked up to see from what friendly hand his preservation and that of the courageous boy had so miraculously come, when to his astonishment he beheld Duncan MacErchar standing before him.

" Och, oich !" cried the worthy Highlander, " Och, oich ! what a Providence !—what a mercy !—what a good lucks it was that she was brought here !"

" A Providence indeed !" cried Hepborne, crossing himself, and offering up a short but fervent ejaculation of gratitude to God; " it seems indeed to have been a most marked interposition of Providence in our favour. Yet am I not the less grateful to thee for being the blessed instrument in the hands of the Almighty, in saving not only my life, but that of the generous noble boy yonder, who had so nearly sacrificed his own in my defence. Maurice de Grey, come to mine arms; take the poor thanks of thy grateful master for his safety, for to thy courage, in the first place, his thanks are due.

Trust me, boy, thou wilt one day be a brave knight; and to make thee all that chivalry may require of thee shall be mine earnest care."

Whether it was that the boy's stock of resolution had been expended in his effort, or that he was deeply affected by his master's commendation, it is not easy to determine; but he shrank from the knight's embrace, and bursting into tears, hurried within the Shelter-Stone.

CHAPTER XXVII.

" By what miracle, good mine host," said Sir Patrick Hepborne to Master Duncan MacErchar—" by what miracle do I see thee in this wilderness, so far from thine own dwelling?"

" Uch! uch! miracle truly, miracle truly, that she's brought here; for who could have thought that the false faitours and traitrous loons would have led her honour this roundabout gate, that they might knock out her brains at the Shelter-Stone of Loch Aven? An it had not been for Donald and Angus, her two cushins, that hunts the hills, and kens all the roads of these scoundrels, she would never have thought of coming round about over the very shoulders of the mountains to seek after them. But—uve! uve! where's the t'other rascals? and where's her honour's men, and beasts?"

Hepborne explained the cause and circumstances of their separation.

" Uch! uch!" cried MacErchar; " uve! uve!

—then, Holy St Barnabas, I wish that the t'others scoundrels may not have them after all; so she shall have more miles to travel, and another villains to stickit yet! Uve! uve!"

And then changing his tongue, he began with great volubility to address, in his own language, his cousins, who now appeared. They replied to him in the same dialect, and then he seemed to tell them the particulars of the late adventure, for he pointed to the dead body of the ruffian on the ground, while his actions corresponded with the tale he was telling, and seemed to be explanatory of it. The two men held up their hands, and listened with open mouths to his narration. He then took up a flaming brand from the fire, and, followed by his two cousins, proceeded to explore the passage leading into the chamber of the Shelter Stone, whence they soon returned with the burden of wolf-skins which the ruffian guide had carried. Duncan MacErchar threw it down on the ground near the fire, and as it fell—

"Troth," said he, with a joyful expression of countenance—"troth but she jingles; she'll warrants there be's something in her. Sure! sure!"

With this he went on his knees, and began eagerly to undo the numerous fastenings of hide-thongs which tied the wolf-skins together, and which, as Hepborne himself had noticed, had been closely bound up ever since they started in the morning, though the other guide carried his hanging loose, as both had done the night before. The knots were reticulated and decussated in such a manner, as to afford no bad idea of that of Gordias.

"Hoof!" said Master MacErchar impatiently, after working at them with his nails for some minutes without the least effect; " sorrow be in their fingers that tied her; though troth she needs not say that now," added he in parenthesis. "Poof! that will not do neither; but sorrow be in her an she'll not settle her; she'll do for her, or she'll wonders at her." And unsheathing his dirk, he ripped up the fastenings, wolf-skins and all, and to the astonishment of Hepborne rolled out from their pregnant womb the whole of the glittering valuables, the fruit of his English campaigns.

"Och, oich!" cried MacErchar with a joyful countenance, forgetting everything in the delight he felt at recovering his treasure—"och, ay! blessings on her braw siller stoup, and blessings on her bonny mazers; she be's all here. Ay, ay!—och, oich!—ou ay, every one."

The mystery of Master Duncan MacErchar's

hasty journey, and unlooked-for appearance at Loch Aven, was now explained. His sharp-eared cousin, Angus MacErchar, had been loitering about the door at the time of the departure of the knight and his attendants in the morning, and hearing something clinking in the Celt's bundle of wolf-skins as he passed, but seeing no cause to suspect anything wrong, as regarded his kinsman's goods, he negleeted to notice the circumstance until some time after they were gone, when he happened to mention, rather accidentally than otherwise, that he thought the rogues had been thieving somewhere, for he had heard the noise of metal pots in the bundle of one of them. Duncan MacErchar took immediate alarm. Without saying a word, he ran to his secret deposit, and, having removed the heap of billets, and the wattle trap-door, discovered, with horror and dismay, that his treasures were gone. It was some small comfort to him, that they had not found it convenient to carry away what he most valued; and he bestowed a friendly kiss upon the black bugle, and the swords and daggers that were still there; but the whole of the silver vessels were stolen. What was to be done? He was compelled to tell his cousins of his afflicting loss, that he might consult them as to what steps were to be taken. They advised instant pursuit; but well knowing the men and their habits, they felt persuaded that the thieves would carefully avoid the most direct path, and guessed that, in order to mislead their pursuers, they would likely take the circuitous and fatiguing mountain-route by Loch Aven. Taking the advice and assistance of his cousins, therefore, Master Duncan MacErchar set off hot foot after the rogues, and he was soon convinced of the sagacity of his cousins' counsels, for they frequently came upon the track of the party where the ground was soft, or wet enough to receive the prints of the horses' feet; and when they came to the ridge of the mountains, they traced them easily and expeditiously over the hardened snow. It was dark ere they reached the brink of the precipice overhanging the lake; but Angus and Donald were now aware of their probable destination, and the fire they saw burning near the Shelter-Stone, made them resolve to visit it in the first place. They lost no time in descending, the two lads being well acquainted with the dangerous path; and no sooner had Master Duncan MacErchar set his foot in the glen, than, eager to get at the thief, he ran on before his companions. And lucky was it, as we have seen, that he did so; for if he had been but a few minutes later, both Sir Patrick Hepborne and Maurice de Grey must have been murdered by the villain whom he slew.

Hepborne now became extremely anxious about the safety of the party under the guidance of the other ruffian. For the attack of one man against so many, he had nothing to fear ; but he dreaded the possibility of the traitor escaping from them before he had conducted them to their destined place of halt for the night, and so leaving them helpless on the wild and pathless mountain, to perish of cold. He had nothing for it, however, but to comfort himself with his knowledge of Sang's sagacity and presence of mind.

Master Duncan MacErchar, with his two cousins, now hastened to cut off a supper for themselves from the bison beef, which they quickly broiled ; and after their hunger had been appeased, the whole party began to think of bestowing themselves to enjoy a short repose. Before doing so, however, Hepborne proposed that they should bury the dead body. This was accordingly done, and from the debris of the fallen rocks a cairn was heaped upon it, sufficiently large to prevent the wolves from attacking it.

The page, wrapped in his mantle, was already sound asleep within the snug chamber of the

Shelter-Stone, and Sir Patrick lost no time in seeking rest in the same comfortable quarters; but the three hardy Highlanders, preferring the open air, rolled themselves up, each in his web of plaiding, and laid themselves in different places, under the projecting base of the enormous fallen rock, and all were soon buried in refreshing slumber.

It happened, however, that Duncan Mac-Erchar had by accident chosen the spot nearest the passage of entrance. The fire had fallen so low as to leave only the red glow of charcoal; but the night, which was already far spent, was partially illuminated by the light of the moon, which had now arisen, though not yet high enough to show its orb to those in the bottom of the glen. He was suddenly awakened by a footstep near him, and, looking up, beheld a dark figure approaching. With wonderful presence of mind, he demanded, in a low whisper, and in his native language, who went there, and was immediately answered by the voice of the other guide, who had gone forward with Hepborne's party, and who, mistaking Mac-Erchar for his companion in iniquity, held the following dialogue with him, here translated into English.

" Hast thou done it, Cormack ?"

" Nay," replied Duncan, " it is but now they are gone to sleep, and I fear they are not yet sound enough. What hast thou done with the party of men and their horses ?"

" I left them all safe at the bothy," replied the other, " and if we had this job finished, we might go that way, and carry off two or three of the best of their horses and trappings while they are asleep, and we can kill the others, to prevent any of them from having the means of following us when they awake. But come, why should we delay now ?—they must be asleep ere this ;—let us in on them—creep towards them on our knees, and stab them without noise :— then all their booty is our own."

" You foul murderer !" cried Duncan Mac-Erchar, springing at him, his right hand extended with the intention of making him prisoner. The astonished ruffian stepped back a pace, as Duncan rushed upon him, and, seizing his outstretched hand, endeavoured to keep him at a distance. Both drew their dirks, and a furious struggle ensued. Each endeavoured to keep off the other, with outstretched arm, and powerful exertion, yet each was desirous to avail himself of the first favourable chance that might offer, to bury the lethal weapon be brandished in the bosom of his antagonist. The ruffian had the decided advantage, for it was his right hand that was free, while MacErchar held his dirk with his left. They tugged, and pushed stoutly against each other, and each alternately made a vain effort to strike his opponent. The brave MacErchar might have easily called for help, but he scorned to seek aid against any single man. They still struggled, frequently shifting their ground by the violence of their exertions, yet neither gaining the least advantage over the other, when, all at once, MacErchar found himself attacked behind by a new and very formidable enemy. This was one of the great rough wolf-dogs, which, having come up at that moment, and observed his master struggling with Duncan, sprang upon his back, and seized him by the right shoulder. The ruffian, seeing himself so ably supported, and thinking that the victory was now entirely in his hands, bent his elbow so as to permit him to close upon his adversary, and made an attempt to stab MacErchar in the breast; but the sturdy and undaunted hero, in defiance of the pain he experienced from the bites of the dog, raised his left arm, and after receiving the stab in the fleshy part of it, instantly returned it into the very heart of his enemy, who, uttering a single groan, fell dead upon the spot. But the dog still kept his hold, until MacErchar, putting his hand backwards, drove the dirk two or three times into his body, and shook him off dead upon the lifeless corpse of his master.

" Heich !" cried he, very much toil-spent— "Foof !—Donald—Angus—Uve, uve !—Won't they be hearing her ?"

His two cousins, who had been fast asleep at the end of the Shelter-Stone, now came hastily round, making a great noise, which roused Sir Patrick, who instantly seized his sword, and rushed out to ascertain what the alarm was.

" Och, oich !" continued Duncan, much fatigued, " oich ! and sure she has had a hard tuilzie o't !"

" What, in the name of the blessed Virgin, has happened ?" cried Hepborne, eagerly.

" Fu ! nothing after all," cried Duncan, " nothing—only that t'other villains came up here from t'others end of the loch, and wanted to murder Sir Patrick and his page ; and so she grabbled at her, and had a sore tuilzie with her, and sure she hath stickit her dead at last. But— uve ! uve !—she was near worried with her mockell dog ; she settled her too, though, and yonder they are both lying dead together. But troth she must go and get some sleep now, and she hopes that she'll have no more disturbance, wi' a sorrow to them."

" But, my good friend," said the knight, " thine arm bleeds profusely, better have it tied up; nay, thy shoulder seems to be torn too."

" Fu, poof!" said MacErchar carelessly, " her arm be's naething but a scart; she has had worse before from a thorn bush ; and her shoulder is but a nip, that will be well or the morn."

So saying, he wrapped his plaid around him, and rolling himself under the base of the stone where he had lain before, he composed himself to sleep again, and the others followed his example. The knight also retired to his singular bed-chamber, and all were very soon quiet.

As MacErchar had hoped, they lay undisturbed until daybreak, when they arose, shook themselves, and were soon joined by Hepborne from within. The sun had just appeared above the eastern mountain-tops, and was pouring a flood of glory down among the savage scenery of the glen. MacErchar and his two cousins were busily engaged in renovating the fire; and as Sir Patrick was about to join them, his ears were attracted by the low moans of a dog, which, beginning at the bottom of the scale of his voice, gradually ascended through its whole compass, and ended in a prolonged howl. He cast his eyes towards the spot whence it proceeded ; there lay the dead body of the ruffian murderer, with the dog that died with him in his defence stretched across him stiff; and by his side sat two more of the dogs, that, having followed some chase as he came up the glen, had not fallen upon his track again until early in the morning, and had but just traced it out, when it brought them to his inanimate corpse. There they sat howling incessantly over him, alternately licking his face, his hands, and his death-wound. Their howl was returned from the surrounding rocks, but it was also answered from no great distance; and on going round the end of the Shelter-Stone, he beheld another dog sitting on the top of the cairn they had piled over the dead body of the first man who was killed, scraping earnestly with his feet, and moaning and howling in unison with the two others. Hepborne went towards him; and did all he could to coax him away from the spot; but the attached and afflicted creature would not move. The howling continued, and would have been melancholy enough in any situation; but in a spot so savage and lonely, and prolonged as it was by the surrounding echoes, it increased the dismal and dreary effect of the scenery. Hepborne called the MacErchars, and proposed to them that they should bury the dead body which lay exposed on the ground. They readily assented, and approached it for the purpose of lifting and carrying it to the same spot where they had deposited the other; but Angus and Donald had no sooner attempted to lay hold of it, than both the dogs flew at them, and they were glad to relinquish the attempt, seeing they could carry it into effect by no other means than that of killing the two faithful animals in the first place, and this Hepborne would on no account permit.

" Verily he was a foul traiterons murderer," said the knight; "but he was their master. His hand was kind and merciful to them, whatever it might have been to others. Of a truth, a faithful dog is the only friend who seeth not a fault in him to whom he is attached. Poor fellows! let them not be injured, I entreat thee."

Some food was now prepared for breakfast, and Maurice de Grey, who had made but one sleep during the night, was called to partake of it. They repeatedly tried to tempt the dogs with the most inviting morsels of the meat, but none of them would touch it when thrown to them, and, altogether regardless of it, they still continued to howl piteously.

Hepborne now resolved to proceed to join his party. Duncan MacErchar had already ordered his cousin Angus, who was perfectly well ac-

quainted with the way, to go with the knight as
his guide, and not to leave him until he should
see him safe into a part of the country where he
would be beyond all difficulty. Sir Patrick was
much grieved to be compelled to part with him
who had been so miraculously instrumental in
saving his life. He took off his baldrick and
sword, and putting them upon Duncan,—

" Wear this," said he, " wear this for my
sake, mine excellent friend—wear it as a poor
mark of the gratitude I owe thee for having
saved me from foul and traiterous murder. I
yet hope to bestow some more worthy warison."

" Och, oich !" cried Duncan, " oich, this is
too much from her honour—too much trouble
indeed. Fye, but she's a bonny sword; but
what will hersell do for want of her ? Ou, ay—
sure, sure !"

" I have others as good among my baggage,"
said Hepborne.

" But thou didst save two lives," said Maurice de Grey, running forward, and taking
Duncan's hand; " thou didst save my life also;
nay, thou didst save mine twice, by saving Sir
Patrick's. Receive my poor thanks also, most
worthy Master MacErchar, and do thou wear
this jewelled brooch for my sake."

" Och, oich !" said Duncan, " too much trouble for her—too much trouble, young Sir Pages—too much trouble, surely; but an ever she pairt with the sword or the bonny brooch, may she pairt with her life at the same time."

They now prepared themselves for taking their different routes, and Hepborne reminding MacErchar of the injunction he had formerly given him, to be sure to claim his acquaintance wherever they should meet, and giving him a last hearty shake of the hand, they parted, and waving to each other their " Heaven bless thee !" and " May the blessed Virgin be with her honour !" set out on their respective journeys.

END OF VOLUME FIRST.

EDINBURGH:
PRINTED BY JAMES BALLANTYNE & CO.

ND - #0061 - 220925 - C0 - 229/152/22 - PB - 9781330910894 - Gloss Lamination